Flintstaff and Cramp:

The Curious Case of the Case.

by

Duncan Howard

Published in 2016 by Createspace for Duncan Howard.

For more information and extra chapters please visit:

www.flintstaffandcramp.com

Acknowledgements.
I would like to thank my beautiful wife, Hanna, with all my heart for her total and unwavering advice and support. I would also like to say a big thanks to Tiernen Trevallion for the cover design. Please visit his website at tiernentrevallion.co.uk. Many thanks to Limor, the two French Nats, Elf and Tom and a few friends who gave me great feedback and advice. You know who you are!

Tibi omnes res.

PROLOGUE

Monday 30th January 1865.

Slime oozed from the thick black stones of the crypt. Vaulted ceilings were held aloft by twisted columns, crowned by the tormented visages of gargoyles; leering at any who dared to enter. Ebony candles cast from human fat and as thick as gallows' poles spat and sputtered, offering an anti-light of creeping shadows. A solitary Death's Head Hawk moth fluttered through the stagnant air, leaving a trail of tiny dust motes in its wake. And then in mid-flight it stopped, hanging, suspended in the air...

'Shaaaaaaaaaaaaaaaaaatooooof!'

'I say!' shouted Major Flintstaff-Membrayne as he suddenly appeared where the moth had just been. In one hand was a leather travelling case and in the other a stocky man with side-burns you could hide a badger in.

'Pie and chips please, Luv,' said Sergeant Cramp staggering sideways before collapsing. He shook his head, straightened his bowler hat and struggled to rise. He wasn't very good on a steam locomotive, let alone travelling through the ether.

Major Flintstaff-Membrayne spun to his left and right, gave the sergeant an encouraging tap with his toe, and stepped back until his shoulders touched the frigid wall. Flags of long-dead nations hung limply along the walls above moth-eaten tapestries. Husks of armour

1

stood at attention beneath each pillar, dented and rust-reddened. The slowly decaying remnants of a thousand years of slaughter drifted to the floor. Sergeant Cramp looked around, gulped, and scrabbled after his colleague. A million tiny feet scuttled towards them in agitation. The floor moved. Seethed.

'That coffin,' said Flintstaff pointing to the southern end of the crypt where a blackened altar held an ivory inlaid coffin, 'can only be one man's, Sergeant. Count Strigoi. One of the most feared Shadows of the Void. And those rats... all of those rats coming toward us, would be...?'

'Rattus rattus?' answered Cramp, unconsciously trying to climb the sheer wall.

'Close, Cramp, close. This 'mischief' of rats is in fact the deadly Rattus Vampiricus.'

'You mentioned the word *deadly*, sir. Will we be needing the case?' asked Cramp.

'Most certainly.'

With a small hiss of compressed air the major opened his case. The horde of rats scuttled closer, razor-teeth bared.

'Ah, here we are,' said the major extracting an enormous V-shaped contraption. He smiled as he depressed a brass lever. 'Never leave home without one: The Cat-o-Vault 3,000 (Patent:7648264)!'

'Weeeeeeeeooooooooooow!' Flew an outraged feline.

'And again, sir!'

'Meeeeooooooooooooow!' screeched a particularly irate tortoise-shell.

'Your eleven o'clock, sir.'

'Weeeeeeeeooooooooooow!' winged ginger death.

'Nothing tougher than a street cat from the London Wharf, Cramp,' shouted Flintstaff over the terrible noise of shredding flesh.

'Twelve stitches on my left arm to prove that, sir,' Cramp shouted back.

The sounds of terrified rats being flensed by London's meanest street cats were music to their ears. Major Flintstaff was about to

2

deposit the Cat-o-Vault in the case when Sergeant Cramp barrelled into him. A dislodged gargoyle came crashing to the floor, narrowly missing the two gentlemen. A figure swept into the air upon translucent, blue-veined wings. Its body was the colour of ash with a scrunched, bat-like face of terrible cruelty. Screeching its displeasure, it hurtled towards them.

'Mind out, Cramp,' warned Major Flintstaff as he rolled to one side firing cats as he went.

The Shadow swept down upon the semi-supine sergeant wrestling him back to the ground. Cramp grappled with the winged beast, using all his skill as a champion wrestler in the Grenadier Guards to stay alive. However, the Shadow had a thousand years of playing dirty and Cramp looked as if he were getting the worst of it. Flintstaff returned the 'Cat-o-Vault' to the case and rummaged within for something of use.

'Could use some help, Major!' Cramp yelled.

'On its way, Sergeant... a towel? No. Box of frogs? No. Ah, a billiards cue! That should do. Hold him, man. I just have to whittle a point on this here stick.'

'Not the cue you thrashed the Earl of Derby with, sir? Surely?' said Cramp – needle-sharp fangs bare inches from his neck.

'Needs must, Sergeant. Needs must,' said Major Flintstaff whistling a ditty as he whittled.

'Awfully kind, sir,' mumbled Cramp as he bit into a leathery wing.

Satisfied with his handiwork, Flintstaff thrust the makeshift stake with an expert accuracy that had won him a hundred sovereigns off the Earl. The vampire, impaled, squealed once, ignited, and vaporized all in an instant. An epoch of evil disposed of – leaving as little ash as a Cuban cigar. Cramp got to his feet and dusted himself off.

''Fraid to say that wasn't Count Strigoi, Major.'

'No,' agreed Flintstaff as he wrote comments in his journal. 'A bit too easy, wasn't it?'

3

'Well, I don't know about that...' said Cramp puffing his chest out like an angry robin.

'I wonder where he is, Sergeant... I don't like it. Best we get back to the house. I don't want it happening again. Leave the cats. The London Docks are teaming with them.'

'Yes, but they're much easier to catch once they've eaten, sir... less vicious,' answered Cramp, instinctively rubbing the stitches on his left arm.

'Exactly my point,' said the major as he pulled a finger-length piece of crystal from the spine of the journal and wrote out five glowing glyphs at his feet. 'Now, come on. Hold onto my hand. Off we go,' he said.

Cramp held the major's hand and smiled at a moggy sat nearby. It was chewing a mouthful of rats' tails and its ginger hair was matted with the blood of a hundred rodents and one careless sergeant. The cat gazed back with feral eyes as the two men and their luggage vanished into the ether. It purred, choked on a rat's tail, threw-up on the floor – and continued purring.

ONE

Friday 30ᵗʰ January 2015.

The pale blue demon was three headed. It was a terror to behold and almost indestructible. Almost. Using his special ability he warped time to slow down the high speed attacks from the demon's two-handed sword. Praying his shield would hold long enough, he ran towards his foe. Just as he reached within striking distance he skidded beneath his enemy's swinging blade and sliced his assassin's dagger through the demon's ankle. The demon roared in agony and collapsed onto one knee. With no time to think he whirled around and plunged the dagger into its heart. The demon wailed as it turned to dust. All that remained was a pale blue stone... he'd be needing that.

'Charlie! What are you doing up there?'

'Damn it,' said Charlie as he quickly saved the game. He shut his PC down and grabbed his school bag. 'Just finishing off some homework, Dad. I'll be right down.'

Charlie checked the clock, hoping he'd only have to sit at the breakfast table for as short a time as possible. His father would be reading the Financial Times as always, trying to find another sure thing to lose all his money on while his mum would be rushing around humming to herself. Charlie would skip breakfast altogether if he could but he was expected to have a proper meal before school; to help him concentrate, apparently.

'Do hurry up, Charlie,' said his mum as she stuck the dishwasher on. 'And remember to wrap up out there. Jack Frost was out and about last night.'

'Jack Frost. Honestly, Sarah,' grumbled his dad. 'You talk to the boy as if he were a child.' He turned another page awkwardly, sighing and grunting behind the pink pages.

Charlie looked down at the congealed bacon and eggs and shook his head. He pushed the plate to one side and spread honey across two pieces of toast. Was it worth mentioning again? For the fiftieth time?

'Mum, I'm vegetarian. I don't want to eat bacon. Have you seen what they do to pigs? Look on YouTube.'

'Don't be ridiculous,' said his dad. 'You should be grateful for what you get. When you're old enough to leave this house then you can make those sorts of decisions.'

'One minute you say I'm not a child and the next you say I'm not old enough to make decisions for myself... I'm nearly sixteen for god's sake...' and as soon as he said it he knew he'd made a mistake.

The pink paper opposite him was lowered to the table and his father's bald head came into view. Charlie felt the colour coming to his cheeks.

'Do not blaspheme, Charles,' said his dad quietly. 'There are countries in this world where you could be put to death for saying such a thing. Show some respect.'

'Sorry, Dad,' mumbled Charlie. But inside he was fuming. How was that a defence against blaspheming? All it showed was that there were a whole lot of idiotic people out there prepared to kill other people for nothing. The news was full of it every day. If anything was proof against the existence of a god it was by looking at some of the crazy people that worshipped them. Charlie bit into his cold toast as the newspaper was raised again, crumbs exploding everywhere. He didn't care if he made a mess and then he felt guilty because it wasn't his dad who was going to clear up the table but his mum. Charlie swept the crumbs into the palm of his hand and brushed

6

them onto his plate. From behind him, his mother gently looped her arm around his neck and kissed the top of his head.

'You're a good boy, cleaning up after yourself,' said his mum. She sniffed and then added, 'hair-washing night tonight. Oh, and that reminds me, remember to pack an overnight bag for the weekend.'

'Please, Mum,' begged Charlie. 'Don't make me go. I can look after myself, honestly.'

'You're not old enough, Charles,' said his father. 'Believe me, if I could find anyone else to look after you while we're away I would. The last thing I want is for you to go and stay with that lunatic of a woman.'

'I wish you wouldn't speak about Aunt Maud like that. It's very mean,' said Charlie's mum.

'Nothing compared to what she's said about me...'

For the next five minutes Charlie ate his toast with the sound of two adults arguing in the background. He relived the last level of his computer game. He didn't even want to imagine what it was going to be like away from his PC for the whole weekend. He glanced up at the clock in the kitchen and got up from the table.

'Have a nice day at school, Charlie-Farley,' said his mum hauling laundry from the washing machine.

'Mum. How many times have I told you to stop using all these rhyming words with my name? It was okay when I was a kid, but if anyone finds out at school, I'm dead meat. What if I started calling you Mumsy-wumsy, or something daft like that?'

'Don't be silly,' laughed his mother.

'Girls are silly, boys are stupid,' came his dad from behind the newspaper.

'Thanks, Dad,' moaned Charlie. 'I'm outta here before I get any more motivation to ride my bike off the railway bridge.'

'Don't be facetious,' warned his father.

Charlie stepped out into a frigid winter's morning. When he breathed through his scarf a great fog of condensation obscured his view. He could just see the orange glow of the sun rising behind the hills overlooking the river valley. Charlie walked over to the garden shed, the sound of hundreds of frozen blades of grass crunched beneath his shoes. For some reason he loved that sound. The shed door opened with a screech of protest. The whole thing leant slightly to the left after a storm at Christmas. His dad certainly wouldn't bother to fix it. He always joked that he was a white collar worker not a blue collar worker. Charlie didn't even know what that meant but his dad thought it was hilarious. He wished he had a father like his mate, Tom. His dad was amazing with electrics and mechanics, and wood and welding.

There were only two places Charlie felt comfortable; the shed and his bedroom. In his bedroom he could lose himself in other worlds playing computer games and in the shed he could mess about fixing broken stuff. He pulled his old bike out and checked the tyres. Amazingly, both were still hard to the touch, meaning that his last puncture repair had been a success. Just as he was pushing off down the drive his pocket beeped twice. Cycling with no hands, Charlie managed to pull off one of his gloves with his teeth, unzip his coat and extricate his ancient mobile. He checked the screen and groaned. A message read:

Picture message received. Unable to open file. Please contact your provider.

It was then that the front wheel of his bike hit the frozen pothole and slipped from beneath him. Without a second to react Charlie slipped and cracked his head against the ground.

Charlie was standing in the centre of a deserted plaza. The cloudless sky was a stunning blue. The sun beat down upon his head with such force that he could actually feel it burning his scalp. It was even hotter than his one holiday in Cyprus. Scrunching his eyes against the glare, he looked around the empty square. Minute dust-devils chased each other around. At one end of the plaza rose what looked to be a kind of temple. The building was whitewashed and shone brilliantly in the sun. It hurt his eyes to look at it. The temple rose up and up into the blue. It must have been ten storeys high, at

8

least, with each level slightly smaller than the one before, giving it a pyramidal shape. On all the other sides of the plaza were huge rust-coloured boulders. Some were perfectly round and as big as a house, others rose in disordered stacks, and some had huge rocks balancing precariously one on top of the other. It looked as if you could prod them with a finger to topple a thousand tons. Charlie lowered his head from the glare and the heat. At his feet were six glowing blue symbols. He'd never seen anything like them. They looked as if...

'Charlie? Charlie, are you okay?'

'Huh?' said Charlie opening his eyes.

'You alright, son?' said the voice again. He was being shaken gently.

Charlie wanted to speak but he could hardly breathe and his head pounded. He gasped some air into his lungs and held down the urge to be sick. What had happened? It was like a dream and he was already losing it. The more he tried to remember the more it slipped from his memory. As his eyes focussed he realised that his rescuer was the postman. He took a hand for support and slowly got to his feet. He was still bent double because if he tried to stand upright he thought he would fall over again. The postman picked up the bike and handed it to him.

'Thanks,' Charlie managed.

'Wanna go back to the house? Get that bump on yer 'ead looked at?' the postman asked.

'No, I'm okay,' Charlie replied, gingerly prodding the bruise on his forehead.

'If yer sure? Then I better get on with me round,' said the postman getting back on his own bicycle. 'Watch out for the black ice on the railway bridge. Bloody nearly had me off just now.'

Charlie checked his bike, and then looked down onto the rutted drive. His phone was blinking. And the glass was cracked. As he picked it up and brushed off the dirt he could just see the time through the broken screen. He frowned. It must be broken because if it was the right time then he had been on the ground for over ten

9

minutes. He put the phone away and jumped back on his bike. He pedalled past the gates of the church and up the lane past a herd of White Park cattle as they munched on stinky silage either side of the lane. Charlie arrived at the school gates just as the bell went. There was the usual anarchy of a hundred 4x4s reversing, honking, parking, double parking and generally getting in the way, as he swerved past them. Out of all those off-road vehicles, only about four belonged to people who actually needed them.

His mate, Tom, was one of them. He was every bit a farmer's son and was his only neighbour and only friend. His dad had actually picked him up from school in a combine harvester once and it was Tom's cattle that Charlie rode past every day on the way to school. Charlie slid the back wheel of his bike to a stop beside a battered, mud-spattered pick-up just as Tom was getting out.

'Oi, watch it!' said Tom hopping out of the way.

'Morning, Mr. Cramp,' said Charlie as he poked his head through the pick-up's window.

'Morning, Charlie,' replied Tom's dad. 'What happened to your head?'

'I hit some ice and fell off my bike.'

'I'm not trying to be funny, Charlie, but you need some ice on that. You still coming over to help me fix the Wheelhorse after school? I could do with a hand.'

'Sure thing, Mr. Cramp. See you this afternoon.'

'So you fell off that girl's bike then?' taunted Tom as they watched his dad drive off.

'It's not a girl's bike, you idiot,' said Charlie going red.

'No, I suppose you're right. Whichever girl owned that would be a grandmother by now!' said Tom, dodging a friendly punch.

'Very funny,' said Charlie and sniffed around Tom. 'Cor, wot be that smell? Smells like someone's been sleeping with them goats again.'

'Hang on,' said Tom stopping abruptly. 'Check that out.'

One of the last cars to pull up in the now emptying school car park was a brand new Aston Martin. It was spotless and gleamed in the wintry sun. The windows were slightly tinted leaving anyone inside invisible. The passenger door opened. And two immaculate shoes touched the tarmac. As the door swung shut a girl stood upright and looked around. She waved once to the departing car and then turned and glanced over at Charlie and Tom. Charlie felt dizzy again as Tom stood gawping at the departing sports car. The girl walked directly towards them. As Charlie glanced in the girl's direction again there were features that set her apart from anyone else at school. Her waist-length hair was jet black and shone with an almost ethereal light against her chocolate-coloured skin. And she had eyes like emeralds.

'Excuse me,' she said walking straight up to them. 'Could you tell me where I might find the principal's office?'

'Urgh,' said Tom.

'There... office... teacher's,' mumbled Charlie pointing randomly.

'Right,' said the girl slowly. 'Perhaps it would be better if you could show me. English obviously isn't your first language.'

Charlie leant his bicycle against the nearest wall and led the way – ignoring the crashing sound as his bike fell over – he pushed open the double doors and walked inside. The corridors seethed with children of all ages rushing this way and that. The teachers' tea room and offices were near the entrance, so it didn't take long to squeeze through to the door of the Head Teacher's office.

'Come on in,' said Mrs. Graham as she organised great piles of files strewn across her desk.

Charlie caught the scent from the new girl as she walked past him into the office; it made his stomach flip. Tom was already grabbing him to leave but Mrs. Graham waved them all inside. Charlie glanced around the room. It was too familiar. There was no worse place for him to be than in the Head Teacher's office. He found everything about it alien and threatening. All six of his detentions had come from here. The fight he'd soundly lost in defence of his

11

dad's stupid job had ended here, with him taking most of the blame. Mrs. Graham was probably in her fifties and never seemed to wear anything other than grey which matched her stern features. Charlie felt the bump on his head throbbing beneath his woolly hat. Pulsating. Like the heat of the sun upon his head... Charlie froze as wisps of images flashed before his eyes.

'So, let's see now,' said Mrs. Graham as she flicked through some files. 'You are...?'

'Aghanashini Nair,' said the girl in her immaculate new uniform.

'And you've come from our neighbouring private school, have you not?' asked Mrs. Graham frowning slightly as she scanned a document.

'That's correct, Mrs. Graham. I was expelled.'

'Well,' replied Mrs. Graham crisply. 'I believe in giving everyone a second chance, Miss Nair. I realize we are mid-way through term three but I thought it better for you to join us now. At least you can familiarize yourself. You will have to knuckle down to get the grades you'll need for Sixth Form College. I'm expecting good things from you, young lady.'

'Afghan... Angan... Astini...?' tried Tom.

'A-ghan-a-shini,' said Aghanashini very slowly and deliberately.

'That's quite a mouthful to remember,' said Tom in his defence.

Aghanashini looked down at the old army bag Tom used to carry his books in. It was covered in graffiti.

'I would assume the band name: 'Puke-Demo Destroy-Boy' is also difficult to remember, yet you do? Don't you?' asked Aghanashini with one eyebrow arched. She sighed. 'You can call me Shini.'

'Well, my name is Tom. T-o-m. And this is Charlie. Charlie?'

'Charlie? Are you alright?' asked Mrs. Graham.

'Gnnn,' moaned Charlie with eyes wide and unfocussed.

'Oi, Charlie!' shouted Tom and slapped his friend on the back.

'What? Where?' said Charlie. 'Oh. Yes, I'm fine. Just felt a bit dizzy. It must be coming in from the cold or something.'

'You look well weird, mate,' said Tom grinning.

'Are you sure you're alright?' asked Mrs. Graham and when Charlie nodded she continued. 'Well, you two boys look like you've already volunteered to look after Shini. She's in the same class, so show her around and introduce her to people.'

Charlie led the way down the empty corridors towards their classroom. They were late but at least they had an excuse this time. Although Charlie and Tom had groaned at the prospect of baby-sitting a new-girl, Charlie was neither blind nor stupid. He wanted to know this mysterious, confident girl but she was way out of his league. And he wanted to know why every time he managed to sneak a look at her he felt sick. But sick in a good way.

TWO

Charlie sat through the class in a daze. His head throbbed with a heavy repetitive thud. He spent the whole lesson tenderly poking the bruise beneath his hair with his fingers. If he wasn't prodding his egg-shaped wound then he was trying to stretch his eyeballs into looking ninety degrees to the way his face was pointing. Shini was sitting beside him at the next table. He could only just see her with his right eyeball. His left eyeball was firmly staring at the side of his own nose. There was a definite problem in facing the teacher, looking to his right and probing his wound all at the same time. As if this were not enough, he had the odd feeling of having been caught in a dream that was not even of his own making. When he'd fallen off his bike something had happened. It was like someone had picked him up and dumped him in the middle of a weird landscape. What it was, he couldn't figure out. The place had been hot. Of that he was sure. But what else?

And then he glanced over at Shini and completely forgot about what he had been thinking of. This new girl had stepped out of an Aston Martin and happily admitted in front of Mrs. Graham to being thrown out of her last school. How could she do that? There wasn't a single girl here who had that kind of front. Sure, there were girls with a lot of attitude, and Charlie avoided them at all costs, but he always thought that was more of an act. And it wasn't just confidence, it was something else. Charlie couldn't even find a word in English to describe it. He wanted to say she had 'balls' – but it felt wrong. All he was sure about was that she was unique. Her family must have originated from India or someplace similar. The way she looked only guaranteed one thing; Charlie and Tom's time with her was limited. From the various glances and whispers of the boys around the class; the sharks were already beginning to circle. Charlie felt the usual trickle of dejection slip down his spine and end up in the pit of his stomach. He was broke and totally out of fashion, lived outside the village and was picked on because of his dad's job. Charlie slipped his phone out of his pocket and checked it under the table. Now it was not only old but cracked. Charlie sighed and placed it back in his pocket wishing he had more money. Couldn't his mum and dad understand what it was like for him? He didn't want to resent them. It was an ugly feeling but they treated him like a kid. Charlie just couldn't understand why everyone else in the school had smart phones while his was about as smart as a brick. Even Tom had the new Strawberry Krush – and he was a farmer.

The class erupted in chatter and the sound of chairs scraping against the floor as everyone made for the door. Charlie shook his head. He had to stop all this day-dreaming. What class had he just sat through? Maths? Geography? He couldn't even remember. Tom slapped him on the back.

'So?' asked Tom.

'So what?' replied Charlie.

'So, are you going to show me round this place?' said Shini standing next to him.

'Alright,' agreed Tom. 'But try not to cramp our style, okay? We have 'respect' round this hood.'

'Tom, you sound like Farmer Giles, the Monster G,' said Charlie. He turned towards Shini. 'Look, Shini. We understand if you want to hang out with other people here. It's no problem, right?'

'We'll see,' said Shini showing a perfect row of teeth. 'Now, are we going to stay in the class all day, or are you going to show me outside?'

Charlie led the way until they reached the door, where Tom pushed him sideways and strutted through. Charlie sighed and shrugged at Shini. He was just about to walk through the door when he was pushed sideways again. Charlie spun around.

'Ladies first,' said Shini as she dashed after Tom down the corridor.

'Bloody hell!' said Charlie. He ran after them, knocking some year sevens aside as he went. Once outside, the chill of winter struck them. They pulled on hats and shoved hands deep into pockets. They found an empty bench looking over the recreation ground where people were booting footballs to and fro.

'So?' asked Tom, annoyingly vague as ever.

'What's the set-up?' asked Shini as she surveyed her surroundings.

'Well,' began Charlie. 'That lot over there are the ones to watch. They think they're hard-core gangsters. They hassle everyone and are cowards when it comes to a fight. They'll never go one on one.'

'Jack Marvin is the worst of the lot,' said Tom. 'We steer clear of them most of the time but we have to watch out for them in the village.'

'The Emo's are over there,' said Charlie pointing towards a group with dyed black hair, 'and for some reason they seem to annoy everybody, although they never do anything to deserve it...'

'So, what d'you get kicked out for?' asked Tom.

'Subtle, Tom. Really subtle.'

'What? She was the one that mentioned it.'

'You really want to know?' asked Shini pulling her hair away from her face. The two boys nodded. Shini sighed and smiled. 'I was kicked out for doing a Ouija board with three other girls...'

'A who-gee board?' said Tom frowning.

'A Ouija board,' explained Charlie. There'd been one in a computer game he'd played last year. 'It's a board with letters and numbers on it and you summon up spirits and ask them questions. Doesn't it spell out the answers with a glass or something?'

'It speaks through a glass?'

17

'Oh, do be quiet, Cramp, for heaven's sake,' said Major Flintstaff as he stepped backwards.

'Aaargh!' gurgled Cramp quietly from ground level. 'Sir...?'

'What now, Sergeant?' whispered the major as he spun on the heel of his Oxonian half-boot.

'Your foot; my hand, sir,' said Cramp between clenched teeth.

Major Flintstaff lifted his boot and Cramp staggered to his feet, sucking his crushed digits. Between the gentleman and his man lay a case with innumerable travel stamps plastered across its surface in languages as far removed as Saan, Gujarati, Mandarin, Slavic and even the fabled lost lingua of Lemuria. If there was ever a travel case that could stand up on its own two brass wheels and say: *I've seen things that would make your nose bleed*; this was the case.

'Coordinates?' whispered the major. He was busy scouting the trees around the glade, picking bits of bark off trunks; sniffing and nibbling them. 'Hmm. The family of Fagaceae. Beech, if I'm not mistaken.'

'Ah, um. Yes, sir,' mumbled Cramp through his sucked fingers. He delved into his Norfolk jacket and produced a minute, brass, valve-powered sextant (Patent Pending). 'North Star visible, moon in plain sight... should have the longitude quite soon, sir.'

'Hurry up, Cramp. We haven't got all night. Out with it.'

'Aaaaaaaaaaarooooooooooooooooow!'

'That wasn't you,' Flintstaff stated. 'Was it?'

'Afraid not, sir. Still busy on the calculations.'

'I would hazard a guess that we are somewhere in the realm of the Dacians. Herodotus. The Histories. Book IV, if I'm not mistaken.'

'And that would be...?'

'Didn't they teach you anything at grammar school? I would say we are in the leafy folds of Transylvania.'

'Moldavia,' crowed Cramp poking a map with one pudgy finger. 'Right in the middle of... oh. Transylvania.'

'Hush, Sergeant,' whispered Flintstaff with a finger pressing against his moustachioed lip. Never one to decry technology, Major

'Oh, do be quiet, Cramp, for heaven's sake,' said Major Flintstaff as he stepped backwards.

'Aaargh!' gurgled Cramp quietly from ground level. 'Sir...?'

'What now, Sergeant?' whispered the major as he spun on the heel of his Oxonian half-boot.

'Your foot; my hand, sir,' said Cramp between clenched teeth.

Major Flintstaff lifted his boot and Cramp staggered to his feet, sucking his crushed digits. Between the gentleman and his man lay a case with innumerable travel stamps plastered across its surface in languages as far removed as Saan, Gujarati, Mandarin, Slavic and even the fabled lost lingua of Lemuria. If there was ever a travel case that could stand up on its own two brass wheels and say: *I've seen things that would make your nose bleed*; this was the case.

'Coordinates?' whispered the major. He was busy scouting the trees around the glade, picking bits of bark off trunks; sniffing and nibbling them. 'Hmm. The family of Fagaceae. Beech, if I'm not mistaken.'

'Ah, um. Yes, sir,' mumbled Cramp through his sucked fingers. He delved into his Norfolk jacket and produced a minute, brass, valve-powered sextant (Patent Pending). 'North Star visible, moon in plain sight... should have the longitude quite soon, sir.'

'Hurry up, Cramp. We haven't got all night. Out with it.'

'Aaaaaaaaaaarooooooooooooooooow!'

'That wasn't you,' Flintstaff stated. 'Was it?'

'Afraid not, sir. Still busy on the calculations.'

'I would hazard a guess that we are somewhere in the realm of the Dacians. Herodotus. The Histories. Book IV, if I'm not mistaken.'

'And that would be...?'

'Didn't they teach you anything at grammar school? I would say we are in the leafy folds of Transylvania.'

'Moldavia,' crowed Cramp poking a map with one pudgy finger. 'Right in the middle of... oh. Transylvania.'

'Hush, Sergeant,' whispered Flintstaff with a finger pressing against his moustachioed lip. Never one to decry technology, Major

THREE

Tuesday 31st January 1865.

Forest leaves glistened like sweat on a fevered brow. The moon had reached the zenith of its eternal arc, pregnant with expectant power. A solitary puff of cloud voyaged across the firmament. Deep within the trackless forest an ancient glade hunched beneath the trees. There was a breathless hush throughout. Moss-clad sentinels of stone encircled dark-bladed grass. A single dead leaf tumbled groundwards, spiralling down like a sun-scorched Icarus. No noise, no movement except the falling leaf. And then, as if all natural laws had been condemned, the leaf stopped its earthbound journey and floated six feet from the forest floor. It hung, twirling in the air. Gradually its speed increased. Faster. Faster. Evermore rapid. Until, until...

'Shaaaaaaaaaaaaaaaaatooooof!'

The sound cracked through the glade like a steam locomotive being sucked backwards into a vacuum. A million skeletal branches shook across the forest momentarily then stopped. A man now stood where a single leaf had once defied gravity. Another heavy-set man lay sprawled at his feet.

'Gadzooks!' exclaimed Major Henry Flintstaff-Membrayne.

'Three o'clock, Wednesday,' mumbled Sergeant Arthur Cramp from below.

'What?' asked the major, scanning his surroundings.

'What?' replied Cramp still crawling on all fours.

With the final bell the normal chaos resumed as three hundred kids tried to get out of school as fast as they could. The three friends walked down the corridor and out into the cold. Tom's dad sat waiting in his battered pick-up. Three cars down crouched the black Aston Martin; Shini's dad talking on his mobile. Clouds of condensation encircled the car as the engine purred.

'By the way,' said Shini, 'Why did that idiot call you preacher-boy?'

'Oh,' grunted Charlie. 'My dad's a vicar.'

'Ouch,' said Shini. 'I bet that hurts.'

'You don't know how much,' said Charlie. 'See you tomorrow then.'

'Uh-huh.'

Charlie picked up his bicycle and cursed. The front wheel had been bent in. It looked like someone had jumped up and down on it and it was pretty obvious who. The spokes were mangled, as was the brake. He picked it up and dragged it over to Mr. Cramp's pick-up and hefted it into the back amongst loops of bailer twine and animal feed. Just as Tom was getting into the front seat he hopped out again and called across to Shini.

'Hey, Shini, you told us how you got kicked out of your posh school – but what happened to Samantha?'

Shini turned. Both the boys were looking at her, waiting for an answer. She looked at them both with her eyes wide and even in the dull winter day they seemed to sparkle.

'She's dead.'

dream of, innit? I like my bitches white or black but I 'int never gonnna do no Taliban rag-head.'

What happened next seemed to occur in slow motion. Tom and Charlie gaped as Shini moved with the speed of a striking cobra. With both hands she grabbed Jack's trousers that were being lewdly thrust into her face as she sat on the bench. With one mighty jerk she pulled them and his underwear down to his knees and then shoved him backwards. Jack Marvin stumbled and toppled backwards onto the frozen grass. Unable to free his hands from his hoodie he writhed on the ground, exposed to the world. Whether it was due to the freezing January morning or not made no difference to those that witnessed the scene. Jack Marvin had the private parts of a gerbil.

'And by the way, *bitch*,' said Shini calmly standing over him. 'Those are not real Calvin Klein. They're fake. Like you.'

No one stopped them as Charlie followed Shini and Tom back to the classroom. The event sped through the school faster than a hurricane. Mobiles vibrated silently, others beeped. Nothing was secret at school. By lunchtime it had appeared on YouTube. Neither Charlie nor Tom knew what to say or do. Never in their time at school had anyone taken on Jack Marvin. The boy had used his size to push people around for as long as anyone could remember. Now it was his lack of size that no one would forget.

After class Charlie and Tom spent lunch alone. Shini had some forms to fill in with Mrs. Graham in her office. Tom couldn't get over what had happened. He went over it again and again. Charlie wasn't so sure it would end there.

'Jack worries me,' he said. 'He's a coward, which means he'll wait till he gets his revenge. And who'll he take his revenge out on? Me? You? Shini? All of us?'

'Look, don't worry about it so much. How many days have we suffered because of that dick-head? Let's enjoy the one day where we're the winners, alright?'

'Okay,' agreed Charlie and then spluttered as he waggled his little finger. 'D'you see the size of it?'

chaplain and asked him to exorcise her. She told him the whole story and I ended up at the Head's study. I didn't deny it, but I never told him why I did it either. So I got expelled.'

'Why didn't you tell the Head that they were teasing you?'

'I wasn't brought up that way. My mum always told me to stick up for myself and not rely on others…'

A football suddenly whizzed through the air, narrowly missing Charlie. It bounced once on the frozen grass before hitting the steel security fence with a rattle. Charlie looked up and groaned. Sauntering towards them with an exaggerated limp, hands stuffed deep into his hoodie, was Jack Marvin. Tom stood up slowly. Charlie stayed where he was with his head down. Shini sat calmly and watched the approaching boy. Charlie glanced up as Jack swaggered towards him. His trousers were slung low in an attempt to look like the prisoners on American reality shows. Walking a few metres behind him were four other boys and two girls.

'Oi, preacher-boy. Gis da ball,' he said to Charlie.

'Why should he?' said Tom. He was the same height as Jack Marvin and he took a step to block him.

'Coz I said so.'

'And who made you the main playa?' asked Tom.

'Look, farmer. You want your dad's barn to catch fire one night then you carry on mouthing me off.'

'Just try it, Jack. My dad'll blow your head off with his shotgun.'

'Excuse me,' said Shini quietly.

'I'll get the ball, Jack,' said Charlie rising.

'Excuse me,' said Shini again.

'Wot you want? Curry or sumfing?' taunted Jack as he faced Shini. He glanced behind him to make sure his followers were laughing at his joke.

'I thought you might like to know that I can see your underwear.'

'Thas right, girl,' replied Jack as he moved in close and loomed over Shini. 'An behind these 'Calvins' is sumfing you can only

'Well, before we all freeze to death,' interrupted Shini, 'let's just say that I called up a spirit and the school were pretty pissed off with what happened next.'

'Yeah, right,' said Tom. 'You really expect us to believe that? You might sucker your posh friends with that kind of story...'

'Hang on, mate. Let her speak,' said Charlie. 'Why were you using one in the first place?'

'Ah. The reason I used one was to teach some girls a lesson. They ganged up on me. They never said anything outwardly. It was notes and texts, Facebook and Twitter; every way they could think of to make my life miserable. They wrote mostly about my mother...'

'What about your mother?' asked Charlie.

'That's none of your business, alright?' said Shini glaring at Charlie. 'She went missing, okay. When I was a kid. I don't want to talk about it.' Shini took a deep breath before continuing. 'Sorry, I didn't mean to snap. Back to the story... They made a mistake. One of the notes they left was written in biro and I matched the writing. I could've gone to a teacher but I decided to deal with it myself. It took a while, but I convinced them that it'd be fun to make our own Ouija board. I told them it could answer anything they wanted to know. We waited up one night and then we went to an empty classroom. I rigged the whole thing. They asked stupid questions like lottery numbers and who fancied them etc. When it came to my turn I asked who of us would be the first to die. Then I moved the glass to spell out the name of the ringleader. Her name was Samantha. I can tell you we only got to the letter 'm' before she screamed and ran out the door. The other two girls were terrified. They looked at me for help and all I could say was that as the circle had been broken without sending the spirit back it was now trapped in the school. We were cursed.'

'Bloody hell,' whispered Tom. 'You did that?'

'What happened after that?' asked Charlie.

'Samantha became the school pariah. No one went near her. The other two stopped eating and eventually Samantha went to the school shrugged at Shini. He was just about to walk through the door when he was pushed sideways again. Charlie spun around.

'Ladies first,' said Shini as she dashed after Tom down the corridor.

'Bloody hell!' said Charlie. He ran after them, knocking some year sevens aside as he went. Once outside, the chill of winter struck them. They pulled on hats and shoved hands deep into pockets. They found an empty bench looking over the recreation ground where people were booting footballs to and fro.

'So?' asked Tom, annoyingly vague as ever.

'What's the set-up?' asked Shini as she surveyed her surroundings.

'Well,' began Charlie. 'That lot over there are the ones to watch. They think they're hard-core gangsters. They hassle everyone and are cowards when it comes to a fight. They'll never go one on one.'

'Jack Marvin is the worst of the lot,' said Tom. 'We steer clear of them most of the time but we have to watch out for them in the village.'

'The Emo's are over there,' said Charlie pointing towards a group with dyed black hair, 'and for some reason they seem to annoy everybody, although they never do anything to deserve it...'

'So, what d'you get kicked out for?' asked Tom.

'Subtle, Tom. Really subtle.'

'What? She was the one that mentioned it.'

'You really want to know?' asked Shini pulling her hair away from her face. The two boys nodded. Shini sighed and smiled. 'I was kicked out for doing a Ouija board with three other girls...'

'A who-gee board?' said Tom frowning.

'A Ouija board,' explained Charlie. There'd been one in a computer game he'd played last year. 'It's a board with letters and numbers on it and you summon up spirits and ask them questions. Doesn't it spell out the answers with a glass or something?'

'It speaks through a glass?'

Flintstaff removed his steam-powered revolver (patent no. 7935415) from its holster.

A small twig fractured in the distance. Flintstaff spun around as trees suddenly cracked, collapsed, shredded, in the wake of something massive gaining momentum. In the centre of the oncoming black vortex were two blood-crazed eyes as big as Royal Worcestershire saucers. The major released the safety-valve of his revolver and offloaded thirty-eight hollow-point rounds into the oncoming torrent. It wasn't enough. Not nearly. The beast took Major Flintstaff in a tackle that would have instantly landed it in Eton's First Fifteen rugby team. The steaming revolver spun a lazy circle in the air, where the major had been an instant before, and fell to the ground.

'Sergeant! The case, man. The case! Aaargh! Silver, quickly now.'

Cramp snapped the two clasps open and rummaged through the travelling case, muttering as he searched.

'Trousers? No. Chinese tea set? No. Golf ball? No. Picture of Aunt Gladys? No... wait! Hang on, sir.'

Within the cloud of dust, leaves, legs, teeth, clumps of grass, a long shaggy tail, and curses that would have left an East-End barmaid breathless, Sergeant Cramp dived forth with all the courage and devotion of a Yorkshire Terrier. The trees shuddered within the great forest. The standing stones trembled. In a terrible moment of violence it was all over. A small clump of grass landed with a 'flump' between the three combatants, marking the end of the struggle – like a full stop at the end of a sentence. As the dust settled Flintstaff looked over at Cramp and shook his head.

'Honestly, Cramp. Look at it,' he said as he lifted his mutilated weapon into the moonlight. 'It's bent to bullduggery. When I ask for a silver weapon I do not expect to have to beat a werewolf to death with Aunt Gladys's silver picture frame.'

'Humble apologies, sir,' replied the scratched and torn sergeant as he doffed a torn bowler hat. 'Seem to be having a slight problem with the organisational side of the case.'

'Something Aunt Gladys was well aware of when she warned me against hiring you,' grumbled Flintstaff as he picked up his revolver. 'Remind me to mix my ammunition with silver-tipped rounds next time, Sergeant.'

'Certainly, sir.'

Cramp looked down at the corpse of the werewolf sprawled between them. He removed a cloth tape measure from his breast pocket and began the task of measuring. Major Flintstaff lit a cheroot and took a leather-bound book strapped to the inside lid of the travelling case. The volume looked like a journal of sorts, often carried by explorers and ornithologists. The beast was over eight feet in length from nose to rump. Its claws measured two and three-quarter inches. The upper canines cut in at an impressive four inches. Flintstaff sat upon a fallen megalith while Cramp called out the figures. After a few moments 'The Change' began.

'We'll have to hurry, Cramp,' urged Flintstaff. 'It's turning back. Quickly, measure the tail. No point putting in the effort if we're not to record it. Ah, well. Um,' said Flintstaff as he watched the beast transform into an extremely large woman. 'I must say, that is the first time I have wrestled with a female of the species.'

'So I can imagine,' muttered Cramp.

'Don't be vulgar, Cramp. Do try to remember this is in the interests of science.'

'Of course, Major. Sorry. Although I'm not sure which shape would've been more intimidating to fight to the death, sir.'

'Good Lord! To think of it! If a naked woman of those dimensions had come at me in a forest in the middle of the night I would have used the revolver on the both of us before she'd come anywhere near.'

'That's what I was afraid of...' said Cramp quietly. Cramp pocketed his tape and walked over to the case. It glowed a sickly

26

yellow from valves pulsing within. The hand-tooled leather of the exterior was scuffed and stained with constant use. Delving into the recesses of the case he found an automated shovel and proceeded to the centre of the stone circle. Setting up the bipod for the shovel he pressed the enamelled green button on its shaft and retreated ten paces. With a hiss of vented steam and the sound of tiny gears gliding into place the shovel bit into the soil.

'There's something bothering me, Cramp. There's something about this body that doesn't make sense,' said Flintstaff tapping the pencil against his teeth.

'Well, me too, sir,' replied Cramp.

'Weren't we here to hunt down a male of the species?' asked Flintstaff.

'Come to think of it, yes, we were. The current head of this order is certainly a male. A Duke Lycaon, if I'm not mistaken.'

'So where are these Shadows? It's unusual for them to leave their strongholds. That's two in two days now, Cramp. '

Cramp made the last few stitches to seal the sheet and they both lowered the body into the shallow grave.

'Mind if I say a prayer, sir?' asked Cramp. 'Seems a bit unjust for the poor lass to be buried here all alone. None too Christian-like, if you don't me saying so?'

'Of course I mind, Cramp,' growled Flintstaff. 'Since when did religion come close to solving a single problem in the history of humanity? We have to dig deeper, Cramp. Far, far deeper than that to find the real Times of Power. If we've been of the order Homo Sapiens for well over thirty thousand years, what is the last three thousand? Ten percent of our wisdom? Nothing compared to the twenty-seven thousand years before that. You have to stop and think once in a while, Cramp.'

'Leave that to you, sir,' retorted Cramp automatically standing to attention. 'Just stick me in the middle of the action, sir. That's where I do best.'

27

Meanwhile, as Cramp collapsed the automated shovel and packed the case, Flintstaff lifted a flap inside the spine of the journal and removed a slender, finger-length crystal. Using the light of the moon he wrote down six symbols on the rock; glowing under their own hidden power. Sergeant Cramp took the proffered journal and re-attached it to the inside of the valise. Once the two men were happy that everything was in order there was only one thing left to do. Cramp coughed uncomfortably and Flintstaff tutted. In one hand Cramp held the valise, and with the other he held the hand of the major.

'We really must find a better way to travel,' said Major Henry Flintstaff-Membrayne.

'Vvvvvvvvvvvvvvvvvvvvvvvvvvvvvvvvvvvvviiiiiiiiip!'

Silence returned to the forest. In the distance, a pair of crimson eyes blinked once and vanished.

FOUR

'Fedududud.'

'...liniment rubbed gently on my temples...'

'Ask Agnes, she might rub it in for you, but I'll be damned if I will,' replied Major Flintstaff as he released Sergeant Cramp's hand and stepped over the neatly embedded glyph set into the white marble floor. Cramp, still clutching the case, gingerly followed suit. Flintstaff walked over to a huge oak work table that dominated the centre of the large room. Cramp placed the case on the table and hummed quietly to himself. Flintstaff frowned, almost managing to merge both eyebrows at the bridge of his aquiline nose. Cramp caught the look of disapproval and stopped humming, leaving his head bobbing gently to his silent ditty. Flintstaff's moustache twitched in irritation.

'We have a problem, Sergeant,' muttered Flintstaff, surveying the room as if in search of an answer. The room consisted of four walls with no windows or doors. There was only a small set of stone steps leading to a hidden door in the ceiling in one corner. However, the room was by no means empty. Apart from the twenty foot table in the centre of the room, three walls were furnished with workshop tables of an industrial persuasion. Brass gleamed and glass glinted under the gaslight. Racks and shelves held equipment, tools and weapons of extraordinary diversity. There were more inventions in this one room than had been revealed at The Great Exhibition of 1851. Most of them had yet to gain patents, yet they served the two gentlemen well.

29

'I suggest we retire to the library, Sergeant. We need to consult The Map.'

'Shall I ring for Agnes to bring us some refreshments, sir? A jellied eel perhaps? Baked oysters? A wedge of stilton?'

'Whatever she has in the pantry, Cramp. Nothing too heavy, though. We need to have our wits about us. There is something fishy going on and I want to get to the root of it.'

'Of course, sir,' answered Cramp as he depressed a button in the wall next to the staircase. Two hydraulic rams began to slide the hatch open as the two gentlemen waited at the bottom of the stairs. A slight hiss of steam announced that they could proceed. Flintstaff, with his journal in hand, led the way upstairs into a brick cellar. The cellar possessed the smell of cellars worldwide; a slightly damp mustiness mixed with lamp oil. Every inch of space held racks of wine and liquors. Cramp walked up to a vintage bottle of Latour, pressed a brick behind it and watched the trap door close with the stone floor slotting neatly back into place, the two men made their way to the next flight of stairs. This led to a very normal oak door which opened into the scullery of No. 35 Chepstow Villas. W11.

Major Flintstaff made his way through the kitchen, along a corridor, past the dining room and into the main hall. He removed his great coat and hung it up. It was only then that he noticed a twelve inch tear across the back. He ran his fingers across it and tutted.

'Blast it!' he said. 'Must have been the werewolf. Cost me a guinea from Fortnum's that did.'

The major then retired to an adjoining library which was lined with mahogany shelves filled with ancient tomes, modern medical journals, scientific treatises, and in a hidden corner some rather savoury volumes on more carnal biological functions. His shoes whispered over the thick pile carpet. The heavy velvet curtains behind his desk had already been drawn, shutting out the choking fog of another winter's night in London. The fireplace crackled quietly, coals glowing amongst the logs like the brooding eyes of a demon. Placing the journal on his study table, the major moved over to the drinks cabinet and took out a lead crystal decanter. He poured two large measures of cognac and with a sigh eased himself into a chair. He was just pulling a cheroot from his silver case when there was a soft knock on the door.

'Enter.'

'I brought a plate of game pie,' said Cramp as he bustled in. 'I thought it a bit late for Agnes to be running around.'

'Excellent. Pop it down here and chuck another log on the fire, will you? I've poured you a glass of cognac.'

'Bless you, Major.'

The two men cut a wedge of pie each and sat in silence while they consumed the mixed remains of pheasant, rabbit, hare and partridge encased in a pastry crust. Once consumed Flintstaff opened his journal and began flicking through the pages.

'So,' said Cramp, 'Not a very successful forty-eight hours, Major.'

'No,' agreed Flintstaff. 'I can understand missing Count Strigoi in his castle. After all, he has been around for quite some time now so he's hardly new to this game. I thought we could surprise him by actually appearing in his chambers. However, either he was warned somehow, or he's gone somewhere.'

'I agree, sir. I don't like it one bit. It's been some time since we missed two in a row. Duke Lycaon doesn't like to leave his forest if he can help it. He spends most of his time peeing on the trees. Do you think they might be meeting?'

'It's a possibility. There are ways we can find out. They're not pleasant, but needs must in situations like these.'

'What do you propose?'

'Before I propose anything I think we should bring out the Map of Baí Zé to refresh our memories.'

'Right-o, sir,' said Cramp as he eased himself from the chair. He walked over to one of the bookshelves on the wall and pulled a rolled chart from a hidden draw beneath the shelves. Together,

31

Cramp and Flintstaff unrolled the vellum and placed Venetian paperweights at each corner. The ancient map was of a world seldom seen by the human eye. Only a few people even knew of its existence and in the past, many of those had not died peacefully in their sleep. There were no borders or nations marked – neither empires nor colonies. The map was topographical in its purest sense. It not only displayed the vegetation and elevation of the world but also human habitation. There were two Sinitic glyphs in the left-hand corner and a sacred geometric symbol called the Flower of Life just like the one set in the floor beneath the cellar. Flintstaff pressed his hand over the first ancient symbol and held it there. Within seconds myriad lines on the map began to glow. The surface moved from two dimensions into three; miniscule mountains rose and rivers flowed. The ocean swelled and the desert winds blew. The planet lived and breathed upon a walnut desk in west London.

'Never tire of watching that,' muttered Cramp as he took a sip of cognac. 'Simply one of the greatest gifts to humanity. Baí Zé really knows his stuff.'

'Hmm,' agreed Flintstaff as he placed his hand over the second symbol. 'This, however, I love.'

The map changed once more. From the corners of the map a ripple of vermillion light spread across the vellum as it entered a fourth dimension. The map now glowed with three hundred and sixty tiny dots the colour of cinnabar – revealing every place of power upon the planet. Pinpricks of light glowed in the deepest jungles of Brazil, the icy wastes of Antarctica, the centre of Australia, deepest Siberia, the Nile basin, London itself, the hills of Jerusalem. Only Flintstaff and Cramp had documented the longitude and latitude of every place. There were many that had never been seen by a white man's eye.

'Now, to know the answer we have to find the question.'

'Exactly, Sergeant. What we do know of the Shadows of the Void is that they are distinctly territorial. Through time immemorial they have carved out their own territories and boundaries. With this in mind, our question must be this: Why now, after millennia, have they up-sticks and gone?'

'If they are on the move, it'll cause all sorts of problems for us to locate them.'

'Agreed. However, we are not the only ones that will face these problems. Humanity might well suffer from such an upheaval in the natural order of things. The people of Europe know how to deal with lycanthropes because they've lived with their threat for many generations, were-tigers in India, were-jaguars in south America etc. etc.'

'Yes, just as those that have knowledge of vampires have the ability to defend themselves against them. The Africans know how to deal with the undead and the tribes of Oceana know how to deal with the Bunyip or Kutji. But if they start moving about, the human population will face unknown terrors.' Cramp stopped gazing at the map and looked up at Flintstaff. 'That's not cricket if you ask me, sir.'

'No it's not, Cramp,' said Flintstaff. 'It's still only a theory. I'd say we need a little more proof before we can act upon our assumptions.'

'Ever the scientist, sir.' said Cramp. 'So where do you think we should look first?'

'I have a feeling that Babba Belani the Bokor will know what is going on...'

'Yes, if ever there was a know-it-all it's him... Haiti then, sir?'

'We've some work to do first, but yes, Haiti it is.'

'We can stock up on tobacco while we're there,' said Cramp. 'Although I do hate those biting insects... never give you a moment's peace.'

'Agreed,' said Flintstaff stubbing out a cheroot. 'I think we should turn in, Sergeant. You get off to bed, I'll finish up here.

'G'night, Major.'

FIVE

'So?' asked Tom, wiping the sweat from his brow.

'So, what?' asked Charlie as he struggled to throw another bale of hay onto the battered pick-up parked in the barn. He loved this place. It was rammed with stuff, including the 'farm pick-up' which Tom and Charlie were allowed to drive in the fields when feeding the cows. 'You always start like that. So? So what?'

'Shini. Do you really think she killed that girl at her school?' asked Tom throwing another bale.

'You're so gullible, Tom,' said Charlie not entirely convinced. 'How's a Ouija board going to kill someone? They don't really work. She's making it up.'

'I dunno, maybe the thought of it drove the girl mad, or she topped herself?' said Tom hefting another bale with ease.

'Nah, I think Shini's just trying to impress us...'

'Er, and since when has any girl, ever needed, or wanted to do something to impress us? Now you mention it, you don't reckon dissing Jack Marvin in front of the whole school was enough then? No one's ever had the guts to confront him.'

'That's because he's a psycho and a coward which is the worst kind of enemy to have.'

'Which *we* have, you mean.'

'Exactly. And maybe Shini's more trouble than she's worth.'

'What?' said Tom turning to his friend. 'You fancy her and you know it.'

'What're you on about, you muppet? 'Course I don't fancy her. She may be rich with a posh accent but it'll take more than that to catch me, Tom.'

'Yeah, sure. I watched you in history and maths. You were staring at her the whole time. I've known you from primary school, Charlie Lawrence, you can't fool me. Still, if you're not interested then maybe I'll ask her out...'

The next bale of hay Charlie picked up never made it onto the pick-up. The bale barrelled into Tom just as he was trying to twist away from it. It bent in two and as the twine loosened it split and fell into slices on the floor. Tom grabbed an armful and dumped it on Charlie's blonde mop. The air filled with dust and flying hay just as Mr. Cramp came back in.

'Oi! What are you two up to? I leave here for five minutes and you're tearing the place apart! Bloody hooligans. Tom, drive the pick-up round to the feeding shed. Come on, Charlie, you can help me with the welding and then we'll fix your bike.'

*****

Charlie locked his bike in the shed and walked up to the flint and brick cottage he called home. The lights were on in the sitting room and kitchen and he could see chimney smoke flowing steadily into the night air as he pulled his trainers off before entering the boot room. He could hear his father talking with someone in the kitchen. It was a voice he didn't recognize. As he walked in all thoughts of a cup of tea and toast vanished.

'I try my hardest, Father, but it doesn't seem to make any difference,' an elderly lady was saying. 'All I can think about is how much he meant to me...'

'In time, Mrs. Burton, I know how much you loved your poodle. But I'm sure you will find that life goes on,' replied Charlie's dad as he wiggled his eyebrows at his son.

Charlie got the hint and walked through the kitchen and down the little corridor to the sitting room. He could see the light on under the crack in the door and pushed it open. The sight that greeted him was almost more than he could bear. His mother was in the process of rubbing oil into one of the hairiest people Charlie had ever seen. Thankfully the man was lying on his front on a collapsible massage bed. Charlie's mum smiled and nodded towards the door he'd just come in. He sighed and trudged upstairs to his bedroom.

Flicking his computer on, he grabbed his headphones and listened to a new track from his favourite band Skindred. As he waited he glanced around his room. It was hardly a sanctuary, hardly *his* at all, and of course it wasn't. The house was owned by the church and had to be respected according to his dad. So there were no posters allowed on the walls because they left nasty marks. The few shelves he had were stacked neatly with second hand games and a few graphic novels. The bed had been made and all his clothes had been washed and folded away in drawers.

Charlie took out his mobile phone. The glass was a spider's web of cracks and he could only just make out the screen beneath it. As usual there was no signal. He had to walk ten paces out into the garden to receive any messages. This was Southeast England in the 21st Century and there was still no signal. Charlie dismantled his phone and swapped the broken glass for some plastic he cut out of an old blister pack. It wasn't perfect but it would do. He glanced up at the computer screen and felt his heart beat faster as he noticed the 'Friend Request' on his home page. It was Shini. Should he accept her as a friend? What he really wanted was to accept so that he could check out her photos. At least then he could look at her without her catching him during class. But if he did accept immediately then it might look like he was too keen. Then again, if she'd made a request to Tom and he'd already accepted then they could be chatting right now… and who knows what Tom might tell her.

Charlie took a deep breath and clicked on 'confirm.' Shini was now a friend. His first message to her was a question. He had to know the truth about Samantha but he felt stupid asking. Shini couldn't be that cold if a girl had died... or maybe she could. Her reply only took a moment.

It read: 'Sucker!'

SIX

Thursday 2nd February 1865.

'Good morning, Agnes,' said Major Flintstaff as he entered the dining room.

'Good morning, sir,' replied Agnes curtseying.

The major took the chair at the head of the table and opened up a copy of the Times. Agnes poured him a cup of tea as he read the front page. The Lithuanians were still in the middle of an uprising and the Americans were finishing off a civil war. Flicking through the pages, Flintstaff scanned the paper for anything unusual, reports of strange sightings or inexplicable occurrences. Agnes filled his plate with kedgeree and placed a rack of toast, butter and anchovy paste within reach.

'Thank-you, Agnes.'

'Good morning, Major,' said Sergeant Cramp as he entered the room. 'Good morning, Agnes. And what delights are we to be treated with this morning?'

'Well, Sergeant Cramp. We have some lovely kedgeree for you and fresh baked bread. Take a seat. That's it. Tea or coffee? Three spoons of sugar and some milk? There we are, Sergeant. Comfortable? Excellent.'

Major Flintstaff glanced up from behind the newspaper and arched a bushy eyebrow. Cramp was beaming with the attention from Agnes until he caught sight of Flintstaff's expression. Cramp cleared his throat and opened up The Illustrated London News. Flintstaff's eyebrow remained raised as he watched Agnes preparing the conserves in individual silver-plated receptacles. Agnes seemed different today. Her usual pallid complexion had been replaced by colour in her cheeks and lips. Flintstaff was unsure if he had ever seen the colour of her hair and yet, this morning, an errant blonde wisp had escaped her bonnet and fallen across her face. He had no idea what age she was and guessed she must be somewhere between twenty to thirty years old. There was something odd about the side of her neck.

'Agnes?' said the major. 'Is that a rash you have on the side of your neck? It looks quite raw.'

'Yes, sir. No. well, it's from…' stuttered Agnes as her face turned puce.

As Flintstaff asked the question Sergeant Cramp had just taken a large mouthful of kedgeree which exploded from his mouth like a mortar and hit the centre of his newspaper. Cramp followed this with a coughing fit so tremendous that Major Flintstaff was compelled to come to his aid. After a vigorous bout of back-slapping Cramp managed to inhale some air that did not consist mainly of rice and fish. Agnes was nowhere to be seen.

'Honestly, Cramp. You really must be more careful,' said the major.

'Well, I thought you were asleep to be honest.'

'Asleep? What on earth are you talking about?'

'I didn't want to do it right in your face. I know how you feel about these things.'

'In my face? Of course you wouldn't want to cough in my face. Especially when you've got a mouth filled with kedgeree. Me, asleep?' mumbled Flintstaff as he returned to his paper. 'You're the one who must have been asleep. It's not hard to eat, you know. Chew, swallow, breathe through the nose…'

*****

It was early afternoon before Major Flintstaff and Sergeant Cramp were ready to leave. They had spent two days in the study pouring over maps and cross-checking references in the journal. Once they had descended into their room under the cellar, the two men busied themselves with choosing what equipment might be needed for the mission ahead. Both men wore frock coat ensembles with knee length boots and pith helmets. Sergeant Cramp opened the travelling case with care. It hissed vented steam and valves glowed from within. Cramp placed their weapons of choice inside while Major Flintstaff removed the crystal from the spine of the journal and walked over to the 'Flower of Life' inlaid in the marble floor. Flintstaff removed a small cover from a cast iron pipe set into the wall about three feet from the ground. A single beam of sunlight shone through the opening and onto the crystal. At first the crystal refracted rainbows of colour which slowly coalesced into four specific glyphs.

Major Henry Flintstaff-Membrayne removed his steam-powered revolver and flipped open the modified cylinder. Spinning it he checked all thirty-eight chambers were filled before snapping it shut and replacing it in its holster.

'Ready?'

'Just about, sir,' replied Cramp. 'I'll pop the journal back into the case and we should be ready for the off.'

Stepping inside the Flower of Life, Cramp grasped the major's hand and waited for his companion to read the glyphs glowing in their own light on the floor in front of them. Sergeant Camp took a deep breath before experiencing a sensation similar to his body being turned inside out with a rusty spoon...

*****

'Feddudduddudd... Splut!'

A stench of death hit the adventurers' nostrils so total, so cloying, it corrupted everything it touched. They stood in a fetid mangrove

41

swamp filled with the hum of blood-sucking Bot-flies, mosquitoes as big as vultures, and toads that croaked their turgid love-songs. There lay black mud that could suck a mule into its very bowels without a sound; the only trace a few fat black bubbles. A place of heat and torpor. A place of magic. A place of Vodou!

'Oh. This doesn't look good,' said Cramp as he fought off a hungry insect the size of a humming-bird.

'Can't see a blasted thing, Sergeant. Wood for the trees and all that. I'll take a hoik up this here mangrove and see which way is out.'

Sergeant Cramp looked down upon the soggy ground. The case lay at his feet, sinking gently into the mud. He glanced up at Flintstaff struggling to gain a hold with his boots on the slimy tap roots. Off to the left he could see an ancient wooden hut on stilts surrounded by a rusty iron railing fence. A few rectangular slabs of stone leaning over. A graveyard. A movement.

'Could you confirm a suspicion of mine, sir? About ten o'clock from where you're looking now,' whispered Cramp.

'Yes, Sergeant. Definitely a member of the undead,' shouted the major from the top of the tree. 'You can tell by the lurching movement. Probably a zombie of sorts. Seems to have heard us too. Heading your way. I'd check in the case if I were you.'

'Marvellous,' muttered Cramp as he bent over the case and flipped the latches. Above his head Cramp could hear Flintstaff's revolver warming up before a barrage of bullets ripped through the foliage. A shattered branch bounced off Cramp's helmet. 'Nothing like the quiet approach,' grumbled Cramp as he sifted through the case. 'Cross-weave thermal underwear? No. Tsarina's tiara? No. Don't even know what that is...'

The bullets had little effect on the approaching zombie as it lumbered onwards. A few extra holes didn't seem to bother it. Flies buzzed around its head, crawling in and out of empty eye sockets.

'Hurry, Sergeant. It's almost upon you,' warned the major, and then added reflectively, 'Lucky they don't seem to know how to run isn't it? He'd have had you by now.'

Cramp fumbled desperately in the valise until he grasped something solid. He hoped it would be dangerous, whatever it was. The zombie lurched at Cramp, knocking his helmet off. Cramp swivelled and presented his unidentified weapon.

'Looks like it'll have to be the secateurs,' he said.

'Ah, yes,' reminisced Flintstaff from the safety of the tree. 'A Gold at last year's Kensington Flower Show... no point cutting off the arms, Sergeant. It's the head you have to go for. You see. Even when you cut them off they still keep a grip on your throat.'

'Just a tick, sir...' gargled Cramp.

'Well, I can see two more on their way, so I'd better come down and give you a hand. I was hoping to stay out of the mud, but there you go.'

Sergeant Cramp had just finished secateuring the zombie's head from its neck by the time the major descended the tree. Flintstaff punted the head between two trees into a bilious swamp beyond. The head floated for a second or two before air bubbles plopped out of the eye sockets and sank. As Cramp dragged himself out of the muck he had been rolling around in he saw that the major seemed quite pleased with himself. Cramp's face infused with blood. Less than thirty yards away the two zombies were wading towards them. Flintstaff caught Cramp's expression.

'Just remembering the footie match against the Fellows of Merton in Mob Quad,' he said as he flipped open the lid of the case. In one swift movement he pulled out a weapon much like a crossbow. He pressed a green button and turned a brass dial to 'Maximum'. Cramp stared at it in bewilderment.

'I was specifically looking for that. I remember placing it right at the top of the case so I could find it easily.'

'You just don't look properly,' replied Flintstaff as the gears wound the torsion bars backwards. 'Disc or Boomerang?'

43

'Very kind to ask, sir. I would like to see the boomerang, if you don't mind.'

'Rather!'

The major placed a slim metal-edged boomerang into the firing groove. The zombies were less than fifteen yards away. Green drool escaped from perforated cheeks as they groaned and snarled at the two gentlemen. Major Flintstaff brought the weapon to his shoulder and aimed. Sergeant Cramp pulled on a chainmail mitten. Flintstaff squeezed the trigger. The boomerang sliced through the neck of the first zombie and disappeared from sight. The only way the gentlemen knew it was still flying was the hum of it cutting through air and foliage. The struck zombie swayed momentarily before dropping in a heap *sans* head where it fizzled into ash. Sergeant Cramp stepped to the side of the major just as the second zombie was preparing to tear them to pieces. The humming sound grew louder and louder. The zombie, attracted by noise, cocked its head and tried to lift an eyebrow that had rotted away months before. Cramp lifted his gloved hand and caught the boomerang two inches away from Major Flintstaff's neck.

Ignoring the zombie, Cramp took out a hankie and attempted to wipe the rotten green juices that had splattered across the major's face. Once completed, he handed the boomerang back and turned once more to the remaining zombie. The head was dangling by a few sinews and the zombie had enough forethought to hold it in both hands and try to slot it back onto its neck. Cramp pulled the secateurs out of his pocket and carefully snipped the last remaining sinews connecting it with its life of undead servitude. The corpse slumped to the ground and turned to ash.

'Let's go and see if there's anyone home, shall we?' said Major Flintstaff as he reloaded the crossbow with a razor-edged disc.

SEVEN

The hut sat upon rotting stilts and leant drunkenly to the right. Around the base of the house grew copious Datura plants with their bell-shaped flowers hanging forlornly. Sergeant Cramp held the case in his left hand as he squelched through the ankle-deep mud as quietly as possible. Major Flintstaff was busy circling the building anti-clockwise, armed with the modified crossbow. From the outside the hut looked to have two rooms and a veranda encircling it. The shutters on the two windows were broken and hanging from rusted hinges. The front door was closed. The pailing roof was quietly rusting away while creepers from nearby trees clambered across the corrugations, seeking ingress. There was a single set of steps to Cramp's left; where the major was heading for. A wire was tied all along the veranda from post to post, upon which hung the remains of snakes, birds, toads, bats, rats and puffer fish among other less identifiable creatures.

'Nice place to sit, of an evening...' remarked Cramp, 'to catch malaria.' He glanced across at his companion and saw Flintstaff give the signal. Cramp moved closer to one of the windows of the house as Flintstaff pulled the crossbow into his shoulder and released the safety catch. 'Hello?' called Cramp. 'Anybody there? I seem to be a bit lost.'

There was a sound of something knocking against the window frame. A curtain was torn down from inside and then the glass shattered before an irate face appeared at the window. The zombie was certainly fresher than the three they had previously encountered.

This one even wore a bonnet and a blue floral dress. The dress could have done with a wash, but otherwise she might have been acceptable company in a London tea shop.

'Hello, madam,' said Cramp lowering the suitcase and doffing his helmet. 'I was wondering if I might be able to speak to your master?'

The zombie flailed her arms out of the window in a vain attempt at grabbing Cramp who was standing ten feet below her. Flintstaff, meanwhile, was using the distraction to creep up the rotten steps on the other side of the house. He tip-toed across the veranda until he was facing the front door. With a mighty 'crack' he kicked the door as hard as he could. The door splintered open and there, silhouetted by the window opposite, was his target.

'Catch!' shouted Flintstaff as he squeezed the trigger of his crossbow. The disc flashed through the darkness of the hut and out the window. He reloaded the weapon with another disc before entering the gloomy interior. The body of the zombie hung half out of the window. Otherwise there was nothing of any danger he could see. He heard Cramp wheezing as he climbed the stairs behind him.

'Been ages since our last cricket match, Major. I do miss my time in silly mid-off. Glad to see I haven't lost the old catching magic though,' said Cramp as he proudly raised the head of the former zombie maid.

'Jolly good,' said the major as he inched his way round the living area and checked in the bedroom for signs of life and death. 'Clear in here. Well, clear, but certainly not tidy. Hurry, we don't have much time before it turns to ash.'

Cramp plopped the head onto the rough wooden table that stood in the middle of the room. The cupboards were mostly bare with a few rusting tins and chipped enamel plates. A blackened cauldron stood beside the fireplace, hanging from chains. Cramp placed the suitcase on the table next to the head and poked his face inside the huge pot. He wrinkled his nose at the smell of putrefaction, instantly regretting his curiosity. Flintstaff flipped the latches of the case open and placed the crossbow back inside. After a few moments of rummaging he pulled out a small bottle of gas, a Bunsen burner, three glass receptacles, glass piping, three vices, a clamp, three rubber bungs and four sealed jars; each identified with an obscure Balinese script. Last of all, he pulled a finely wrought brass box the size of a small carriage clock. Sergeant Cramp began constructing the apparatus while his companion measured out a green liquid into the first receptacle, a blue powder into the next and a fine white powder into the third. Each of them was connected to the other by a glass pipe and their tops sealed with a rubber bung. Cramp leant over and peered at the various chemicals.

'I say, what on earth is that one, might I ask?' said Cramp enthusiastically.

'Salt.'

'Oh.'

Flintstaff finished the apparatus by slipping the last glass tube through the brass case and into the right ear of the severed head. He nodded as Cramp struck a match and lit the Bunsen burner. A dagger of blue flame cradled the glass containing the green liquid. Soon enough it began to bubble and evaporate before cooling and dripping into the jar containing the blue powder. The blue powder effervesced and expanded until it began dripping onto the salt in the next jar. This in turn reacted energetically forming an orange liquid that bled through the last glass pipe. As it poured through the brass box it exited the other side as clear as water where it decanted into the ear of the decapitated head.

Closed eyes opened. Lips parted and a grey-green tongue flopped onto the table. Opened eyes looked down at the tongue and opened wider.

'Would you look at that,' muttered Major Flintstaff. 'How on earth are we going to understand a bloody thing she says?'

Cramp sighed, turned off the Bunsen burner and pulled the glass tube out of the ear of the severed head. The woman's eyes swivelled left and right and her mouth opened and closed like a beached fish. Flintstaff tapped his fingers on the table until the eyes of the woman finally closed once more. Cramp hunted in the case until he produced a curved needle and thread. After a few minutes of cursing and sweat the tongue was more or less stitched back in situ. The Bunsen burner lit and the chemicals bubbled and fizzed. Dead eyes opened once more.

'Well blogger ble blackwards,' said the head. 'One minute I'm doing the bleeding ironing for old Mista Fancy-Pants and I'm thinking to myself what a right old day this is with all this heat and little Roger with the flu and my dead-weight husband running after cabin boys when he should be planting cabbages cause lord knows what we're meant to eat in this godforsaken flea-pit out in the middle of some blooming great ocean and a million miles from home and a decent drop of gin and...'

The tube was rapidly pulled from the jabbering head once more.

'A trifle less heat this time please, Sergeant,' implored Flintstaff as he put a pinch more blue powder in the second container.

The eyes opened once more. They glared up at the sergeant.

'What've you done to me?' asked the woman.

'We cut off your head, madam. Not for any personal reasons, except that you would have tried to kill us had we entered this hut unarmed. You see, you're dead.'

'So how come I'm still talking? Can't talk if I'm dead now, can I?'

'Yes, good point. The thing is you *were* alive and then you died and then you were risen from the dead...'

'Like Jesus?'

'Well, technically he didn't actually rise from the dead as a zombie but was resurrected... it's an allegory...' said Cramp.

'Listen, you mad old bint,' interrupted Flintstaff impatiently. 'You were turned into a zombie by Babba Belani, a Bokor. A practitioner of the forbidden religion. He should be here in this house, but he isn't. Instead, he hired you and three other goons to guard the place while he's away. What we want to know is where did he go?'

'I'm a zombie?' asked the maid looking crestfallen.

48

'Don't worry it's extremely temporary,' said Flintstaff. 'Now, where is he? Think, woman, think.'

'I… I remember the taste of almonds. Pain and darkness. The sound of earth hitting wood. A tall man in a top hat with white teeth and the devil's smile. He had a ticket in his hand…'

'Anything else?'

'Something about a journey, leaving the island…'

'We're running out of salt, Major…'

'Any mention of a country?'

'Indies… Indians… Indus…'

The eyes closed slowly, and with it the last words and memories of an unknown serving maid, mother and wife. Major Flintstaff began dismantling the equipment, lost in thought.

'What do you think, sir?'

'I'm not sure yet, Cramp. Dispose of this head, while I pack this away, will you.'

'Sir,' replied Cramp automatically. He grimaced at the head and delicately picked it up by the ears. He looked around the room, dithering. Cramp knew he had less than a minute before the Major would remark on his tardiness. Spotting the cauldron he popped the head inside and finding the lid, covered it.

The two men sat at the table and each lit a cheroot. The dense smoke eventually dissuaded the constant assault from a variety of blood-sucking insects.

'The Indies makes the most sense,' stated Cramp. 'It's local.'

'And yet, for some reason, my intuition is telling me the least likely. It does not take into account that we have now been to confront the Duke in Transylvania, the Count in France, Babba Belani here, and none of them are home. I think we might need to go and have a look at the map. There's something going on and I believe India may be our next destination.'

'Jolly good, sir. Agnes told me we're out of pepper; we can pick some up while we're there.'

49

EIGHT

Saturday 31ˢᵗ January 2015.

'I still don't see why I had to come,' grumbled Charlie as he gazed out at the passing countryside. Trees whipped past the passenger window of his mum's old Ford. The branches were still bare and spring was a dream away. Winter dragged on and on. His mum hummed along to some old song from the seventies.

'I know you're upset, but it's not my fault the Cramps are away this weekend.'

'Just my luck,' muttered Charlie. If Tom wasn't off to a farm show up north somewhere they could've had a wicked weekend gaming.

'Look, Charlie, Aunt Maud's really not that terrible. Be polite and help her out a bit.'

'It's going to be the longest weekend of my life.'

'If you got out of your bedroom and made friends then you'd have more options wouldn't you? And just remember that one day you'll get very old too, Charlie-Barnes, and then you'll live for the days when people come to visit you. You know she gets lonely in that house of hers.'

'I'm not surprised,' he said. 'The place looks like it's straight out of a horror movie. Anyway, how come dad hates her so much?'

'Aunt Maud never really thought much of your dad, I'm afraid,' said Charlie's mum. She gathered a stray lock of her blonde hair and tucked it behind her ear.

'Didn't she look after you when you were my age?'

'Yes. She did. My mummy and daddy died when I was sixteen. It was the summer of '86 and they went sailing around the Scilly Isles while I was at a summer camp in Eastbourne. Aunt Maud came to pick me up and gave me the news…'

Charlie looked over at his mum and suddenly regretted asking. He could see that his mum was no longer seeing the road ahead, although that was where she was looking. The sadness in her face grew as all the years since her parents' death disappeared. She was back to being a vulnerable teenager, taken to one side during an activity at summer camp. A girl who was led into the manager's office where Aunt Maud was waiting for her – to change her life forever.

'I lived with her for about two years and then I took a year out between school and university. I travelled mostly during that year and then went to study at Lancaster, where I met your dad.'

'Was she nice to you?'

'Yes, she was. In her own way. She told me to question everything and believe in nothing unless I could see it for myself. But she was a bit paranoid and a bit eccentric. We didn't exactly fall out, but me marrying your dad meant I had to choose sides, I'm afraid.'

'So why doesn't she like dad?'

'It's complicated, Darling. Maud's not a religious person. When I brought your dad down to meet her he was fresh out of studying theology and very serious about his calling. Maud and he fought like cat and dog over lunch and both of them realized that they had nothing more to say to each other. Maud was just being protective over me and wasn't sure your dad was up to the job. She said I'd be second best as the church would always come first.'

'I guess that makes me third best then,' muttered Charlie.

'What?' asked his mum as she took a right turn down an overgrown single-track lane. About half a mile in the distance sat the farmhouse.

'Nothing.'

The diminutive farmhouse nestled at the bottom of a coombe surrounded by fields; its roof bowed under the weight of years. Charlie looked at it with some distaste. He'd only been here a couple of times in his life and never to stay the night. He imagined a young couple driving across the country and suddenly running out of petrol. They walk to the farmhouse for help. The door creaks open as the young man knocks... etc. etc. until there's the sound of chainsaws and buckets of blood wash across the movie screen.

'How old is Aunt Maud?' asked Charlie. What he was really thinking was how on earth an old woman managed to live in the middle of nowhere on her own with no transport. He didn't want to say that though as his mum had mentioned her moving in with them when she got too old to look after herself. That was the only time he'd ever heard his dad use the f-word.

'Um, I think she was born in 1930. Yes, that's right. She'll be eighty-five this spring,' said his mum as the car thumped into a pothole; an arc of mud splashed into the brambles on the side of the road.

They parked the car next to the dilapidated barn beside the house. The wind was blowing the rain diagonally across the gravel drive as they both took a breath and ran from the car to the stable door of the farmhouse. Charlie reached the door first and struggled with the latch. His mum gently nudged him to one side as she put her weight against the bottom half of the door and pulled the top half towards her. The latch sprung open and they both tumbled into the warmth of the kitchen.

'It's a knack,' said his mum. 'The wood swells up in winter.'

'Why not replace it with a proper door,' said Charlie as he shook water out of his tangled hair.

'That door, young man, has kept the weather out of this house for over a century,' said Great Aunt Maud as she stood in the doorway of the pantry. She was wearing an old pair of wellie boots that were covered in mud, brown corduroy trousers and a thick knitted jumper that almost hung down to her knees. It had gaping holes in the

53

elbows. The kitchen was awash with old newspapers, letters, scraps of paper, old cartons and a hundred other things. The place was a dump.

'Exactly,' said Charlie turning towards his oldest living relative. 'Time for a new one.'

'Oh, I see, we have a smarty-pants coming to visit do we?' said Maud. Her eyes glanced from Charlie's mum and back. They were chestnut brown and sparkled with intelligence.

'Hello, Auntie,' said his mum as she embraced Maud.

'Don't worry, Charlie, I'm not going to ask you for a hug and a kiss,' said Maud. 'I know it's the stuff of nightmares for a young man to have to kiss an old lady, especially with a hairy mole on her cheek.'

'Auntie!' admonished Charlie's mum.

'Please, Auntie Maud, don't go on about it,' begged Charlie as he tried not to focus on the growth erupting from his aunt's cheek.

Maud filled a kettle from the tap and placed it on the Aga. An ancient-looking German Shepherd was lying as close to the heat as possible. She popped open one of the oven doors and a smell of heaven filled the room. Even Charlie couldn't stop from licking his lips as the smell of fresh-baked bread wafted past his nose. Maud cleared a pile of newspapers from the kitchen table and pulled chairs out for them to sit.

'How have you been, Maud?' asked his mum.

'Fine, dear. Fine. I take Ruben out every day and collect firewood from the copse in East Field. The cats keep the rats out of the house and Mr. Stevens comes by with my supplies once a week.'

'Mr. Stevens? Is he a home help or something?'

'Home help? Don't be silly, girl. He supplies organic food from the local area. A box of whatever's in season delivered to the home once a week. I found him in Blewbury. Very nice man. He has long hair, you know. Reminds me of the Sixties,' then she added conspiratorially, 'I think he might be a hippy.'

'And you're not too lonely?' asked Charlie's mum as she sat on one of the wooden chairs at the kitchen table.

'Lonely?' repeated Maud as if tasting the word. 'Alone doesn't mean lonely, Sarah. You should understand that. Anyway, I have Ruben and the two cats and the field mice in the walls when it gets very cold. Outside is the whole world, so why should I be lonely?'

'You just seem so isolated here.'

'Do you know that every morning I can spot over twenty species of birds in the garden and hedgerows? I have a badger's den in the copse and the foxes live in the woods past West Field. There are squirrels and rabbits galore and the red kites glide above the house every day. I even saw a weasel the other evening.'

'Well my offer still stands, Maud,' said Charlie's mum.

'Now then, a nice cup of tea for all and fresh bread with homemade jam,' said Maud dismissing the last comment.

'I can't, Maud. I have to rush. We've got to catch the train from Reading. Be good, Charlie,' said his mum ruffling his hair. 'I'll pick you up tomorrow evening.'

And with a click of the latch his mum was gone and Charlie was left alone with a very old woman and a very old dog in a very old farm. Maud eased herself into a seat opposite him and poured two cups of tea. She pushed one cup across the table with her eyes fixed on Charlie. He looked at his hands trying to ignore her and wondered just how uncomfortable he could possibly feel. This was worse than being in the Principal's office...

'Don't worry, Charlie,' said Maud quietly as she spread jam on the bread. 'I understand.'

'Understand what?' said Charlie checking his mobile. No signal.

'How little you want to be here.'

'Well... no, it's not... you know. I...'

'Your mum's told me you're not very good with people, Charlie. It's okay to be shy.'

'I'm not shy, I just... like being on my own.'

'And so do I,' agreed Aunt Maud. 'Yet here we are, both wishing we were alone. But we're not. So instead of moping about we can either sit in different rooms, or you can help me chop some wood for the night and I'll treat you to some of my spiced cider.'

'Okay,' said Charlie, thinking that sitting in different rooms might've been the better option.

Charlie spent the rest of the morning in the open-sided barn splitting logs with an axe and then using a smaller one to chop kindling. Maud left to cook them lunch. He soon removed his jacket and then his hoodie as he swung the axe back and forth. He couldn't help enjoying what he was doing. He didn't like sports but this was different. It wasn't long before he was chopping the blade through the heads of demons, orcs and knights like he had in Skyrim. It was a good way to pass the time. His mum and dad hated his love of gaming. They said he was 'an addict' and thought he should be *doing something useful* instead of wasting his time. It was pointless trying to explain.

'Lunch!' Maud shouted from the door.

Charlie let the axe thud into the chopping block with satisfaction, pulled his jacket on and hefted the log basket back to the house. As he was opening the door he noticed three symbols engraved in the wood above. They were faded and weather-worn.

'What're those marks cut above the door?' asked Charlie as he placed the wood basket next to the fireplace in the sitting room.

'I have no idea,' said Maud as they sat down to eat. 'They've been there for as long as I can remember.' They both sat in silence while they ate. Eventually Maud spoke. 'Charlie, tell me, how are things at school?'

'Lame,' replied Charlie between mouthfuls of veggie casserole.

'You can do better than that... you're mother mentioned you getting a hard time there.'

'You try being the son of a priest.'

'No, thank you! Is it really that bad?'

'It can be... It's okay, I suppose.'

'Do you have many friends there?'

'Well, there's Tom Cramp. He's my best friend, I suppose. His dad owns the farm next to the church.'

'Did you say your friend's name is Cramp?' asked Maud. She looked startled.

'Yeah... stupid name isn't it? He gets loads of grief at school.'

'How long have you known him?' asked Maud. She'd put her knife and fork down and was staring at him intently.

'Since primary school,' replied Charlie. The colour seemed to have drained from Aunt Maud's face and she was definitely looking at him in a strange way. 'Are you alright?'

'I don't know,' she replied standing. 'I need some air, Charlie. Do you mind looking after the house? I'll not be long.'

And with that she grabbed a coat from the back of her chair and stepped outside. Charlie stared at the door and shrugged. Old people were well weird.

*****

'I'm not going up there,' said Charlie as he wobbled at the top of an old step ladder and shone a torch into the dusty loft. 'Why can't you just tell me...'

'Well, well,' interrupted Maud from below. 'I never thought a relative of mine would ever be such a lily-livered cry-baby. It must come from your father's side.'

'My dad is not a coward,' replied Charlie angrily. 'He looks at dead people all the time.'

'Is that after they listen to his Sunday sermons?' asked Maud.

Even Charlie burst out laughing. Charlie swung the torch around the opening of the loft. The step ladder wasn't tall enough and he'd have to climb up inside. He wanted to be sure there were no huge wolf spiders ready to jump on him. He wasn't scared, but no one wanted spiders running over their face. With a sigh of resignation he pulled himself up into the loft. Once he had one leg up he managed to haul himself into the space.

'There should be a light switch near the opening,' Maud said from below.

Charlie found the switch and turned it on. The light came on, barely piercing the darkness around him. The bulb was covered in dust. A clutter of Christmas decorations and empty cardboard boxes surrounded the hatch. As he turned he nearly fell back through the opening because in the corner of the loft was a ghost. His body surged with adrenaline just as he realised it was a huge old wasps' nest. The swirls of grey-papered mulch transformed the nest into an amorphous ghostly apparition. Making sure he trod on the eaves, Charlie found what he'd been sent up there for. A case. Upon closer inspection it was more of a large trunk. It had a name printed on the lid in faded white paint.

Capt. R.L.W. FLINTSTAFF.

'Found it.'

'I wouldn't risk trying to getting it down, Charlie, but if you find anything interesting inside then bring it,' said Maud. 'There should be some letters...'

'Okay,' replied Charlie. He brushed a finger across the top and glanced at the thick crescent of dust stuck to his finger. Below the name was an insignia depicting two fat-bladed knives crossing one another with a number '7' above them. Wiping the dirt on his jeans, he placed the torch beside the trunk and then studied the two clasps. They were stiff but unlocked. The clasps snapped open on their hidden springs and made Charlie jump. He pushed the lid open until leather straps inside took the weight off it and he stared in wonder at the contents.

A tray sat snugly in the top of the footlocker with a bundle of letters, a green leather-bound diary dated 1942 and a small box with a medal in it. There were also some black and white photographs, a compass and other military paraphernalia. Charlie flicked through yellowed photographs of a Edwardian-looking family dressed completely in black with white frills. Another showed a handsome young man with two lightly-armed Asian soldiers; another of a fighter plane banking in the sky, and one of the same man on a camel with the pyramids in the distance.

Charlie put it all beside him and lifted the tray out, using the finger holes on each side, and lowered it to the floor. There was a delicate white sheet of crepe paper covering the contents. A pristine uniform lay folded within, smelling of age and some kind of chemical that made his nose itch. Charlie assumed it was an officer's dress uniform from what little he knew of such things. Feeling beneath the uniform he found a wooden box about a foot long and eight inches wide and four inches deep. It had two small hooks which he opened.

Inside was a rosewood-hilted knife tucked inside a worn leather scabbard with two smaller, black-handled tools tucked in beside it. Charlie lifted the weapon out of the box and was surprised at how heavy it was; at least until he pulled the knife free. The thick blade glowed a dull red in the light of the attic bulb. The curved cutting edge was heavily weighted towards the tip. At the bottom of the blade, next to the hilt, was an ellipse with a single tooth. Charlie carefully placed a thumb against the edge. He felt the hairs on the back of his neck rise and a chill spread down his spine. He shivered and glanced down at his thumb. A droplet of blood stained the silver sheen of the blade. Charlie's vision swam as he stared at his own blood, dizziness sweeping through his mind, his breathing ragged.

There was a loud humming in Charlie's ears and every time he drew breath he could smell diesel and gun powder, burning rubber and tin. A flat, intense heat struck him like a physical blow. He could see black smoke streaming across a wasteland of sand and bleached rock. The wreckage of tanks and trucks with bodies blackened and bloated hanging from barbed wire stretched as far as the eye could see in the shimmering heat. A stiflingly sweet smell of decomposition

59

invaded his nostrils making him retch. Clouds of flies swirled in the wind. At the edge of his hearing he could hear the slow, deep rumble of something laughing. It was the worst thing Charlie had ever heard in his life. He could feel his teeth chattering and his spine shrinking; every bone turning to powder in the face of such terrible, callous joy. There was a presence surrounding him, enveloping him, crushing him until he was paralyzed and suffocating.

'Charlie, Charlie! Snap out of it, this instance!'

'Mum, help me. I don't know what's happening to me...' moaned Charlie as he slumped to the floor.

'It's not your mother, it's Maud.'

'Where's Mum? I need to go to hospital. I've got a brain tumour or something...'

'Charlie, listen to me. You're okay. You're mother's gone, remember? You've been up here an hour already. I want you to bring down the journal and the letters. I can't stand on this step ladder any longer; I'll fall off. Now come down carefully and I'll make you a nice cup of tea. We need to have a little chat.'

Charlie's vision swum in and out of the desert and the cobwebbed world of the attic. He placed the Kukri knife back into its sheath and jammed it into the back of his jeans and covered it with his hoodie. With the letters and the book he crawled through the narrow space until he reached the loft hatch. Below him was the concerned face of his aunt staring up at him. She smiled encouragingly and raised her hands to take hold of the things he'd brought. Charlie passed everything down before gingerly lowering his legs until they touched the top step of the ladder. He turned off the torch and the light and pulled the trap door shut.

Charlie followed Maud downstairs to the sitting room. A pot of tea and two cups were already sat on the table, steam curling into the dusty air. Maud sat in the armchair and placed the letters and book on the table beside the tea. She poured two cups of tea and dosed them with a liberal amount of sugar and milk.

'I want you to tell me what happened,' said Maud. 'Then, I'll tell you everything I know.'

'Where's Mum? I need to go to hospital...'

'I told you. She'll be back tomorrow. You're okay, Charlie. I think I know what's happened. Now, come on. Out with it.'

'I was just looking through the trunk when I felt hot and dizzy. I thought I was in a war, in a desert. Everywhere I looked were dead people and burning tanks. I was going to be sick, but then I felt there was someone nearby... or something. It... it was laughing. It was happy that all these people had died. The stench of death...' Charlie couldn't continue. He dropped his head into his hands and ran his fingers through his hair; to try to stop them shaking.

'The footlocker up there belonged to my brother, Robert. He was a captain in the Ghurkhas,' said Maud softly. 'Unfortunately, he died during the second battle of El Alamein. The medics found his body without a single scratch. They assumed he died of a heart attack on the battlefield, but it wasn't true... it was the desert that killed him. Or something in the desert...'

'Auntie, you're not making any sense. In fact, you're scaring me a bit.'

'That's good, Charlie,' said Maud looking into his bright blue eyes. 'You need to be.'

Maud opened up the back of the diary. She squinted at the pages, moving it back and forth from her face to focus on the writing inside. Charlie sat and watched, feeling the hidden kukri digging into his tailbone. Finally, Maud passed the open book over to Charlie.

'Read this,' she said.

'21st October. 1942,' began Charlie as he deciphered the precisely inked words. 'I fear this will be the last night I am able to write. Another vision this morning, when I was scratched by one of the many robber cats that hide amongst the boxes and tents. I found myself spontaneously transported to what looked like a huge stone

61

shaft. I was looking down upon two men and they seemed to be trying to communicate with me. I couldn't understand what they were saying but it seemed as if they were warning me of something. It was then I felt a presence behind me. Something terrible, something that induced utter despair. Just as I turned I glimpsed a three-headed devil, pale blue in colour... it was then I awoke. One of the corporals found me nursing the scratch and staring into nothing. Fortunately, out here, it is quite common to see soldiers staring into space, so I am seen as no more mad than the rest.

We are ready for the big push and my boys can hardly wait to take revenge on Jerry for Mersa Matruh and Gazal last June. I wish I could feel the same, but I know there is more in this desert than first meets the eye. There is something hidden in the shimmering heat upon the horizon and it is neither German nor Italian. It is far older, and hungry for destruction. I fear the curse of the Flintstaffs has followed me here. Whatever it is out there in the wastes, it has found me. Should I not survive, I have given orders for my belongings to be sent home to my beloved little Maud.

How I miss your smile. Our summer days on the farm. I miss you, sweet sister of mine. When you read this, Maud, stay safe. Use every trick in the book to keep them away. One day our family will overcome the tragedies that *dog our every generation. All my love, Robert.'*

Charlie remained staring at the last entry of the diary. His heart was thudding erratically. He re-read one sentence again. *Three-headed devil, pale blue.* Hadn't he just killed one of those in his computer game? That was too weird. He looked up from the book and saw the tears running down his aunt's cheeks as she dabbed at them with a crumpled hankie.

'I'm sorry, Auntie. I didn't mean to make you cry.'

'You didn't make me cry, Charlie. It's Robert. I miss him. You know, he used to make me cry laughing growing up here with Mother and Father, and your grandmother, Rose... They're all gone now, Charlie. Only me left.'

'I still don't understand what's going on. So Robert had visions too?'

'When he reached puberty it started. Not often, but hurting himself seemed to trigger it.'

'I had one yesterday, when I fell off my bicycle,' he said showing the purple bump high on his forehead. 'I was in a hot country, but it was very different from the desert I just saw. It seemed more tropical... and there was a big white temple and huge red rocks everywhere.'

'It seems one person in every generation of Flintstaffs has these visions. Robert wrote most of his down in the journal you're holding. There's a section titled: Dreams.'

'But I'm not a Flintstaff... My name's Lawrence.'

'And yet you're a direct descendant of the Flintstaff family through my sister and now your mother. The blood runs true. I remember your mother had visions for a while but I doubt she'll talk about them. They started after her parents died and she came to live here. I told her they were hereditary and she even made some attempts to understand them. That was, until she met your father...'

63

Charlie could hear the scorn she felt for his father in her words and he experienced a hot flush of anger against her. He managed to keep his mouth shut and waited for her to continue.

'He convinced her they were psychotic episodes or something. I knew they weren't but your father dismissed anything I had to say out of hand. That's why we never speak.'

'Dad says you've lost it,' admitted Charlie, feeling he was about to go the same way.

'I can't blame him. Who wouldn't?'

'So what can I do? There must be a way of stopping them.'

'First, let me tell you everything I know. You mentioned earlier that your friend's name is Cramp. I can tell you now that this isn't the first time I've heard that name, although it's been many years since I heard it last.

'About a hundred and fifty years ago two gentlemen went missing. It wasn't big news, although enquiries were made and it was mentioned in a newspaper or two. You see, those two men were adventurers and it was quite easy to fall off the edge of the world without anyone knowing how, why, or where in those days. The reason it did make the news was that rumour had it they were overly interested in the occult.'

'So? What's that got to do with anything?' asked Charlie exasperated.

'Their names were Major Henry Flintstaff-Membrayne and Sergeant Arthur Cramp.'

'So you're saying our relatives were friends?'

'It does seem so.'

'And they both disappeared a long time ago.'

'Yes. From the family stories handed down by my grandfather it's believed they died fighting some kind of evil entity.'

'Yeah, right,' scoffed Charlie. 'I'm not stupid, Auntie. They don't exist in the real world. And the names are just a coincidence.'

'People like to believe in coincidences,' said Maud. 'We, as a family, cannot. There are no coincidences. Oh, I don't expect you to grasp it all now, this instance, Charlie. Someone, or something, is trying to make you aware of its presence. You had a vision describing where my brother died in the desert and you *felt* what killed him. I have spent my life hiding here, Charlie; living with an inadequate amount of knowledge that I could do very little with. You mention the name Cramp to the only living person that knows there is a connection between our families. What are the chances? All I know is that there is something out there and 'They' are destined to be our enemies.'

'But how's it all possible? None of it makes any sense.'

'When your grandparent's died in that sailboat I knew it wasn't an accident,' continued Maud. 'They were killed, Charlie. Murdered. My beloved sister, Rose. By what or whom, I don't know. It's why I've hidden here my whole life... those symbols above the front door are my only protection; carved by my grandfather a hundred years ago.'

'Listen, Auntie,' said Charlie trying not to shake. 'I don't want to talk about it anymore, okay? Life's tough enough without listening to this kind of crap.'

'I'm sorry, Charlie. I didn't mean to frighten you...'

'I'm not frightened!' shouted Charlie. Dumping the letters and photos on the floor, he stormed out of the house to the woodshed. Closing the door behind him he slumped onto a stack of logs. He savagely rubbed the tears from his eyes. It was only then he realised he was still holding the diary. He flicked through the pages until he found the one titled: 'Dreams.' He read the first entry describing a plaza surrounded by huge boulders and a vast white pyramid-shaped temple...he snapped the book shut, too scared to read on. He felt hot and dizzy and there was a strange ringing in his ears. None of this was possible. He'd never felt so helpless or confused in all his life.

NINE

'Something's' wrong.'

'To be honest, I never feel right after travelling like that,' said Cramp as he let go of the major's hand and placed the case on the table in the basement.

'Shhh! Take a weapon, Sergeant,' advised Flintstaff as he pulled his revolver from its holster and cocked the hammer. The basement was exactly how they had left it. Not a single item had moved in the time they had been away. But Flintstaff's nose was twitching. He could sense that something had changed. 'Unless I'm mistaken, Sergeant, I can smell alcohol. Is it at all possible that Agnes has been at the bottle?'

'Certainly not, sir,' retorted Cramp. 'She is of a nature never to indulge before her duties are complete and the household is at rest.'

'Then, Sergeant, we have visitors.'

Cramp strode to the weapons rack and pulled a massive 6-bore hunting rifle manufactured by William Chance. Ten minutes later, the rifle was loaded and ready for anything in size from an African elephant downwards. Leaving the case behind them, Cramp pressed the hidden button and climbed the stairs to the cellar above. The cellar was a disaster. Flintstaff's moustache began to quiver feverishly as he saw broken bottles and caskets strewn across the floor. Cramp groaned and moved as quickly and quietly as he could across the wreckage towards the scullery.

Flintstaff's eyes narrowed as he followed behind. Through the scullery door they went, where dried pulses and flour carpeted the

67

floor. Flintstaff knelt down and studied the prints left behind. There were pug marks, a size six ladies shoe print and a size eighteen foot print from something with extremely long talons. Cramp cocked his rifle and darted into the kitchen.

On the ground, counting grains of rice spilt from an overturned sack, sat a minion of the Shadows of the Void. Its face resembled that of a furless wolf, its skin grey and leathery; almost desiccated. The body was humanoid but gnarled and twisted with tufts of wiry black hairs breaking through the skin sporadically. It pushed a grain of rice from one pile to another with clawed fingers.

'32,057... 32,058... 32,059... 32,060.'

'You missed one,' said Cramp levelling the rifle at the creature's chest.

'32,062?'

'No, I make that 32,068,' said Flintstaff as he flanked Cramp.

'32,000 and... and...Argh! How could you? Now I'll have to start again,' hissed the creature.

'Where's Agnes, you wretch?' demanded Cramp.

'Then I'm not the only one missing something, am I?' said the creature slathering with pleasure.

'If you touch a hair on her head,' said Cramp. 'I'll... I'll...'

'You'll what?' said the minion. 'Hunt us down? You're already doing a bad job at that. It took us a long time to find you, it did. Searching and searching and still nothing. But we have time, don't we? All the time in the world!' the minion laughed baring long yellowed fangs and a blackened tongue.

'Keep it here,' Flintstaff said to Cramp as he made his way to the door leading to the rest of the house.

Flintstaff, pistol raised, walked through the hallway and checked the drawing room and then the library. Everything had been overturned and ransacked. Once he had checked the bedrooms upstairs and Agnes' quarters he returned to the library. With a feeling of dread he knew that they had discovered The Map. The secret draw under the book shelf was splintered and broken.

Flintstaff placed his revolver on his desk and removed his pith helmet. He ran his hands through his blonde hair and tried to think. He picked up his revolver and returned to the kitchen. Cramp remained where he had left him with the hunting rifle trained on the minion.

'43... 44... 45...'

'Where did you take Agnes and the map?' demanded Flintstaff.

'I didn't take them anywhere, did I? 46... I'm still here,' snarled the beast as it stood up on its hind legs, its talons clicked on the tiled floor. 'However, 47, you are expected in the ruined city of Vijayanagara, 48, where my masters will be willing to come to some sort of arrangement in return for your servant. The map, however, may take a little more bargaining. Little did Duke Lycaon know you owned so powerful an artefact. 49. He always wondered how you knew the whereabouts of our strongholds and now we know. What has pleased him most with this discovery is that he can now locate all of our brothers and sisters across the globe.'

'When are we expected in Vijayanagara?' asked Cramp getting to the point.

'You're servant will arrive within two weeks. Our methods of travel are not quite as immediate as yours. Do not attempt to follow. You are expected at midnight fourteen days from now, any earlier and she will be sacrificed in your honour.'

'Is there anything else we should know?' asked Flintstaff as he pulled a table cloth from a draw and proceeded to lay it on the floor behind the creature.

'Bring the case and the journal. Nothing more.'

'And that's it then? Nothing else? No useful tid-bit of information we might need?'

'Er, no. That's all I was told to tell you,' replied the beast frowning.

'Well, thanks awfully for your message. Now we really must tidy up, if you don't mind.'

'But I haven't finished counting the rice yet...'

'Sergeant?'

'My pleasure, sir.'

The roar of the hunting rifle shook the entire house. The creature reached molecular level instantaneously and was displayed rather artistically across the table cloth Flintstaff had just placed on the floor. Cramp pulled himself out of the scullery where he had landed from the recoil and gently placed the smoking rifle in one corner of the kitchen. The major was already placing broken crockery onto the blood-stained table cloth.

'What amazes me,' yelled the major. 'Is why those in the service of evil have to gloat all the time? I mean, they could have left a note.'

'They want to see the look on your face,' shouted Cramp in return. 'Still, nothing like the look on its face when it realized I was pulling the trigger, what!'

'We're in a pickle though, Sergeant. I mean with Agnes and the map.'

'More than you think, sir.'

'Oh?'

'Agnes is… Agnes and I… Well, Major. The truth is; we're married. Agnes and I. Not only that... she's pregnant.'

'Good Lord!'

'I didn't want to tell you like this. However, I need to continue our lineage if there is to be any hope in this world. I'm an only child, whereas you have a brother and sister to continue if anything happens to you.'

'Well, I must say, you could knock me down with a goose feather,' spluttered Flintstaff. He gathered himself, walked over to his companion and shook him by the hand. 'Congratulations, Sergeant. I did wonder why you always got three Yorkshire puddings on a Sunday compared to my two... all makes sense now.' Flintstaff smoothed down his moustache and frowned. 'And even more reason why we need to get Agnes out of harm's way.'

'Hear, hear.'

70

TEN

Monday 2nd February 2015.

'What are you on, Charlie?' asked Tom as he handed back the Kukri Charlie was showing him. 'It's a wicked knife but you're not making any sense. Did your Auntie slip you some of her medication?' He was frowning and tugging at his curly brown hair.

'Don't ask me, mate. All I know is what she told me. She thinks our great, great, who knows how many, relatives were friends. Devil worshippers, or something. Apparently they were adventurers and they went missing in the 1860's. She's totally paranoid. Thinks our family is cursed and there's someone out to get us.'

'Cursed with insanity if you believe her, that's for sure,' taunted Tom.

They leant on a fence at the end of the recreation ground staring across the road towards the housing estate. The usual groups of teenagers hung in different areas during the morning break; laughter and shrieks and the beeping of mobiles filled the area with noise. Tom and Charlie had found a vacant spot and occupied it.

'So are you related or something?' asked Shini.

'Bloody hell!' said Charlie. 'You nearly gave me a heart attack. You shouldn't sneak up on people like that.'

'Sorry, but I wasn't sneaking up on anyone. You two wouldn't notice if a herd of elephants were behind you,' said Shini. 'I couldn't help hearing what you were saying…'

71

'About Charlie having visions?' said Tom grinning, 'Or the bit where he thinks a great uncle was killed by a genie in the desert? Or that our relatives knew each other a hundred and fifty years ago?'

'Actually, not all of that, just something about relatives…'

'Nice one, Tom,' said Charlie glaring at him. He looked down before continuing. 'Look, Shini, it's not really any of your business…'

'I didn't come here to listen in on your conversation, if that's what you think, Charlie Lawrence. In fact, I came here to give you this,' said Shini with molten steel in her voice. In her hand was an original Strawberry smart phone. The first touch phone they'd brought out eighteen months ago. Some argued that it was a classic, better than the Strawberry II or the Krush. The phone was covered in a garish pink neoprene skin that claimed to make it waterproof. Charlie just stared at it, biting his lip in embarrassment. Even on eBay these things were still fetching well over a hundred quid. Charlie slowly raised his head until he was looking straight into Shini's emerald eyes. He wanted to die, he knew that. It would be preferable than seeing the anger in her face.

'I'm… I'm sorry, Shini,' said Charlie and then carried on in a state of shock. 'But it's not mine. I can't afford one of those.'

'It's not your phone, yet,' said Shini and then her voice softened as she handed him the phone, 'but it is now.'

'But you could sell it. They're worth a fortune. I can't just take it. I'll pay you back when I get a job in the summer. I promise.'

'Charlie,' said Tom. 'Just shut up and take it.'

Charlie wanted to kiss her. More than anything else he wanted to kiss her. Even with the hood of her coat up, hiding her silky black hair, she still looked amazing. He was struck with a mixture of fear and elation and unfortunately the former negated the spontaneity of the latter. In the end he managed to pat her shoulder. Shini grinned at his discomfort.

'Well, you're always complaining about getting no signal with that old brick you carry round. I had this sitting in a draw at home and thought it might be nice to give it to a friend…'

'I think we can trust her, don't you?' said Tom grinning.

'Sure,' said Charlie and in the last fifteen minutes of break he told Shini everything that had happened during his visit to his aunt. As they were walking back to the classroom Shini suddenly stopped to face the two boys.

'There is one way to find out the truth behind this mysterious disappearance of your relatives,' she said.

'I already tried Googling them and nothing came up. I mean absolutely nothing,' said Charlie.

'No, not Google. There were other ways before the internet… I was thinking of a Ouija board.'

*****

Charlie did his best to make some space in the tool shed. His bicycle was now hanging from two hooks he'd attached to the wooden frame of the shed and the engineless lawnmower was pushed to the back so that he had more space to strip the engine. He'd put sheets of cardboard down on the floor so he could start with a clean workspace. He'd learnt that trick himself. If a nut or a bolt dropped on the floor it would undoubtedly disappear. It was like an unwritten law of physics. It was not something his mentor, Mr. Cramp, ever worried about. He'd take stuff apart in the middle of a puddle if that was where it'd broken down. Charlie blew onto his frozen hands. The heater was struggling to turn the arctic temperatures into positive single figures. He was cleaning a spark plug with a wire brush when he received his first text on his new phone. It read: **Hi m8. Tlkd 2 dad about our relatives. No family history. Never heard of Flintstones!! lol. Said family stuff all lost in fire in London in war. Wot with Shini? We still meeting up?**

Charlie snorted. Then he texted back. These touch screens were amazing but he felt awkward with the new technology: **Sh. coming here, then we come to you. @ 8.30.** Once he'd finished he pressed the send button and watched the screen as it ran a cool App which showed a raven grasping a letter and taking off into a stormy sky. **Message sent.** Charlie grinned. He'd already taken off the pink neoprene and had put it up for sale on 'eBay' as well as bidding on a Draggenskin to replace it. He hoped the one would pay for the other.

Outside he heard the crunch of tyres on gravel. The sound made him feel queasy and he unconsciously ran his hands through his hair and rolled his shoulders. The light from the car's high beam illuminated the shed and yew trees separating the back of the garden from the graveyard. Charlie poked his head out of the door and scrunched his eyes as he walked towards the car. An electric window wound down from the passenger's side.

'Hi Charlie, do you want us to wait here for you? Or shall we come in?' asked Shini.

'God, no!' replied Charlie a little more forcibly than he meant. 'Just a sec.' He ran to the front door and yelled into the house. 'I'm going to Tom's. Back at elevenish. Bye.' And without waiting for a reply he shut the door and ran over to the waiting car.

'This is my brother, Raj. Raj, this is my friend, Charlie.'

'Sick wheels,' said Charlie.

'Ta,' replied Raj smiling. 'So where am I taking you two?'

'I'll show you,' said Charlie. 'It's only a mile or so.'

'Fasten your seat belt' advised Shini. 'My brother's a nutter.'

'Cool,' said Charlie.

The car sped down the country lanes connecting the church to Tom's farm. Charlie sat in the back looking at the blue lights that lit up the interior of the car. He guessed that Raj was probably around twenty and he already had a brand new Audi. He couldn't help feeling envious. How could anyone that age afford a car like this? Would he ever earn enough money to own something as expensive as this? If he didn't get decent results and get to college he wouldn't stand a chance. He had to try harder in school, not only because he feared the disappointment in his parents' eyes if he didn't, but because he had to give himself the best chance of 'Making It'. He wasn't even sure what that meant but he could tell from a single glance who had and who hadn't. Shini's dad? Made It. His dad? Not Made It. Tom's dad? Hmm, that one was harder. Mr. Cramp certainly seemed happy and yet he didn't own anything less than ten years old. Maybe he'd ask him one day. The car cruised between the farm buildings until it parked in front of the flint and brick house.

Raj turned in his seat and winked at Charlie. 'Have fun,' he said. 'I'll be back around ten-thirty, okay?'

'Thanks, Raj,' said Shini giving him a kiss. She hopped out the car with a large plastic bag in her hand just as Tom came to the front door.

'Nice motor,' said Tom as the Audi reversed and took off down the lane. 'Right then, let's go to the den.'

Charlie allowed Tom to lead them to a row of disused stables. The last one of the row still retained glass in the windows and a door that didn't hang at a drastic angle from rusted hinges. This was 'The Den' and out of bounds to all humans except Tom and Charlie and very occasionally Tom's mum when she couldn't find things that had disappeared from the house. Charlie sidled up beside Tom before they reached the stables.

'I hope you cleared up,' whispered Charlie.

'Didn't have time,' replied Tom as he opened the door. 'Ta da!'

'Oh. My. God.' said Shini as she walked in.

Charlie winced and then followed Shini inside. The place was spotless. The mountain of sweet wrappers and plastic bottles had disappeared, along with t-shirts, socks, muddy trainers, boots, tin cans and tea cups. It had never, ever been this clean before. He glanced over at Tom who was looking smug. The Playstation and Xbox were tucked away under the TV and all the games were back in their sleeves. Magazines were piled up and various bits of balsa wood and modelling tools were placed neatly on a table in the corner. There was even a plant pot holding a Christmas Rose on the coffee table.

'What a great place,' said Shini sitting down on the sofa.

'How…?' asked Charlie.

'Mum doesn't have to feed the cows for a week…' admitted Tom. 'Although I think she went a bit over the top with this,' he said as he picked up the plant pot. Charlie and Shini burst out laughing.

The two boys leant forward and watched Shini as she revealed the Ouija board. It was made of wood and about the same size as a board game. The face was marked with all the letters of the alphabet, numbers from '0-9', there was a 'Yes' and a 'No' and also the word 'Goodbye'. There was also a wooden pointer and this was where the three of them would each place a finger.

'I checked this on the net and they say its rubbish,' said Tom nervously. 'You're not going to kill us like you did with Samantha?'

'It was a joke,' said Shini. 'Didn't Charlie tell you?'

'Oops,' said Charlie sniggering. 'She only needed six months counselling...'

'Anyway, whether you think it's a con or not will soon be answered. This is how it works. You place a finger here. Only a light pressure and never push the pointer or it won't be worth doing. Then we start by asking questions that no one else knows the answer to. This is the best way to test it. Now, whatever you do, don't remove your finger from the pointer until we say goodbye to the spirit.'

'But how will it know the answers to our questions?' asked Charlie. He was feeling less sure about the whole thing.

'Because they exist in more than one dimension?' said Shini. 'I don't know, really. To be honest, I've never used one seriously. The last time was just to scare those bullies.'

'Only one way to find out.'

'Okay, shall we start? If you could light some candles Tom, and Charlie sorts the drinks out, we can get going.'

The boys did as they were told as Shini polished the board with a tea towel and laid it on the coffee table within reach of everyone.

Three cans of lemonade were opened and the bar heater turned up to the max. Tom and Charlie lay a finger on the pointer and smirked at each other. Shini added her delicate brown finger alongside.

'Okay. Close your eyes and open your minds,' instructed Shini. 'Is there anyone out there? We humble humans ask for any benevolent spirit to enter this room. We have important questions that need to be answered. If there is anyone out there, please answer by pointing to the word 'Yes'.'

The pointer remained in the centre of the board. Charlie peaked through his eyelids at Tom and then over to Shini. Her hair had fallen across her face so that only the tip of her nose and mouth were visible. He could see her nostrils quivering slightly as she breathed. Her lips were pursed. He guiltily closed his eyes and focused on the closeness of her fingertip to his. She had beautiful, slender fingers compared to Tom's great clod-hopping fingers and his own nail-bitten sausages. Even if this didn't work it was worth it, just to be able to sit so close to Shini.

'Is anyone there?' Shini asked once more.

The pointer juddered forward a fraction and stopped. Everyone opened their eyes to see who had moved it. Tom shook his head. The pointer moved again. This time sliding towards the '**Yes**'.

'Welcome,' Shini said in a detached voice. 'What is your name?'

I-D-I-S

'Please tell me what day it is today, Idis.'

The pointer slid towards the splay of letters. **M-O-N-D-A-Y.**

'Thank you. Tom, you can ask a question now. Something neither of us will know would be best.'

'What was the name of my first cat?' asked Tom.

C-A-T.

'That's right!' whispered Tom. 'No one knows that.'

'Charlie.'

'Okay. How did my great uncle...'

Before Charlie could finish, the pointer moved rapidly across the letters. His finger was hardly able to stay on top of the pointer as it moved. It spelt the word: **A-P-E-P**.

'That doesn't mean anything,' scoffed Charlie.

Shini was ahead of him. She had already tapped the letters into her phone with her free hand. She tapped on the screen and then said: 'It does. It's an Egyptian Demon. Called the Eater Of Hearts.'

'But I didn't even finish the sentence…'

'Your turn, Shini.'

'Why did my mother leave me?'

T-O-P-R-O-T-E-C-T-Y-O-U

Charlie watched her bite her lip as the pointer moved across the board. He could see the pain etched into her face, just like his mother's had been when he'd asked her about her parents. It was horribly sad to see in another person; especially someone he cared for.

'Okay, I've got one,' said Tom reading from a scrap of paper Charlie had given him at school.

'What about our relatives? Where did Sergeant Arthur Cramp and Major Henry Flintstaff disappear?'

I-N-D-I-A.

'And what happened to them?'

T-A-K-E-N

'Who by?' asked Charlie.

S-H-A-D-O-W-S

'Eh?'

S-H-A-D-O-W-S

'Who?'

A-R-E-Y-O-U-D-E-A-F

'Okay, okay. So why were they taken by these Shadows?'

T-O-S-A-V-E-H-U-M-A-N-I-T-Y

'Humanity?'

'Well, that's that then,' said Charlie. 'There's nothing we can do about something that happened a hundred and fifty years ago.'

T-H-E-R-E-I-S

'What?'

S-A-V-E-H-U-M-A-N-I-T-Y

'Who asked you?' grumbled Charlie. 'Anyway, where would we start?'

2-3-3-4-8-7.

Shini jotted the numbers down with her free hand. She copied everything the board spelled out so they could study it later. As she was writing the marker began to move once more:

D-A-N-G-E-R-T-H-E-Y-C-O-M-E.

'Who comes?' asked Shini.

S-H-A-D-O-W-S-O-F-T-H-E-V-O-I-D

'Thank-you, spirit, for your help. We would like you to leave now,' she said quickly. 'As the pointer moves onto the word 'Goodbye' you will go back to the spirit world.'

All three of them began pushing the pointer towards the 'Goodbye'. An inch from it and the pointer moved away again towards the letters. **T-O-O-L-A-T-E**

'Okay, Tom, if that's you, you can stop messing about right now,' said Charlie.

Time slowed like the grinding down of gears. The candles in the room flickered. The light dimmed. The friends stared down at the board. Great clouds of condensation filled the room as they breathed. Ice began to form around the plant pot. A crimson tentacle as thick as a finger wriggled out of Charlie's can of lemonade, flopping blindly this way and that. Charlie tried to pull away from the pointer but it was stuck and no matter how hard he pulled he could not free himself. The pointer moved again. **W-E-W-I-L-L-F-I-N-D-Y-O-U.**

As Charlie struggled he knocked the plant pot over. The Hellebore tipped over and as the flowers hit the Ouija board the plant melted like molten plastic across the letters. Tom was immobile, staring at the tentacle in utter shock. Charlie kicked the table as hard as he could. The board, drinks, plant pot and pointer crashed to the floor. The candles went out and the room was plunged into darkness.

ELEVEN

'What the hell just happened?' asked Tom turning on the lights. He grabbed a broom from the corner of the room and brandished it like a sword. 'Where's the octopus? Where is it?

'I don't know,' said Charlie as he booted the Ouija board out the door.

'It's gone,' said Shini breathlessly. 'It melted when the plant fell over.'

'I am never, ever, using one of those things again,' said Charlie. He felt his face had flushed with fear and he was shaking with adrenaline. 'You could've warned us, Shini.'

'I'm sorry but how could I possibly know that it would get so out of control?'

'My whole life's been out of control since you turned up.'

'What did you just say?' asked Shini glaring at him.

'Nothing,' mumbled Charlie. He hid his face by bending over to pick up the plant pot.

'Don't start blaming me...'

'Can you two shut it for a moment?' interrupted Tom. 'Let's clear up and see if we can work through some of this, okay?'

Charlie grunted agreement and carefully picked up the can of lemonade. Holding it under the light he peered inside. Nothing.

'I've never seen anything like it,' said Shini standing beside him. 'What was that thing?'

'I have no idea, it looked like a tentacle, or snake-thing,' said Tom. 'I mean it came out of your can... how am I ever going to drink out of a can again?'

'It was definitely a tentacle,' confirmed Charlie as he placed the empty can on the floor and crushed it with his shoe. 'It just appeared and disappeared.'

'But how?'

'Whoever sent it said they were looking for us,' said Charlie. 'What are we going to do? I mean, if they can make tentacles appear; what else can they do?'

'I don't know,' said Shini. She picked up the piece of paper she'd been writing on. 'But we need to calm down a bit. Let's see what the spirit told us.'

'I don't care,' said Charlie. 'I think we should stop what we're doing right now. I don't want to mess around with this anymore.'

'Come on, mate,' said Tom slapping Charlie's shoulder. 'We might as well look at what Shini wrote down.'

'I just want to go home.'

'Do you think this only affects you, Charlie?' blurted Shini.

Charlie spun round to reply. He was so angry. At least he thought it was anger but he knew it was mostly fear. His world was crumbling around him and he needed to blame it on someone. His quiet life of computer games and hanging out with Tom had been turned upside down by Shini. But as he opened his mouth to speak he saw the gleam of tears in Shini's eyes. It transfixed him and pierced his heart. His teeth clacked as he snapped his mouth shut.

'My mum disappeared when I was six years old, Charlie. Can you even imagine that? One day she was there and the next she was gone. That spirit just told me she vanished to *protect me*. But how? I've needed her to protect me every day since she left, but she hasn't...'

'Listen, Shini,' said Tom. 'Charlie doesn't mean it. He's scared. And so am I. I think that's fair enough, considering.'

'I'm sorry,' said Charlie. He slumped down onto the sofa and ran his hands through his hair. 'Everything's going wrong at the moment and anything I do just makes it worse.'

As Charlie sat there with his head in his hands he felt someone sit beside him and place a hand on his leg. He looked up and into Shini's eyes. He felt like he was looking over the edge of an abyss with a singular urge to jump. She placed the piece of paper on her lap and pointed at her neat handwriting.

'Apep. Google it,' she said. 'Tom can you check our spirit: Idis.'

'As you said, it's an Egyptian devil. Mostly in the form of a snake and a bringer of chaos...'

'Idis is some sort of female spirit, Anglo-Saxon but probably originates from the Norse. She's meant to be benign. What's benign?'

'It means good. The Shadows of the Void only seem to be mentioned in World of Warcraft... so that doesn't really help does it?'

'So that leaves us with Flintstaff and Cramp being caught in India to save humanity.' said Tom.

'Why? It doesn't make any sense,' replied Charlie. 'Who was saving humanity? The Shadows by capturing them, or Flintstaff and Cramp by allowing themselves to be caught?'

'Let's assume for now that they saved humanity from the Shadows by being caught,' said Shini.

'Okay. So they save humanity and that's that. Mystery solved,' said Charlie hopefully.

'That's a point,' said Shini, grabbing her phone. 'There are those numbers the spirit told us about. 233487. I'll Google it. Hmm, it's a colour of paint... a positive integer, whatever that means. There's not much else... oh, wait a minute. It's also a sort code for a bank. Here, look. 'Davenport Bank. No.23a. Henrietta Street, London. WC2. It has other branches in... Cayman Islands, Switzerland, New York, Paris, Mumbai, Tokyo, Beijing, Moscow, Rio... the list goes on...

they're all major cities around the world. It's owned by the O'Void Corporation.'

'I can't see how that helps at all,' said Charlie.

'Only one way to find out,' said Shini writing something down. 'It has a phone number.'

TWELVE

Thursday 16th February 1865.

No. 35 Chepstow Villas, W11 gleamed from attic to basement; the smell of carbolic soap, incense, and beeswax pervaded every room. Cramp was still fervently polishing the family silver with a mixture of kaolin and quartz when Henry Flintstaff emerged from his bedroom and descended the stairs wearing a full-length vermillion kimono. Glancing out of the large bay window in the hall, Flintstaff was greeted by darkness still dully illuminated by gas lamps in the street. Upon entering the kitchen Cramp looked up from his vigorous rubbing of a silver samovar, placed it carefully upon a baize table before him and stood to attention.

'At ease, Sergeant,' Flintstaff responded automatically as he inspected the glimmering collection of valuables on the table. 'Is it utterly necessary to be polishing the silver two hours before reveille?'

'Absolutely, sir,' replied Cramp returning to the samovar.

'The polishing I can understand, Cramp. It's the necessity of wearing Agnes's pinafore that concerns me more.'

'Ah, er, well,' replied Cramp his red face shimmering in the silverware. 'Just making sure there's no extra work for Agnes when she returns. I'll not have her scolding us for living like errant bachelors during her absence.'

'Quite so, Cramp. Couldn't agree more. Breakfast?'

The limpid streets of London turned from monochrome to a singular grey as the two gentlemen ate a hearty repast of kippers, blue cheese, half a pheasant and a bottle of port. Outside the city was barricaded from the sun by a sickly layer of smog over a mile high. They retired to the library where the sound of carriages led by wheezing horses and the rasping coughs of passers-by filtered through the window.

Flintstaff produced a mythical Linghzi mushroom sealed in a mason jar and placed it upon the study table. Henry Flintstaff had been reading most of the night, making notes in his journal, tapping his teeth with his fountain pen and frowning. Cramp had spent his time downstairs beneath the cellar making an inventory of everything they might need for the day ahead. The moment of action was upon them; for the day had come to get Agnes back.

'Did you get to the market yesterday?' asked Flintstaff.

'Yes, sir. A hundred-weight of fruit.'

'Excellent. With any luck our little surprise will be enough.'

'It's a simple plan, sir. But I do feel we're relying on the unreliable.'

'We shall see, Sergeant. We shall see.'

Major Flintstaff popped the mason jar open and tipped the mushroom onto a silver platter. It was a young sporocarp with colours ranging from a fiery red at its base through a sickly yellow and ending with a snow-white tip – a unique variety of Zhi that had been sought after by every Emperor of China for the last four thousand years. Adventurers from across the planet had searched in vain to find the Mushroom of Immortality. The major took a pair of silver tongs and prodded it thoughtfully.

'What do you think, Sergeant?' he asked. 'Do you want to live forever?'

'Couldn't think of anything worse, if you want my honest opinion, sir.'

'I tend to agree. Having the knowledge of millennia is hard enough… having to live with it forever would be a chore. However, we are about to walk straight into a trap and it is our duty to do everything we can to disrupt the enemy.'

'And the safety of Agnes is paramount... As is the valise.'

'Precisely, and in that order. What do we know of this fungus?' asked the major rhetorically. 'Very little indeed. I would say to achieve immortality one would have to consume a significant amount, otherwise there would be a variety of immortal mushroom-eating insects buzzing around certain legendary mountains in China and we would have heard of them.'

'Ye-es,' replied Cramp, less than convinced. 'So what do you propose? We do a half each? Gain a short-term invulnerability?'

'Splendid idea!' agreed Flintstaff. 'Which half do you want?'

Cramp eyed the mushroom with a renewed sense of caution. Its red base looked positively deadly and the yellow part couldn't look any more poisonous but the innocent white part at the top could be the worst. He glanced up at Flintstaff.

'Split it lengthways?'

'Done,' replied Flintstaff and opened his penknife.

*****

An hour later the two gentlemen were sat underneath the kitchen table re-enacting the Battle of Waterloo using bars of soap, a sock, three tomatoes, a letter opener, ninety-six buttons of various sizes and a toy schooner. It seemed whichever way they played it Napoleon kept winning...

*****

Three hours later the two gentlemen were beneath the cellar packing the last of their equipment inside the case. They were both dressed in full military regalia and ready for battle. Sergeant Cramp had brushed his sideburns and Major Flintstaff had waxed his moustache, as all warriors are prone to pampering themselves before a slaughter. Every brass button and buckle gleamed, not a single wisp of lint adhered to the red coats or the dark trousers. Once every item had been double-checked the case was closed and Flintstaff and Cramp made their way to the centre of the transportation glyph etched into the floor.

'Ready?' asked Flintstaff holding out his hand.

'Feel a bit strange, to be honest, sir.'

'Hmm,' replied Flintstaff and read out the appropriate glyphs...

'Fedduddudddudd!'

'Skin like flower petals. I tell you, sir.'

'You've a mind like a regiment's latrine, Cramp.'

'Was I speaking out loud, sir?' said Cramp as his face matched the colour of his jacket. Must be that mushroom we ate...'

'Immediate situation appraisal, Sergeant,' said the major as he swivelled from one side to the other with his trusty steam-revolver in hand.

Cramp looked around, his elephant gun held at the hip. 'Midnight. Moon waning gibbous. India. Vijayanagara, sir. We call it Hampi. Bazaar road, facing the pyramid temple of Virupaksha. No sign of movement and even the locals seem to have cleared the area.'

'Indeed,' agreed Major Flintstaff. In the light of the moon he could see that the street was over two hundred paces in length. It would have been used for ceremonial processions to the temple and also as a place of trade. Low stone structures with colonnades running the entire length lined either side of the street. In its day it must have been a place of splendour. But those days had gone; destroyed by a Deccan horde three hundred years previously. The only movement now was from dust devils tugged this way and that by a hot night wind. Nearest to them the avenue led to the temple of Virupaksha, the other end of the road led to ruined temples and plaza systems.

'If memory serves me well, there's a temple to Hanuman within the locale.'

'True, although some distance from here.'

'Irrelevant, Cramp. Be a good chap and fetch a rocket from the case.' Flintstaff handed the case over to Cramp.

Cramp popped the case open and dug into its depths while the major opened the journal and began drawing two circles on the ground in fine white chalk. He added various runes and astrological symbols. He pulled the crystal from the spine of the journal and using the light of the moon transcribed the glyphs onto the stone. They glowed a soft blue. Cramp kept delving, his pink tongue poking out as he concentrated.

'Astrolabe, no. Coptic funeral jar, no. Steam-saw, no. Ah! Here we are, I think. Will a Mongol rocket do? Not quite as reliable as the Chinese...'

'Fine, Sergeant. Pop it in this hole and let her off when you're ready.'

'Won't we be alerting the enemy, sir?' asked Cramp.

'That is precisely what I want, Cramp. I'm also relying on a certain animal's curiosity.'

Cramp struck a match and lit the fuse. The rocket had been built as an artillery weapon five hundred years before but age had not dampened its content. The missile lifted off with a 'whoosh' and lit the night's sky with an enormous explosion that echoed across the valley, bouncing from rocky hill to river valley. And then a movement was caught in the light. In the distance. Barely visible at the far end of the bazaar road stood a solitary figure.

'There,' Flintstaff said removing his cavalry sabre and pointing. 'The cheese and the trap on the same plate.'

'Agnes!' shouted Cramp. Muttering curses he shut the case, removed a twenty-four inch bayonet from his hip belt, slotted it into place and cocked the elephant gun.

The two adventurers walked slowly down the centre of the street. In the distance, caught upon the wind, they heard the transcendental strains of a sitar. As they passed the colonnades ghastly figures emerged from the shadows; the only sounds were the grating of claws upon stone and the dripping of saliva from gaping maws.

'Reminds me of our rugby match against the 8th Irish Dragoons,' murmured Flintstaff.

'Or a night in Glasgow...' added Cramp, keeping eyes fixed forward.

'I'll have you know the Membrayne side of the family is from the Clyde, Sergeant,' replied Flintstaff stiffly.

'Apologies, sir. Heat of the moment.'

As the two men drew closer they could see Agnes chained to a stone pillar. She wore a blindfold and gag. Cramp growled.

'Easy, Sergeant. It's what they want.'

'Actually, no.' said a voice in the darkness. Count Strigoi, the Lord of the Vampires, emerged into the moonlight beside Agnes. 'What we want is in your servant's hand.'

'Servant?' said Cramp. 'Outrageous! I've never been paid a farthing.'

'Slave then,' snarled Duke Lycaon, the Lord of the Werewolves, as he appeared from behind a ruined temple. He was a huge man with a jutting jaw and deep-set eyes framed with a mane of long grey hair. Beside him also came the sorcerer, Babba Belani the Bokor. He bowed; his grin spread wide, top hat tilted and sword cane tapping on the stones.

'Well, well. What a fine picnic we have here,' Major Flintstaff said as he turned full circle. 'From the selection of buffoons behind us I do believe there may be even more of you. I see werewolves, vampires, zombies, goblin-faced redcaps, and the twisted figures of Rakshasas. You have been busy.'

'There are more,' rumbled a voice as heavy and cold as granite. A giant rose from the darkness that the two gentlemen had assumed was a massive rock. He was an immense demon with porcupine quill hair, amber eyes and a continual stream of blood running down his face. He carried a vast flint axe.

'So, we have Atasaya the demon of the Zuni too. All the way from the Americas, eh?' said the major. 'I see you invited the locals,' he continued, pointing to the cannibalistic, goggle-eyed Rakshasas, 'Lord Cofgod must be here too, all the way from North England with his redcaps.'

'Evening,' said Lord Cofgod appearing from behind one of Atasaya's tree-like legs.

'Quite a collection of scum, Count Strigoi.'

'And you thought your beloved science could only better mankind's position on this planet. How naïve of you, Major Henry Flintstaff-Membrayne.'

'I would have you believe that, Count,' replied Flintstaff. 'Science will always work for the good in the end.'

'Really? As you see, the invention of steam has allowed us to travel and make new friends,' added Duke Lycaon. 'Now the Shadows of the Void can finally unite! Nothing can stop us!'

'Yes, well I'm sure you all have a lot to chat about, but I do believe we're here to negotiate a transfer of property for your hostage, were we not? You desire the case and my journal and we desire the safe return of Agnes, our house-keeper.'

'First, your weapons,' said Count Strigoi, his eyes gleaming in the moonlight.

'First your minions,' replied Cramp.

Neither side moved.

'How about this…' said Flintstaff. 'I will meet you, Count Strigoi, in the middle of the street with the case and journal and you bring me Agnes. Once there, I will open the case wherein the journal is kept, and you will unchain Agnes. We will go our way and you can go yours. Agreed?'

Count Strigoi smiled, his fangs glinting in the moonlight. He nodded towards his companions. Duke Lycaon growled in agreement and his pack of werewolves backed away. Lord Cofgod signalled for his redcap goblins to move beside him. The Rakshasas hissed with disapproval but slipped away past the colonnades. However, Babba Belani had less luck controlling his zombies which tended to bump into each other and trip over things. While Cramp checked their path was clear back to the chalked glyphs a hundred paces away, Flintstaff glanced around the roof-tops of the ruins surrounding them. Figures were silhouetted against the night's sky, and there were hundreds of them. Flintstaff holstered his revolver and placed his sabre back into its scabbard.

'As soon as they have what they want they'll try to stop our withdrawal,' whispered Flintstaff. 'Sergeant, be sure to clear the path for Agnes.'

'My pleasure, sir,' replied Cramp lowering the elephant gun. 'Good luck, sir.'

Two goblin redcaps unchained Agnes and led her up the road towards the waiting gentlemen. The Shadows of the Void and their slathering minions followed, step by step. Many slipped around them through the ruins. With a gap of twenty paces the Shadows halted. One of the goblins untied Agnes's blindfold and gag. She gasped a lungful of air and caught sight of Cramp.

'Arthur,' she cried.

'Stiff upper lip, lass. We'll have you home in a jiffy,' Cramp replied. 'That's a promise.'

'I'm sorry, my love. They tricked their way into the house...'

'Never your fault, Aggie,' said Cramp gruffly. 'We're here now...'

'Enough of this,' hissed Count Strigoi. He grasped Agnes by the arm and dragged her forward.

Flintstaff walked to meet the vampire with the case in his hand. They met in the middle. Flintstaff looked the vampire directly in the eye. The count returned his gaze and for a moment the world stood still. The tropical air cooled, breath condensed, frost appeared on the major's moustache and the tips of the count's fangs. A tiny crease appeared on the forehead of the count at which point Flintstaff smiled and lowered the case onto the dusty street.

'Open the case and you can have the girl,' demanded the count. The Shadows and their minions inched closer.

The major smiled and calmly produced a cigar. He took his time lighting it and puffed it into life before bending down to flip the two catches of the case. The silence would have been unbearable had it not been constantly interrupted by groaning zombies. As he slowly opened the case orange light slipped out and a hiss of steam escaped from a hidden valve. The interior of the case glowed. Attached to the inside of the lid was the journal, otherwise the case was completely empty.

'My house-keeper, if you please,' he said talking hold of Agnes's hand.

'Is that it?' Strigoi asked, peering down at the empty case. The rest of the Shadows moved forward.

Flintstaff pushed Agnes gently towards Cramp who came forward and hurriedly gathered her into his arms. Agnes clung to him.

'No time for that now,' he whispered into Agnes's ear. 'I want you to be ready to run straight for that chalk circle when I tell you. Take this piece of paper and read the glyphs out loud once you're in the centre with the case. Don't wait for us, do you hear me? I've left you a list of instructions on the kitchen table.' Cramp placed his free hand on her stomach and looked into her eyes. 'Look after the little one, Agnes. This child is the hope of the future.'

'I'll put the kettle on,' replied Agnes as a tear slipped down her cheek.

Flintstaff was still standing beside the case, and instead of moving away he bent down to tie his shoelace. The Shadows moved closer to look inside the case. The count was scowling. On the rooftops of the temples hundreds of silhouettes were straining to see what was going on. Beneath them the demon Rakshasas were crouching in readiness.

'Where are all the weapons?' growled Duke Lycaon.

'It's a trick,' said Lord Cofgod.

'Kill them all!' roared the count.

Just at that moment the chiming of a bell began ringing somewhere inside the case. Everyone froze. The floor of it opened and a large iron bowl inscribed with Chinese symbols emerged. Flintstaff remained crouching beside it and touched his cigar to a hole drilled into the side of the bowl. Suddenly Cramp and Agnes ran off towards the chalk circle. There was a dull 'thump' that shook the ground and toppled several colonnades. From within the depths of the iron bowl a hundred-weight of bananas exploded into the sky.

'Monkey-mortar!' yelled Flintstaff as he drew his revolver in his left hand and his sabre with his right.

Bananas flopped and plopped back to earth like rain. Count Strigoi moved with unnatural speed and struck Flintstaff across the face before he could raise his revolver. The major went down, rolled and jumped to his feet. Before he could raise his pistol goblins, zombies and werewolves set upon him. Cramp glanced back and saw him go down. A group of vampires had taken to the air and landed in front of the chalk circle, cutting off Agnes's escape. They were joined by hissing Rakshasas. Cramp kept running. He moved a dial on the side of the elephant gun for choice of ammo.

'Silver-tipped flechettes,' he said grinning manically, and pulled the trigger.

The blast echoed across the hills and valley; a temple collapsed from the shock wave. The flame erupting from the muzzle was enough to instantly incinerate three of the Indian demons while a thousand needles travelling at the speed of sound shredded everything within a forty-five degree arc. Cramp pushed Agnes forward. 'Get into the inner circle. You'll be safe there,' he yelled. 'Go!'

Turning round, Cramp held the smoking gun in front of him and raced towards the major and mass of whirling limbs; the bayonet glowed red-hot. Count Strigoi had his back to him standing over the case. Cramp charged home aiming the point of the bayonet at the heart of the Shadow. A zombie stumbled in the way, lost its head with a sideways sweep from Cramp but he slipped on a banana and crashed to the ground. A werewolf bit into his calf before Cramp could swing the bayonet around and skewer it through the head. Dropping the gun, the sergeant rolled once and leapt towards the case. The count was just about to release the journal but the bristling side-burns of an enraged Cramp emerged over the raised lid.

'Touch my girl, would you?' said Cramp before head-butting the count neatly on the bridge of the nose. The count yelped and went down. Cramp thrust his hand in the case hoping for a weapon. He grasped onto something and yanked it free just as a goblin jumped on his back and bit his ear; it was a tube of lipstick. Cramp shoved it into the goblin's eye. The goblin yelled, half-blinded but prettier to look at. Cramp delved into the case once again and grasped something more solid...

Henry Flintstaff was surrounded. He loosed off all thirty-eight rounds of his revolver dropping goblin, zombie and werewolf alike. He had been wrestled to the ground again by a Rakshasa when he heard the air parting with a whistle. He rolled sideways just as an enormous stone axe buried itself into the road. Atasaya towered over him. Flintstaff got to his feet, brushed himself off and offered up his sabre. Atasaya grinned. Swinging his axe in a figure of eight motion he advanced on the major.

'You're dead,' said the Zuni demon.

The silhouettes on the rooftops had watched in wonder as the mortar released its ordinance. Their king and god lived in a temple on a hill a few miles away. When they had seen the Mongol rocket split the night's sky they could not escape their instinctive curiosity, and from the ruins of a hundred temples, shrines and palaces that littered Hampi they had made their silent way through the mango trees and rooftops of the dead city to see what was going on. They had seen the Rakshasas and remembered their great wars with them in the past; when gods had fought gods. But what really grabbed their interest were the thousand bananas erupting into the air and onto the street. Because when it came to good, evil, or a banana, the choice was obvious. Every time a zombie or Rakshasa trod on one it made hundreds of watching monkeys wince, and very, very angry. And of all the creatures on the planet, the hardest thing to fight is an enraged monkey. And the toughest monkey on the planet is the Indian Macaque.

Flintstaff dodged an enormous swipe of Atasaya's axe and stepped inside the giant's reach to slice at its throat. The porcupine bristles deflected the blow, so flowing with his momentum Flintstaff swept past the demon and kicked him behind the knee. The demon went down. Skewering a vampire on the way, the major fought his way back towards Cramp just as the night came alive with monkeys. They leapt upon goblins, Rakshasas and anything else that moved, beating them relentlessly with their bandy arms. The Rakshasas, remembering the wars of Rama, fled screeching.

Cramp, afforded a second of relief, wiped his brow before pulling out the Cat-o-Vault 3000 and pumped out thirteen furious felines in all directions. Slamming the case shut, he grabbed it by the handle and barged his way past a zombie staggering under the weight of three monkeys. Cramp bumped into Major Flintstaff and was nearly impaled by his sabre.

'Ah, there you are, Sergeant. I was wondering where you'd got to,' said Flintstaff. He slammed a fresh clip of ammunition into his revolver.

'Got the case, sir. Time to withdraw.'

'Excellent fellow.'

The two gentlemen fought their way back towards the chalk circle where Agnes still stood. Lord Cofgod paced around the chalk circle, a few piles of ash showed where other less intelligent minions had tried to cross it to reach her. The redcap lord was busy drawing another circle around their own. A dozen werewolves and vampires stood guard.

'We'll never stop him finishing that damned circle in time, Sergeant. Our luck's running out.'

'Yes, sir. Only one last hope, if you could clear the way.'

Flintstaff dropped to his knee and fired as fast as his finger could pull the trigger. Cramp ran towards Lord Cofgod. Vampires and werewolves dropped dead either side of him. Cramp swung the case and hurled it towards Agnes.

'Catch!' he yelled before being dragged to the ground by claws and talons.

Just as Major Flintstaff was knocked to the ground by Atasaya, the demon giant, he saw the case fly through the air end over end. Werewolves leapt for it, goblins threw themselves towards it and vampires swooped down to intercept it. End over end it span. One delicate hand reached up through the throng. Agnes grasped the case and vanished.

'Now that's cricket,' Flintstaff gasped as the demon grasped his throat.

THIRTEEN

Thursday 5th February 2015.

'Go on then, you call it,' said Charlie as the three of them stood on the periphery of the playground.

'You're such a chicken,' said Tom. 'It's been three days since we got this number and we still haven't done anything with it. Give it here.'

'Try to sound grown up; like a businessman.'

'Hello?' said Tom as his voice cracked. He reddened, coughed and started again in a deeper tone. 'Hello? It is? Good. I was wondering… my name is…' Tom wobbled his eyebrows at his friends, suddenly stuck for a name.

'Flintstaff,' whispered Shini.

'My name is… Thomas Cramp. Yes. That's right. Hold? The manager?' Tom held his hand over the phone and whispered: 'They're getting the manager… Hello? Yes, that's right, a direct descendant of Arthur Cramp. Something for me? Really? You're absolutely sure? What is it? Oh. Okay then, when can I come and pick it up? Okay… I.D. of course. Is a student card and a passport alright? On Saturday? Won't you be closed? Refurbishment… fine. Around midday then. Goodbye.'

'So?' asked Charlie.

'He says there's something for us in the vault. Said he couldn't tell me over the phone.'

'I wonder what it is?' said Shini.

'Let's hope it's gold!' replied Tom grinning.

'I just hope it doesn't get us into any trouble,' said Charlie fiddling with his phone.

After school Charlie rode his bike along the lanes and over the railway bridge back home. Tom and Shini had wanted to meet up again to discuss what to do next. Charlie had disagreed and told them he wanted to think things through for himself. They'd all been nervous since the Ouija board but everything had been quiet and no tentacles had appeared anywhere. They were all starting to think they had imagined it. Anyway, when it came to thinking he found Tom could confuse matters because he talked so much and Shini, well, she just stopped Charlie from thinking at all. He also had to admit to himself that it was an excuse for him to play his computer game in peace.

His dad was over at the church preparing a young couple for their nuptials and his mother was out giving a treatment somewhere which suited Charlie well. He stomped up the stairs, a mug of hot tea in his hands, went to his bedroom and fired up the computer. While he was waiting he unpacked his overnight bag. There, resting on the top of his clothes was a note. It was from Aunt Maud.

```
Dear Charlie,
I'm very sorry I upset you. I'm afraid the
truth hurts. Keep the knife. I think Robert
would have been happy for you to have it if
he'd ever known you. But remember, a blade
should never be drawn lightly; it demands
payment in blood.
Much love. Maud.
```

He stared at the letter for a long time, eyes fading in and out of focus. He felt like a thief. Sighing he stood up and went back to his computer. He had to work stuff out. What could be in the bank? That was one of the questions he needed answered. Another was who these Shadows were and exactly how dangerous they might be. The only person who might have any idea was probably Aunt Maud.

Should he call her? After giving it some thought he decided against it until he'd been to the bank with Tom and Shini. He would only have to wait two days. Right now he needed to do some research on the internet about self-defence of the paranormal kind. After an hour of searching he discovered that the net was filled with ten-year-old fantasy gamers or paranoid schizophrenics.

What Charlie did not want to do was talk to his parents about it, even though he knew they might have more knowledge about the occult than most people due to their respective professions. Of course, what they'd seen the night of the Ouija board could have been a collective hallucination. The more time passed the less Charlie trusted his own senses. Maybe whatever the Davenport Bank was holding would answer their questions.

*****

Saturday 7th February.

'I don't know if this is such a great idea,' said Charlie standing by the ticket counter at Goring railway station.

'What d'you mean?' asked Tom as he passed his money and student card under the glass screen. 'There's something waiting for us in a bank... and what do they keep in banks?'

'Money.'

'Correct!'

'We just seem to be getting deeper into something that we know so little about,' said Charlie biting a finger nail. 'And what we do know is hardly filling me with joy...'

'You're such a whinger, Charlie,' said Shini as she bought her ticket. 'It's better than being stuck at home, isn't it?'

'I dunno,' replied Charlie thinking about the next level of his computer game. He sighed and handed over money he couldn't afford to spend.

Charlie, Tom and Shini caught the slow train that ran from Oxford to London. Charlie stared out of the window as they rattled along the

Thames Valley following the flow of the river until buildings took over from green fields and the train finally slowed down and stopped at Paddington Station. He hoped everything would go smoothly but he kept feeling a stabbing pain under his ribs whenever he thought about the night of the Ouija board. If only it could be money. Just money, with no ties or strings attached.

Exiting from Covent Garden tube station they followed the flocks of tourists past Jubilee Hall and the street performers until they reached Henrietta Street.

'Hang on,' said Charlie. I want to buy some snacks in case they make us wait for ages.'

'Hurry up, mate,' said Tom. 'We might be able to buy the shop in a minute.'

'Mentos?' offered Charlie after he'd placed a litre of coke in his daypack.

'Mint? No thanks,' replied Tom.

'Here we go,' said Shini as they reached the end of the street. They stopped in front of an ornately carved oak door with a small green plaque which had: 'Davenport Bank. Est: 1800' embossed on it and painted white. There was a brass knocker depicting a wolf's head. Shini grasped the knocker and banged against the door.

Just as Shini was about to knock again the door opened and an ancient little man peered out at them behind half-rim spectacles.

'Can I help you?' he asked breathing heavily.

Shini smiled brightly and spoke in her best 'private school' accent.

'We called you on Thursday. This is Thomas Cramp, and this is a direct descendant of the Flintstaff-Membrayne family. His name is Charles Lawrence and I am Aghanashini Nair. Pleased to meet you.'

'Oh my-oh-my,' said the old man rubbing his hands together. 'What a day! Do please come in.' he opened the door and the three of them filed past the old man as he closed the door behind them and slipped three bolts across it. Tom turned as he heard the noise and the old man smiled at him. 'We are a bank, son. Best not to leave doors open when you're a bank.' He chortled. 'Now, follow me.'

Charlie had never seen a bank like this one. It didn't look like it'd seen a single customer since it had opened in 1800. The bank clerk's desk was of mahogany inlaid with ivory, the carpets were a plush burgundy and the walls were filled with old paintings. Charlie imagined that there were a very limited amount of very influential customers.

'Now,' said the old man, 'may I see some identification from all of you? I'm afraid it is the protocol for relatives of deceased customers to produce some form of identification before we can sign over any items contained herein.'

Tom produced his passport and Charlie and Shini showed the manager their student I.D.'s. The old man peered closely at each one, waving it back and forth in front of his face until he found the right distance to focus on the writing. Shini suppressed a giggle, the manager hardly reached her shoulders.

'Everything seems in order. Would you all follow me, please?'

'I thought you were having building work done,' said Tom as they followed the old man down a long passage.

'Building work? What building work? ... Oh, building work! Yes, they're starting round the back.'

The old man hobbled down the corridor, turned a corner and then descended a long flight of stairs. As they descended the air became mustier. The stairs led to another long corridor with a single door at the end. The walls were bare rock now rather than painted, and the floor was made from stone. Charlie noticed how worn they were in the middle, as if a million feet had padded down this way through the ages.

'Here we are,' panted the old man. 'Probably the safest vault in the world. I must say that after all these years as manager I'm very excited to be here today, on this historic occasion. You see, it's not every day that relatives of famous adventurers come to retrieve a family heirloom.' With that he pulled out a large bunch of keys from his waistcoat pocket and jangled through them before placing a big brass key in the lock. The door swung open into a vault carved from the bed-rock. Charlie was the last to step inside the room which held a single steel security cabinet beside the door and in the centre a dust sheet covered something sat upon a table.

'There you are,' said the old man as he ushered them inside. 'I have been looking after this from a boy to a man to this very day.'

'What is it?' asked Tom.

'Let's take a look,' said Shini as she carefully pulled the dust sheet away.

'Oh.'

'Is that it?'

'A case?' asked Charlie staring at the object sat on the middle of a carved stone slab.

'Oh my,' said the manager. He was giggling to himself. Almost uncontrollably. 'Not any case, my dears. *The* case.'

'What's inside it?' asked Charlie. The brown leather was scuffed and scratched with a hundred old travel stamps plastered across it; some of them were of places he'd never even heard of. And yet there was something inexplicable about it that drew his attention. Charlie couldn't put it into words except that it had 'presence'.

'Never opened it. Couldn't. Wouldn't. Against our policy,' said the old man. 'We'd almost forgotten about you. Not me, of course. But if I did have one favour to ask it would be to take a tiny peek inside once you've opened it. Would that be too much to ask? Would it? Would it?'

The three friends ignored the old man for a moment as they surrounded the case. Tom glanced over at Charlie, disappointment showing in his face. At most the case could carry enough clothes for a weekend away or at a push, a week-long summer holiday.

'You do it. It's you that got us this far, it's only fair that you should open it,' said Tom.

'Yes, open it, young sir,' urged the old man. 'A peek. A glance. Just a little lookie. All this time. Waiting. Yearning. Not allowed,

104

they told me. Guard and wait, they said. Stuck here for an age... that's why I haven't told them about you coming... open it. Go on!'

'Um, I think you should calm down,' said Shini.

'Don't mind me, young lady,' said the manager as he turned towards the door of the vault.

'You might have a stroke.'

'A stroke?' snarled the old man as he locked the door. 'I don't think you have any idea, do you? Now, open the case.'

'Look,' said Charlie. 'I think you're getting a bit over-excited about this. I realize you've been here looking after it for us and we're grateful for that. But, it belongs to us and we don't have to open it here at all. In fact, I think we should take it home before we open it.'

This was not what the old man wanted to hear by the look of his face. His head began to swell in all directions, inflating like a balloon. It became redder and redder. Charlie heard Tom retch beside him as he stood transfixed. He thought he should help. Was this what happened when you had a brain haemorrhage? The old man's body twisted this way and that, growing in stature with every seizure and spasm; his tweed suit tearing apart. The groans became a roar as bones elongated; teeth and nails grew. Whatever it was, it wasn't the little old man anymore. It turned the colour of blood and bared its sabre-like teeth with a hiss of fury. Two bone-white horns erupted from its crimson head. Charlie instinctively placed an arm in front of Shini. He could hear her breathing rapidly beside him. He swallowed heavily as the seven foot monster loomed over him.

'Now that I have your attention,' said the demon as he placed a razor sharp talon against Charlie's throat.

'Wha... what are you?'

'Never seen a demon before?' the demon snarled. Its breath came out in a dark greasy cloud. 'Now empty your pockets and drop your pack on the floor. Then you, Mr. Cramp, will open the case for me. Do you understand?'

The three friends nodded dumbly. Charlie handed over his pack and emptied his pockets onto the floor. Tom picked up the case.

'Slowly does it, boy,' warned the demon.

'What's so important about the case?' asked Shini as she backed against the wall.

'You don't even know, do you?' said the demon. 'This is the case Flintstaff and Cramp used in their war against us. A weapon so great that they were willing to sacrifice themselves in order to protect it from us.'

'But you've already got it...' said Tom. 'Why do you need us?'

'Because we cannot open it, fool. Many died trying, believe me. So, instead, I was placed here to guard it and I waited and waited. And to my astonishment you called me, out of the blue.'

'But it's only an old case,' said Charlie. 'Let us go and you can have whatever's inside it.'

'Hmm. Nice offer but unlikely,' mused the demon as he searched through Charlie's bag. The demon pulled out the litre bottle of coke, unscrewed the top and drunk the whole bottle in one gulp. 'Seems a bit merciful, doesn't it?' it said belching a great cloud of gunk.

'But we're innocent!' implored Charlie. 'Whatever our ancestors did, it doesn't mean we're the same...'

'Oh, but it does. It's in your blood, otherwise you wouldn't be here,' said the demon, its eyes gleaming like black pearls. 'Until today we thought we'd rid the world of your bloodlines but obviously we were wrong.'

'Look. This isn't fair. I'm just a teenager,' said Charlie. 'I can't even get out of bed in the morning, let alone fight demons.'

'And I'm just a demon and I can't stop myself from feeding off the fear and suffering of others; let alone be merciful to three idiot children.'

'We're not children,' stated Shini. Charlie noticed her staring at the packet of Mentos lying on the floor next to the demon. She seemed to be wiggling her eyebrows. 'And now we're going to be killed by a demon with stinky breath and a bad sense of humour. I

106

don't suppose you could eat one of those delicious mints before you kill us. I'm sure Tom will open the case for you then.'

The demon glanced suspiciously at the packet of mints and then looked towards Tom. It frowned and hesitated.

'Forget it,' said Charlie making a dash for the Mentos. 'Those are mine and I'm damned if you're going to eat them all before killing me.'

The demon backhanded Charlie across the face knocking him to the floor. Shini ran to help him as the demon stepped over to the mints, picked them up, tore off the wrapping and dropped the whole pack down his throat.

'Mmm,' grunted the demon. 'Tasty.'

Shini, Tom and Charlie all stared at the demon. The demon stared back. It frowned.

'What?' asked the demon.

'Mentos and coke. I don't suppose you watch YouTube...' said Shini.

'?'

And the demon exploded.

*****

Charlie got to his knees and spat. Tom had already been sick and was wandering around the vault trying to find something to wipe his face with. Shini had taken the full force of the exploding demon and was still lying prone on the floor, moaning. Charlie crawled over to her and lifted her head. She coughed and opened her eyes. Even though Charlie was deep in shock, and maybe because of it, he was pretty sure Shini had never looked as beautiful as she did lying beneath him, the ash on her face irrigated by her tears. His heart nearly burst with fear for her safety. She looked up at him and the emerald wells of her eyes grasped his soul.

'You okay?' he asked.

'Yup, I think so,' she whispered. 'You're bleeding.'

'I didn't even notice,' said Charlie as he wiped blood from his split lip. 'God, it stinks in here...'

'With a hint of mint,' muttered Tom as he tried to open the cabinet by the door. 'One of those Mentos nearly broke my nose.'

'I think we need to get out of here as soon as possible,' said Charlie as he helped Shini to her feet.

'If we walk out into the street covered in this stuff we might attract attention,' she said. 'Better we clean up a bit and then get the hell out of here.'

Tom walked over to the remains of the bank manager. All that was left was its shredded human clothes and a large pile of ash. Tom rifled through the pockets and pulled out a wallet, a set of keys on a chain and an address book. Opening the wallet Tom found thirty pounds in cash, a tube ticket, three credit cards and a selfie of a grinning demon beside an erupting volcano. Charlie watched Tom pocket the money and drop the wallet. He looked up and saw Charlie staring at him.

'What?' asked Tom. 'He tried to kill us!'

'And we need to pay for our train tickets,' agreed Charlie as he lifted the case and shook it gently. 'This thing's empty.'

'So why are the Shadows, or whatever, guarding it underground with a seven foot demon? They think it has magical powers or something and they seem quite willing to kill us to open it. It can't be empty,' said Shini.

'Let's clean up and get home as fast as we can. I don't want to open it here. There may be more of these things on the way,' said Charlie.

They took turns using the dust sheet to wipe each other down and grabbed their stuff before making their way along the passageway. Just before the stairs Charlie and Shini turned round to see that Tom hadn't followed.

'Tom!' shouted Charlie. The word echoed back and forth down the passage.

'One sec. I dropped my mobile,' echoed his voice.

Charlie and Shini waited in the entrance of the bank until Tom came panting up the stairs and through the clerk's office. They unbolted the front door and Shini peered out to make sure there were no surprises. Signalling the two boys to follow she stepped out into the street and ran towards the bustle of Covent Garden Market.

Three hours later they were back in Tom's converted stable with the case sat on the coffee table. Charlie was still shaking from his experience. A demon. A demon in his video game, a demon killing his great uncle and a demon trying to kill him and his friends. The world had changed forever. How was he ever going to sleep again? Would he ever be able to walk outside at night? Maybe they'd hallucinated all of it. Except he had a split lip...

'So who's going to open it then?' asked Shini interrupting his thoughts.

'I'm not bothered,' said Tom nonchalantly.

'Yeah, me neither,' said Charlie.

'You're both scared,' said Shini, shaking her head.

'You open it then,' challenged a red-faced Tom.

Shini looked across at Charlie who nodded in agreement. She leant forward on the sofa as Charlie and Tom leant backwards. Grasping both catches she pulled them sideways and jumped as both clasps sprung open. Gingerly, Shini opened the lid. The three friends peered inside the case.

'Can you smell bananas?' asked Charlie.

'And a faint smell of curry,' added Shini.

Lying in the bottom of the case was a plain envelope. It was sealed. Written on the envelope in long flowing handwriting it said:

TO WHOM IT MAY CONCERN.

Shini took the envelope out of the case and turned it round in her hand. There were no other markings and it was plain to see that there was only a single sheet of paper inside the envelope when she held it up to the light. Charlie pulled the case towards him and began to examine it. Although the case was empty its interior was lined with paper, and in one corner of the lid was a block of printed symbols. Attached to the lid were two leather straps crossing one another. They were held in place by brass pins. Next to the hinges were two valves and a tiny, ancient-looking bulb bolted next to a small brass box.

'What d'you think that box does?' asked Charlie.

'Not sure,' said Tom leaning forward to inspect it. 'It must have power, otherwise why would it have a bulb and those valves?'

'Maybe that writing in the corner will explain,' said Shini.

'That's writing?' said Charlie.

'I recognize it,' replied Shini. 'It's definitely not Hindu, but I think it might be Nepalese or Tibetan. There's an easy way to find out,' she added as she pulled out her phone and took a photo of it. She tapped away for a few seconds and then sat back on the sofa and smiled. 'You have to love these translation apps. Some of them are so bad! Okay, this one is better... it says:

'Congratulations on your purchase of the 'Valise Adventurer Mk.IIA'. The ultimate travel accessory for the discerning explorer. Handcrafted in Tibet by Master-craftsman: Ran Wan Limpo. 500-year guarantee. Please read instruction manual before use.''

'Right,' said Tom. 'So we know where it was made and who made it, but we don't have the instruction manual which looks like it should be attached to the lid using those leather straps. I think we should open the letter...'

'You do it, Shini,' said Tom. 'I'll never be able to read that handwriting.'

'Okay,' she said opening the letter carefully. 'It's dated 4th June 1923. And reads:

To Whom It May Concern,

   My name is Agnes Matilda Cramp, the beloved wife of Sergeant Arthur Bartholomew Cramp, mother of Felix Arthur Cramp and former housemaid of No.35 Chepstow Villas. W11. I have spent most of my life in hiding from a cabal called The Shadows of the Void, guarding this case and the journal hidden within for nigh on sixty years. I am now too old to continue.

I decided to withhold this information from my only son, Felix. He never knew his father and I did not want the same fate to befall him.

I hope that you, the one who has finally opened the case, can discover its secrets and renew the war against the enemies of humanity. To do so you will need to find the journal. The journal and the case are inextricably tied; one cannot work without the other. I have removed the journal and placed it in safe keeping with an old friend of the family. It is held by Colonel Askew-Manly of the Royal Geographical Society. A good soul and unknown to the Shadows. He will help you. Remember: They must never take possession of the case - even if your life depends on it. May the Ancients protect you.

Yours sincerely,

Agnes Matilda Cramp.

'So what do you think?' asked Shini placing the letter on the table.'

'I can't see where this thing gets its power from. I mean this brass box is tiny...' said Charlie.

'Looks like we'll have to find this bloke at the geography thing,' said Tom.

'Except that he'd be more than a hundred years old by now,' said Shini as she tapped the screen of her phone. 'But... wait... there is a

Professor Manly who's the Director of Research... He's about the right age to be his son or something.'

'I don't know,' said Charlie raising his head out of the case. 'We were lucky today. I think we should quit now while we still can.'

'Really?' said Shini. 'But we could just give this guy a call and see what he says.'

'Sounds like a plan,' said Tom. 'Wouldn't you like to see if we can get the case working?'

'Are you two really that stupid? That demon was going to kill us! Do you *want* to die? Because I don't. They own banks across the world. They had the case and they were waiting for us. Who's to say that this Manly bloke wasn't caught by the Shadows? Maybe it's another trap...'

'Alright, mate. Chillax,' said Tom. 'We can be careful.'

'I agree,' said Shini.

'At last,' said Charlie turning to Shini. 'Someone with some sense...'

'No. Like Tom said. We should be careful. Calling warned them. I think we should go back up to London and try to find this Professor Manly and see what he's like.'

'Now that's a plan,' said Tom.

'We're all going to die,' said Charlie placing his head in his hands.

FOURTEEN

Sunday 8th February 2015. City of London.

The office in the penthouse suite of the crescent-shaped 'Ellipse' building in London's Canary Wharf had obviously been designed by a person with an utter revulsion for curves, or possibly a hatred for the architect of the Ellipse. Everything within the office space was angular, sharp, aggressive and minimalistic; the materials used were stainless steel, chromium and heavy plastics. The black-tiled floor gave the impression of walking in space as flecks of diamonds glistened beneath the feet. The seven metre long table was made from platinum and topped with acrylic glass which had been injected with a deep red liquid; two rows of chairs matched the design of the table. The window over-looking London covered one entire side of the room. Beside that window, gazing across the financial centre of the United Kingdom, the River Thames, and the city streets stood a solitary figure. He was tapping his foot. Next to the figure was a gilded bird cage containing a pair of near-extinct Tasmanian Orange-bellied Parrots. Soundless, the parrots huddled together in the far corner of the cage.

Seventy-five floors down, at the entrance to the building that had been nicknamed 'The Mango' by the press, shuffled a rather short, dishevelled man in his late fifties. He was balding and suffered from terrible dandruff that heaped upon the shoulders of his ill-fitting tweed jacket like newly-fallen snow. The security guards standing outside the entrance to the building grimaced at each other as the man approached. Each guard reached an impressive two metres in

113

height, wore paramilitary black and had bulges in pockets that were not bags of sweets. They both angled towards the shuffling man as he approached.

'Who are you?' ordered one of the guards, towering over the man.

'And what d'you want?' asked the other.

'I'm here to see Count Strigoi. And who I am will mean little to you, I'm afraid,' said the man in a posh English accent.

'Yeah, right,' said a guard. 'Let's see your I.D.'

'Bend down a little closer and I'll show you,' said the old man calmly. The two guards folded themselves in half to reach the gentleman's level. In a blink, his looks transformed from that of an alcoholic history teacher to a visage filled mostly with razor-sharp teeth, a forked tongue, rotten green skin, and jet-black eyes. The two guards jumped back a step and were faced by the gentleman from before. 'I doubt Count Strigoi will be overly pleased if I'm kept waiting... and your names are?'

Twenty seconds later, Lord Cofgod stood in the express elevator hurtling skywards towards the seventy-fifth floor. *Kindertotenlieder* by Mahler was playing from hidden speakers. The music made Lord Cofgod smile – music about the death of children always did. The doors whispered open and led down a hall, past other closed doors, to the office. Lord Cofgod raised his hand to knock when the door opened silently. Cofgod rolled his eyes, cleared his throat and entered.

'Lord Cofgod,' said the count, although he did not turn and was still staring out of the window.

'The very same,' replied Cofgod, unimpressed. He walked over to a section of brushed steel and depressed a button that revealed a well-stocked drinks cabinet. He helped himself to an ancient whiskey and added a frozen cube of blood from an ice box beneath. 'I have some rather unsettling news.'

'And what news is that?' asked Strigoi, turning to face his visitor. The count was immaculately turned out in suit and tie. His pale features were angular, accentuated by his slicked-back hair. His shirt buttons were black pearls and his shoes were made from the skin of a baby Black Rhino.

'The case has gone,' said Lord Cofgod.

'What case?' asked Strigoi frowning.

'*The* case, remember? Flintstaff and Cramp? It was stolen from our bank in Covent Garden. I believe we arrived a minute too late.'

'But where was the Guardian?' asked the count as he clenched his fists. He walked over to the bird cage and gently lifted the golden catch to open the wire door. The two parrots waddled away from his hand. The count grasped one, yanked it squawking from the cage and bit its head off. He drained the blood from the still-fluttering corpse and lobbed it at a waste-paper basket in the corner of the room. The body hit the lip of the bin and flopped to the floor. Count Strigoi frowned. 'Was the demon still there?'

'Oh, he was there alright, and over in the corner, on the ceiling, the door, the floor.'

'Any clues to who it might have been?'

'The only evidence we found was an empty bottle of cola, a pool of vomit... and a strange smell of mint. The Guardian obviously believed he was able to deal with whoever it was by himself. Looking for a bit of glory, I should think.'

'So,' said Count Strigoi glaring balefully at Lord Cofgod. 'You're telling me that we don't know who took the case, how many of them we're looking for, or how they managed to defeat a Guardian Demon who was placed there specifically to entrap anyone who came for the case?'

'Um,' said Lord Cofgod closing his eyes, mentally ticking off the questions. 'Yes, that about sums it up. We did find a single footprint.'

'And all our other security issues are accounted for?'

'Absolutely,' said Cofgod. 'I checked with the security firm about the CCTV cameras in the area but they were shut down for maintenance, I'm afraid.'

'Have you informed anyone else?'

'By anyone else, I assume you mean Duke Lycaon?'

'Yes.'

'I thought it best if we dealt with it.'

'Good. He has enough on his plate setting up the meeting in Davos,' said Count Strigoi as he pulled a chair from under the table and sat. He beckoned Lord Cofgod to do the same opposite him. The count tapped on the tabletop. The window over-looking the city instantly blacked out and became a vast screen. Numerous panels opened on the glass as the count tapped out information. Messages were sent across the globe, orders given, demands made. In an instant, messages returned.

'Anything I can do?' asked Cofgod feeling a bit left out. He'd never really got the hang of the whole computer thing.

'Yes. In the meantime, you can release your minions to sniff out who stole that blasted case. I want the case back and whoever took it. If they can open it, all the better. I will not have everything we've worked for jeopardized. Do you understand?'

'Perfectly,' said Cofgod and drained the rest of his whiskey. 'Do you want the culprits alive? Or can I dispose of them as I see fit?'

'Alive. Dead men tell no tales and I like a good story. Information is key in this.'

'Shame,' replied Cofgod nonchalantly. 'My minions find it so hard to restrain themselves.'

FIFTEEN

Sunday 8th February 2015.

Charlie sat at the dining table as he cut into a steamed carrot and wedged it onto his fork with a slice of veggie sausage. Sunday dinner was the one time his dad said they should always eat together as a family. Charlie tried to get out of it but he'd already missed two Sundays in a row and knew his dad would sulk for the rest of the week if he didn't attend. The 'family time' was usually spent in silence with an intermittent question coming from his mother about school or a story about one of her healing circles. Charlie's dad would grumble about some bishop, or the reprehensibility of the Catholic Church. Charlie didn't even know the difference between the two religions and couldn't care less. He'd been a secret atheist for a couple years now.

However, for once, he was in desperate need of advice from his father and was shocked at how difficult it was to broach the subject. He'd rarely, if ever, asked his dad for anything other than stuff like money, computers, phones, trainers, etc. His dad was a wallet. A very tight wallet. He was not someone you went to for advice unless you wanted an hour-long sermon.

'Er, Dad,' began Charlie. 'I'm doing an R.E. assignment at school about evil spirits and that sort of thing. You know... demons and stuff. Do you know anything about it?'

'Well,' began his father as he happily munched through a large mouthful of roast potato. 'The Christian faith has varying views upon the matter. Jesus was known to have exorcised many people

117

possessed by demons. For example Luke 8.2: *'and also some women who had been healed of evil spirits and infirmities: Mary, called Magdalene, from whom seven demons had gone out.'*

Matthew, Mark and Luke also mention the famous moment when Jesus casts the demons from two men – some believe one man – into a herd of pigs which all run into the sea and drown...'

'Natural healers believe that it's just negative energy, Charlie,' interrupted his mum. 'Many believe that demons were just another way to describe illnesses.'

'For once, I tend to agree with your mother,' replied his dad. 'I've never encountered a possession. Schizophrenia, panic attacks, drugs – these can all be misinterpreted as possession. Take the Roman Catholics. They're so medieval they still have exorcists running around...'

'Now, now, Peter,' said his mum as she placed her hand on his dad's arm. 'We don't need to get onto that subject.'

'They're still medieval, whatever you say,' grumbled his dad as he impaled a Brussels sprout.

An hour later Charlie was up in his room searching the net for anything that could help them in preparing for what might come. Shini and Tom were online and they shared whatever they found that might be useful. Charlie wanted to tell his mum and dad what had happened at the bank; to shock them. *I killed a demon. Not a possessed man, not a negative energy, but a huge slathering beast with teeth like daggers.* They'd escaped with their lives by sheer luck. Charlie doubted that kind of luck could last. All they needed was the journal and then they could quit. From the research they'd done they knew the professor was the son of Askew-Manly and that he worked at the Royal Geographical Society. They'd have to wait until the end of term on Friday before doing anything. It was a half day so they should be able to make it up to London before the R.G.S. closed.

Charlie spent another hour surfing and then rushed through some maths homework he'd forgotten about before loading his computer game. After completing another level he gave up. Somehow he just couldn't get into it. Not like before. And that was the problem he was facing now; the Charlie he'd grown used to who lived in the time 'before' the Ouija board and the Charlie who lived in the after. And he wasn't sure he wanted to be the new Charlie.

He crawled between the cold sheets of his bed just after midnight, closing his eyes and re-living the moment when the elderly man transformed into a demon, again and again. His tongue probed his split lip proving to him that he couldn't escape the reality of the situation. He'd told his mum and dad that he'd cut it working at Tom's farm.

It wasn't easy getting comfortable and sleep wouldn't come as spurts of adrenaline shot through his body whenever he thought of the demon, or the case, or what they were getting mixed up in. Charlie heard his parents turning out the lights and closing their bedroom door, the soft mumble of a conversation and then silence. An owl hooted in a nearby tree. A glimmer of moonlight came through the window that overlooked the graveyard. Shadows played across the surface of the suitcase from the beech tree outside. A soft orange glow came from the side window. Charlie turned in his bed and scrunched the pillow up to make it more comfortable. He must have slept if the dawn light was already coming in but he didn't feel like he had. Slowly, his brain jerked him awake. How could there be moonlight and daylight coming from two different windows? He hopped out of bed and peered through the side window. It wasn't daylight… it was fire.

Charlie raced out of his bedroom door and ran down the stairs, yelling to his parents as he went. Into the kitchen, he yanked on a pair of trainers and unlocked the front door. He hesitated just for a second then swung it open and ran outside into the frigid night. The garden shed was completely in flames. The tar roof was ablaze, billowing acrid black smoke into the night's sky. Charlie ran to the outside tap beneath the kitchen window and dragged the hose pipe towards the shed. He knew he was too late, far too late to save anything of value in the shed, but he still aimed the jet of water at its base and played it across the fire. His dad ran into the garden, leaving his mum to phone Emergency. His dad tried to take the hosepipe off him but he resisted.

Charlie watched the flames dance and jump as oil cans caught, the dull thud of the mower exploding under a pile of dust sheets and cardboard boxes, the blackened frame of his bicycle hissing every time the water hit the tortured metal. He thought he could see faces in the flames; they seemed to be laughing. All of his stuff was in there. All the things he was building and fixing and his only mode of transport – his stupid girl's bike. Just when he thought he could feel no worse his dad gripped his shoulder and said,

'I've told you again and again not to leave that bloody heater on.'

Monday 9th February 2015.

Charlie was dropped outside the school gates by his mum. He'd hardly slept. His dad had really hurt him by blaming him for the fire and although he knew he hadn't left the heater on, he wouldn't listen. After all, Charlie was the only person to go in the shed in winter and that was proof enough. By the time the fire engine had arrived there was nothing left of the wooden shed; it was a steaming, smouldering ruin. Charlie's mum had offered the firemen cups of tea and apologized over and over again. The fire officer had taken Charlie aside and told him he'd done a good job of tackling the blaze, reacted quickly and contained the damage.

'Remember,' he'd said 'It's only a shed and it's only got stuff in it. There's nothing in there that you can't replace. If it was your house that would be a different matter, eh? Just make sure you disconnect your electric appliances in the future...'

The last words had stung. His dad had got to the fireman first. Charlie had trudged back to his bedroom and sat at his desk with his head in his hands. What was he going to do now? He'd have to work twice as much to buy another used bike and he was pretty sure, eventually, his dad would make him pay towards a new shed. And then Charlie shook his head, trying to clear it. *I know it wasn't the heater that started the fire. Why am I even thinking about my bad luck? The fire was started by someone else... that's what's important!*

And so Charlie had shut off his light and opened his curtains and divided his attention between the window overlooking the graveyard and the one facing the side of the house where the shed had been. Terror gripped him in the cold hours of the night. If the Shadows had tracked him down so quickly, there was a good chance that his house would be next. He'd phoned Tom but got no reply. Shini had answered, her voice thick with sleep, and had listened to Charlie's news and his theory. Shini had told him not to worry about her because her house had a wall around it armed with security cameras and alarms. She'd told him how sorry she was and that they'd work it all out tomorrow at school. Shini's smoky voice had filled a part of his brain with warmth but he'd still spent most of the night on guard duty.

Charlie told Tom before lessons began but had to wait until break before all three of them could stand out in the cold and discuss this turn of events. There were still so many questions concerning the case that the burning of the shed just seemed like a distraction, except that Charlie was convinced there was a connection.

'Listen,' he said. 'So far we've discovered that relatives of mine and Tom have attempted to hide the case and this journal, or whatever it is, from these Shadows of the Void. We then locate the case by using a Ouija board. However, we also awaken something that appears in Tom's stable and tries to attack us from inside a can of lemonade. They say they'll find us and yet when we arrive in London to get the case there's only a single demon there to stop us.'

'Only one!' exclaimed Tom. 'I think that was quite enough, thank you.'

'And yet it wasn't,' added Shini frowning. 'How many are there and where do they come from?'

121

'I dunno. But that letter mentioned a war. Not a fight - a war,' said Tom.

'Let's assume that the demon was intending to imprison us or kill us,' continued Charlie. 'Had it managed to keep us there we'd now be in the hands of the Shadows.'

'I agree,' said Tom. 'We need that book. If it can tell us how to defeat these Shadows then we might stand a chance.'

'But if they already know where I live then how much time have we got before they catch one of us... or kill us?' asked Charlie.

'Why would they burn your shed and not your house if they wanted to kill you?' replied Shini.

'A warning?' said Tom. 'Maybe they want to scare us into bringing the case back to them. Maybe they knew Charlie had the case in the house and didn't want to damage it.'

'It's in my bedroom. Under the bed.'

'Great hiding place, mate,' said Tom punching Charlie in the arm.

'Fair point, Tom.' Charlie said as he glanced at a murder of crows squabbling in a nearby beech tree. 'We've got to hide the case. And we need that journal, but I'm not sure it can wait till the weekend.'

'So what do you suggest?' asked Shini.

'Sometimes there are more important things to do than go to school.'

'Excellent,' said Tom. 'Let's bale.'

'Not today. Not yet,' said Shini. 'We need to get prepared for this. It would be stupid to go to London without a plan. Let's stick to Friday after school breaks up. Then we have a time to organize; do some research.'

For the rest of the day Charlie could hardly keep his eyes open. He'd never felt so tired. Each lesson dragged on forever as he stared out of a body that hardly seemed to belong to him; voices echoed in his head as teachers garbled on senselessly. His eyelids had become the heaviest part of his body and his head dipped and bobbed as he fought to stay awake. Finally the bell went and he could get a lift home with Tom's dad. Just as he was climbing in the passenger door Jack Marvin sauntered past with a few of his 'crew'.

'Oi, preacher-boy,' he sneered. 'Where's your girl's bike?'

Charlie glared at Jack but was too tired to react any further. Tom wasn't.

'Oi, Marvin,' said Tom waggling his little finger. 'Where's your little chode?'

Marvin stopped abruptly, causing one of his crew to bump into him. He turned and pushed his mate out of the way and walked straight up to Tom. Tom didn't back down an inch. He stood by the door of his dad's pick-up and faced his aggressor. Jack Marvin pushed his face close to Tom's.

'Watchit, Sheep-shagger, or you'll be next,' he whispered and then grinned, showing off his silver tooth.

'I'll be waiting, chode-boy,' replied Tom.

SIXTEEN

Friday 13th February.

'Are you sure you want to do this?' asked Shini as she held Charlie's shoulder. Shini's eyes sparkled in the last of the winter sun. London traffic surged past them.

'No. It is Friday the thirteenth, you know,' answered Charlie. 'But I'm here now. Let's get on with it before I change my mind.'

'All sorted?' asked Tom. 'Skype me now and remember to leave the camera facing out so we can see where you're going and what's happening. Any sign of trouble and we'll come running.'

'I think calling the police might be better,' said Charlie. 'Just don't leave me.'

'Never,' said Shini.

With those words swirling around his mind, Charlie walked along Exhibition Road. He Skyped Tom and got the okay. Charlie felt his heart beat faster as he approached the R.G.S. This was certainly the most stupid thing he'd ever done and he prayed it wouldn't be the last. He still wasn't sure how it had ended up being him going in alone.

He'd spent the whole week in a foul mood after hearing what Jack Marvin had said to Tom. This had almost been a declaration that Charlie's shed hadn't been burnt down by the Shadows as he'd originally thought but by the village hooligan instead. It'd been Shini that had kept the situation under control. She'd persuaded Tom that marching into the estate where Jack lived and demanding justice would be suicide. Shini had also put things in perspective for her two friends. She'd asked them what was better: an idiot bully with zero brains burning the shed down or a demon? Shini reminded them to stay focused.

The last light was dying as he walked into the entrance of the R.G.S. Inside was a lady at a reception desk, she was already in the process of packing up for the day. She glanced up at Charlie as he came in.

'Sorry, dear, we're closing for the day. We're open to visitors from ten till five, Monday to Friday.'

'Actually, I'm here to see someone,' said Charlie presenting a headed piece of paper with a name printed below. Charlie hoped the forged letter would work. 'I have an appointment.'

The receptionist squinted at the paper and picked up a phone. She punched in a number and waited. 'There's a young man here to see you, Professor. Says he has an appointment. Really?' said the receptionist frowning. She placed a hand over the receiver. 'He says he doesn't have any appointments.'

'Tell him my name is Flintstaff,' said Charlie. 'Henry Flintstaff-Membrayne.'

Charlie thought he heard a kind of squawk from the phone once this piece of information had been relayed. The receptionist's head was bobbing up and down and then she replaced the receiver.

'Through this door. Down the corridor until you reach a set of stairs on your left, then up two flights and it's the first door on the right. The professor requests that you knock on the door and wait until he receives you. He's an extremely busy man and will need to finish his meeting before seeing you.'

Charlie did as he was told. As he walked down the corridor he whispered into his phone.

'Did you get all of that?'

'Yep. Good luck.'

Once Charlie reached the top of the stairs he checked the strap holding his Kukri that he and Tom had made from an old horse bridle. It held the knife against his back and meant that he could pull it free with his right hand. It was his only protection if this was a trap. Although the building was cold inside sweat was running down his back. He couldn't understand why he'd agreed to such a stupid plan. This was plain crazy. In the next few minutes he was going to be captured, tortured and killed. And yet there was one piece of the jigsaw that didn't fit. If the Shadows had the journal and the case then why hadn't they tried to combine their powers? Unless there were separate groups within the Shadows working towards different ends... Charlie took a deep breath, cursed and knocked on the door.

'Just a minute,' said a voice from behind the door. Charlie waited. The voice didn't sound threatening, but nor had the little old man from the bank. 'Okay, you may enter.'

Charlie opened the door and peered inside, the room was gloomy and wreathed in smoke; it smelt of pipe tobacco. Glancing down there seemed to be chalk markings on the floor. Suddenly a hand grasped the collar of his jacket and hauled him inside.

'We have him, Professor!'

Before Charlie could utter a word he was hit in the face by a bucket of cold salty water. Spluttering for breath, a pound of garlic swung through the air crashing into the side of his head, knocking Charlie sideways just as he caught a glancing blow from a crucifix. Half-stunned he dropped to the floor. He fumbled for his Kukri but couldn't release it before he was face down with a knee in the small of his back and his arm twisted painfully behind him.

'The stake, Professor. Get the stake...'

'Stab him with the silver letter-opener...'

'The tin of pilchards. Use the pilchards, for pity's sake!'

'I'm not one of them,' grunted Charlie with his face pressed against the parquet floor. 'I'm a human.'

The person holding him down didn't loosen his grip. He heard someone come round from behind the desk and then he felt a sharp pain in his hand.

'Ow! You bastard,' yelped Charlie. 'You bloody stabbed me.'

'He doesn't seem to be dissolving, Professor. Maybe he's speaking the truth.'

'So how does he know about Flintstaff then?'

'You're right, Professor. Better safe than sorry; let's stake him.'

'Whoa!' yelled Charlie. 'Please, wait. There's a letter in my trouser pocket. Read it. It's from Agnes Cramp. The case. We have the case!'

Charlie felt someone dig around in his pockets and then after a few seconds the grip on his arm was released. A man immaculately dressed in tweeds and brogues pulled him to his feet. He must have been about thirty years old but his clothes made him look fifty. Standing beside him, still armed with a wooden stake and a tin of pilchards was an elderly gentleman with puffy red cheeks, a straggly smoke-stained beard and a bulbous nose sporting horn-rimmed glasses. He also wore tweeds; although his were threadbare, and he wore fluffy slippers that resembled a pair of dead cats.

'My name is Charlie Lawrence,' began Charlie, sucking on his hand where he'd been jabbed by the letter-opener. He was dripping wet. The room he was standing in was a large study with chairs, bookcases, a table and a rack of glass jars containing specimens of odd-looking creatures. Runes and circles had been chalked over the floor where he was standing but most of it had been washed away by the bucket of water. 'And I'm a relative of Major Henry Flintstaff-Membrayne. The letter you're now holding was discovered in the bottom of an old case, and as you can see, it says the journal is being held in safe-keeping here at the Royal Geographical Society.'

The old man placed the stake and the pilchards onto the study table behind him and picked up a battered and chewed pipe. He struck a match and puffed away until a deep glow emanated from the bowl of the pipe and great bellows of smoke issued from the side of his mouth. He stared at Charlie. 'You have the case?' he asked.

'Yes,' said Charlie frowning. 'But not here. Somewhere safe. Do you have the journal?'

'Yes,' said the professor frowning. 'But not here. Somewhere safe.'

At that moment the door behind them flung open, propelling Charlie headlong into the professor. The pipe flew into the air sending burning tobacco across the room. The young man in the tweeds was barrelled over by Tom as Shini stood in the doorway, case in hand. 'Nobody move!' she shouted. 'This case is armed and dangerous.'

Shini's command was ignored. Charlie and the professor were flapping their arms around in a desperate attempt to put out numerous small fires that covered their clothes, while Tom and the man wrestled on the floor. Once the fires had been smothered, Professor Manly and Charlie extracted the two rolling around on the floor.

'Please, please,' begged the professor. Let us all just sit down and discuss this like normal human beings. It's quite obvious that you three are *not* from The Void and I think you can safely say the same of us. Let us introduce ourselves and see if we can't share information that might be beneficial for one and all. I am Professor Manly and this is my associate Dr. Edison Frobisher.'

'This is Tom Cramp and this is Shini,' said Charlie.

'Well, well,' said Dr. Frobisher smoothing down his jacket and staring at Shini. 'Is your name short for Aghanashini by any chance?'

'Yes, it is,' replied Shini smiling in surprise.

'You do know that it is Sanskrit for Destroyer of Sins. That is quite a remarkable and beautiful name,' said Dr. Frobisher with a winning smile.

'Well, what does my name mean then?' asked Tom jutting his jaw out.

'Not much,' replied the doctor glaring at Tom. 'Quite boring really, means 'twin' in Aramaic.'

Shini placed the case on the floor beside her as Charlie was handed a crumpled handkerchief by Professor Manly to dry himself.

Shini informed them that they might want to speak to security as Tom and Shini had rushed past the receptionist as soon as they'd seen Charlie being attacked from his phone camera.

'Sorry about our precautionary tactics, young man,' said Manly refilling his pipe. 'Holy water, by the way…'

'And the tin of pilchards?' asked Charlie handing back a sodden handkerchief.

'Apparently imps hate fish,' replied Manly a little lamely. 'Now then, I assume Ms. Shini has the case beside her. I would very much like to see it.'

'As we would the journal,' replied Shini smiling innocently.

'Fair enough,' agreed Professor Manly rising from his chair. 'You'll have to come with us though.'

SEVENTEEN

The taxi stopped outside a small row of houses in Albion Mews situated on the other side of Hyde Park. Professor Manly, Dr. Frobisher and the three friends squeezed out of the taxi. Charlie couldn't believe there were any streets like this left in London; there were gardens and even a small wooded area and no traffic. Apart from the noise of the city it could have been a street in a village. As Dr. Frobisher handed the cab driver the fare the others followed the professor to the large front door; beside the steps leading to the door an arch led through to the gardens at the back of the houses. The interior of the house was richly furnished with mahogany, plush Persian rugs and gold-framed oil paintings.

They followed the professor into the kitchen where he made them all a pot of tea and then led them through to his drawing room where he beckoned them to take a seat. Shini was still holding the case and placed it between her and Charlie. Dr. Frobisher entered a few minutes later with what could only be the journal bound in a silk cloth. He unwrapped the silk cover to reveal a leather-bound book which he reverently placed on the coffee table. He then took out a small notebook and pen from his pocket and took a seat. The professor sipped his tea, placed it back on its saucer, relit his pipe and steepled his fingers.

'May I be the first to ask a question? Then I believe we can take it in turns.'

'Sure, why not,' agreed Charlie after glancing at his friends.

'Where did you find the case?'

'In a bank,' replied Charlie.

'A Bank? Where?' asked Dr. Frobisher.

'Our turn,' said Tom belligerently.

'Does the journal tell us how to use the case?' asked Charlie.

'Not per se, although it does mention the use of a crystal as a sort of pen. It's more of an explorer's log,' began the professor. 'It describes events, gives measurements, dates, times, methodology. There are numerous languages used, glyphs, runes, codes, hieroglyphs etc. etc. Edison has a PhD in linguistics and glottochronology which has been extremely useful in studying this book. It is not a 'how to' book, if you know what I mean. So, my next question is how did you get your hands on the case?'

'We found it by using a Ouija board,' said Shini. 'Through the information we were given, we traced it to Davenport's Bank in Covent Garden...'

'Davenport Bank? That's incredible. But it must have been guarded...?' interrupted Edison.

'It *was*,' said Tom proudly. 'Our turn. We want to look at the journal.'

'Then let's clear the table of cups and we can study the book and the case together.'

Once the cups were cleared Shini placed the case on the table beside the journal. Although there were no visible signs, Charlie felt a distinct change in the air around them; a feeling of distant thunder – the static moment just before a lightning strike. Charlie picked up the journal carefully, the tan leather warm in his hands. The spine of the book was very thick and the book felt heavy. He opened the front cover and read the first page:

Dear Major,

25 December 1858.

Have a Jolly Merry Christmas and a fruitful New Year.

Yours sincerely,

Sergeant Cramp.

If found, please return to No. 35 Chepstow Villas, W 11. London. A reward of one gold sovereign will be paid upon delivery.

The next page was less personal but certainly more interesting. It described, in detail, how to use three moon-infused flint blades to disarm and dis-leg a Slavic demon called a Chort. As Charlie was flicking through the pages with Tom one side and Shini on the other, he noticed that the professor was having trouble opening the case.

'You just flick the catches to the side,' said Charlie. 'They were a bit stiff but we sprayed WD40, so they should work fine now.'

'Seems to be stuck,' replied the professor as he pressed and pulled. He pushed the case towards Edison who then began his own struggle with the catches.

'Honestly,' said Tom as he moved over and flipped them open with ease.

Edison and the professor opened the case with extreme caution. Charlie watched the look of confusion cross their faces as they saw it was empty. Edison took his notebook and began jotting down the Tibetan script while the professor brought out a magnifying glass and inspected the brass box, bulb and valves.

'The journal always mentions that the case is filled with valuable and useful items,' began the professor. 'It enables instantaneous travel around the globe and can carry unlimited items within whilst remaining light enough to carry... this brass box; it looks to me like a sort of...'

'Energy source,' finished Tom. 'But what powers it? That's what we can't figure out.'

'As it was built in the mid-nineteenth century one can assume that it will be steam-powered... and yet it's tiny... where would the coal and water go? Ah, here's a little tray and next to it a hole for pouring water...'

'Er, excuse me,' said Shini holding a hand up. 'Did you say that this case allows you to travel wherever you want?'

133

'Well, something like that,' said the professor still poking the brass box. 'But it hardly seems likely. Flintstaff and Cramp were renowned within the R.G.S. for their eccentricity. This little device is fascinating…shall we try to power it up?'

'We have some smokeless coal,' added Edison rising from his chair.

While the two scientists were busy preparing the case, Charlie kept examining the book. There was something odd about the spine. It was too thick just to bind the pages together. Turning the book on end he noticed that a small corner of the leather binding had become dog-eared and beneath the leather was a glint of gold. Glancing up to make sure the two men were not paying him any attention, he peeled the leather back which revealed a tiny gold catch. Slid to one side the catch revealed a secret compartment within the spine. Holding the book upright, a pencil-thin shaft of crystal dropped into his hand. It was broken in two pieces. Charlie glanced at Shini who had been watching his every move. She shook her head slightly. Tom was busy with the scientists. Charlie replaced the crystal, slid the gold catch across and pressed the leather back into position. No one else had noticed.

'Are we ready chaps?' asked the professor. He had a pair of tweezers and was placing a smouldering chip of coal on the brass plate. Dr. Frobisher had used a syringe to squirt a few drops of water in the hole and then went back to jotting down notes. The professor slid the plate back into the brass box and everyone gathered around to see what would happen. There was the slightest glimmer from the bulb and a tiny wisp of steam from the hole where the water had been poured. And that was it.

'Oh,' said Tom. 'Not much good then.'

'Except that it proves we are correct in our assumptions. This is a steam engine of sorts, although it seems to need a more powerful source of fuel than coal.'

'What like?' asked Tom leaning forward.

'I'm not sure, but it would have to be more concentrated. Denser than coal by the look of it.'

'Hmm,' agreed Tom.

Charlie was still looking through the journal. The pages were filled with the elegant writing of Sergeant Cramp and the precise notes of Major Flintstaff. There were sketches, tables and graphs, mathematical equations, algorithms, glyphs and measurements. Charlie flicked to the last page of writing. Sergeant Cramp gave a rundown of items packed into the case for their last journey to a place called Vijayanagara in Karnataka in India. As he read the name, Charlie felt heat upon his scalp and his vision swam for a second. He felt dizzy. He could almost taste something and yet it escaped him. The list of items included various strange weapons and a hundredweight of bananas. The last paragraph was something more personal and some of it was written in Latin.

We have discussed our predicament at length and believe we are walking into a trap with our eyes wide open. Being of the Empire, and soldiers to boot, we shall face whatever horrors have been prepared for us. Our only goals are for Agnes to be rescued and our most prized possessions NOT to fall into enemy hands. With the emergence of the Industrial Age our hopes were for the advancement of humankind and the search for its true destiny towards enlightenment. However, the dark cloud of the Shadows has also benefited from such advancements. Once they were separated by great distances that can now be crossed with ease. They are unifying. If the Shadows collude it will be the greatest threat humanity has ever faced. I fear our services will be sorely needed in a time of great upheaval. Should we not survive the coming battle the world may be brought to its knees...

'Eram quod es, eris quod sum.

Manus in mano.

Quod si inveni placeat reverti transporter.'

Below the writing were four glyphs. Charlie and Shini glanced at each other as he closed the journal and placed it on the table.

'Do you know how it all works?' asked Charlie.

'We've ascertained from our studies,' said Edison, 'that the case and the journal are fairly useless apart. Flintstaff and Cramp used some type of crystal to transcribe glyphs, or symbols, that allow the case to travel. Holding hands would enable more than one person to travel at the same time. Many of those symbols are written down in this book. There is also mention of a map they used that includes all the places of power on earth. However, there is a reference late in the journal of it being stolen when Agnes was taken hostage. It seems the map gave the locations of all the places of power both for the light and the dark.'

'Do you mean light and dark, as in there may be entities out there that are not Shadows?' asked Shini.

'Exactly,' replied the professor. 'There are entities that Flintstaff and Cramp actually called upon for help.'

'I still think the most important question is who are they? The Shadows. Where do they come from and what do they want?'

'There's a page in the journal that explains something about them. The war against them seems to have been waged over thousands of years, so it doesn't explain much. They seem to have been summoned or created, possibly from another dimension, by the darker side of human nature. Apparently, all the legends and myths of mystical beasts and demons may well have elements of truth within them.'

'Are you saying that because humanity created these things in its imagination they became real?' asked Shini.

'It's a bit chicken and egg, I'm afraid. Which came first?'

'So have you met any of them?' asked Tom.

'Who?' asked Dr. Frobisher.

'Shadows. Have you come across any of the Shadows?'

'Not as of yet,' said Dr. Frobisher. 'We've been refining our research to the journal itself. The rest is just hypothesis.'

'You've had the book all this time and all you've done is read it?' asked Charlie amazed.

136

'We've studied it. What else could we do? We only had a journal written by two men who went missing a hundred a fifty years ago and were later accused of occult practices. And as far as we knew the case had been lost or destroyed. This whole thing could have been a fantastical hoax, a fiction. But now we have the case we might try a few experiments...'

'What do you mean? Now you have the case?' asked Tom.

'We'll need to study its properties...'

'Actually that's why we're here,' said Tom leaning forward to take hold of the journal. 'I'm very grateful that you and your family have kept the journal safe for us for so long, but it's getting late and we need to get home. I'm sure you can come and visit us on Sunday or something, and then we can talk about how to use the case properly...'

Dr. Edison Frobisher laughed, while the professor smiled.

'If you think I'm giving up this journal just as the case appears, you've got to be mad,' said Edison. 'I think you'll find it much safer if you leave the case in our possession so that we can study this in a secure and scientific environment.'

'It's probably for the best,' agreed Charlie. 'We could always come up again, you know, when things die down a bit...'

'Charlie!' said Shini glaring at him.

'What does that letter from Agnes Cramp say?' shouted Tom as he stood up. 'It says that you're looking after it. *Not* keeping it. It's ours and you know it.'

'But you're only children,' said the professor. 'How on earth do you think you can achieve any sort of results without our help? We're scientists. We have the backing of an historic institute. If the Shadows of the Void are real, they'll come looking for you, the journal, and the case. If they take the case and the journal together then heaven help us, apparently.'

'What do you mean: *if* the Shadows are real?' asked Charlie.

'Well, it's all hypothetical so far. What we need is a thorough investigation into the case and that would be safest and wisest to study here in London.'

'You think the Shadows are hypocritical... hypothermic... hypo... not real?' gasped Tom. 'We killed a seven foot demon to get this case, and if you think we're going to hand it over to a couple of old-fashioned idiots like you, you've got another thing coming. Haven't you people heard of jeans and trainers?'

'Erm, good point, Tom,' said Shini. 'We're leaving. Now. With the case and the journal. And if you want to study anything to do with them then you'd better let us go now, or I'm calling the police.'

'My dear,' said the professor. 'You're in my house. Who do you think the police would believe were the thieves?'

Charlie realised he'd made a mistake. These scientists were clueless. He lunged for the case, grabbing it before Edison could stop him. Tom managed to block the doctor before being flung to the floor, giving Charlie enough time to grab the journal and throw it inside the case. He slammed the lid shut. There was a feeling of static running through his fingers as he grasped the handle with one hand and fumbled for his Kukri with the other. Then he remembered what Aunt Maud had told him: *a blade is never drawn without paying the price in blood.* How could he threaten these men with a knife?

'Stop it! Everyone!' said Charlie placing the case on the carpet. 'We've got to work together. We have no idea who or what these Shadows are but we do know that one of them tried to kill us. Instead, we killed it. We're in this way over our heads, but I think you would be too. If we work together we might stand a chance of beating the Shadows. They were *our* relatives and they trusted *your* family to help us. And that's what you're going to do. Maybe the case is better off here. Maybe it is safer. Instead of treating us like kids who stole something, maybe you should start treating us with a bit of respect. We need the journal to learn how to defend ourselves and without the case you only have a book of notes. Can't you see that?'

The silence that followed Charlie's plea was broken by the ringing of Tom's mobile phone.

EIGHTEEN

A black Bentley crawled through London's rush hour traffic, behind the luxury car a black transit van followed. Inside the limousine Lord Cofgod sipped on a rare blood type. He was dressed in a pinstripe suit handmade by one of his tailors in Regent Street, although it did little to help Cofgod's unkempt appearance. Reclining on the rear seat he deliberated over his current course of action and how he had arrived there in the first place. He was outraged by Count Strigoi's demand that he discover the perpetrators of the Davenport Bank job. And yet here he was having to run around taking orders from a count whose peerage was certainly no greater than his own and happened to be foreign, which made it dubious in the first place. However, Count Strigoi was extremely powerful and had to be respected. So Lord Cofgod had set his minions to work, starting from the beginning.

Since the battle of Vijayanagara in 1865 where Flintstaff and Cramp had finally met their match, the Shadows had raced to London to retrieve Agnes, the case and the journal. Number 35 Chepstow Villas had been broken into by Cofgod's redcaps only to discover the entire building to be empty. Not a single scrap of information had been left behind. Every wall and floor had been tapped, sniffed, bashed or broken, and yet the house had revealed nothing as to the whereabouts of Agnes, the case, or the journal. Cofgod had later bought the house because he enjoyed the irony.

It was only seventy-five years later, during the London Blitz that fortune had swung the way of the Shadows. The East End had been hit by incendiary bombs and entire districts had been reduced to ash, along with thousands of residents. Amongst the cinders and piles of rubble a suitcase was found completely untouched by the inferno surrounding it. A young air raid warden had discovered it but he'd never made it home that night. He'd been intercepted by a vigilant minion.

The Shadows were jubilant. Once opened, they could retrieve the journal and learn the secrets of Flintstaff and Cramp and the case itself. Cofgod had watched the first minion try to open the case. It had been one of Strigoi's vampires. The minion had shown no fear as it grasped the catches. No one had expected the vampire to survive but neither had anyone believed the thing could liquefy so immediately. Others were pushed forward; a minion from every clan. None survived. Humans were told to open it but it remained stubbornly locked, although humans didn't die as a result... at least not due to the case. Tempers flared and blood was spilt until Count Strigoi, Duke Lycaon and Cofgod decided to use the case as a trap. If anyone came for the case the Shadows would be ready. But decades had passed and interests had moved on. New technology had intrigued and overridden the desire for the workings of the case.

Since the fall of Flintstaff and Cramp many of the Shadows had unified and manipulated humanity to twist it towards their own end. Lord Cofgod had done remarkably well in the mills and mines of the Midlands and the North. He built slum after slum and filled them with humans and joyously watched as their wretched children choked on the fumes and furnaces, the dust and dirt until they were old enough to take over from their dying parents. It was a marvellous and unremitting system. He placed his minions amongst them, sniffing out dissent and devised terrible accidents for those that stood against him.

Eventually he shut down his factories in Britain and sent all his manufacturing overseas. He was impressed by the ability of developing countries to work in such horrific and suicidal conditions. He never wore a single article of clothing made in one of his sweat shops in Asia; the quality of material was so poor it hardly survived its first machine wash. It meant that Cofgod could mark down his clothes to an unbeatable price, destroying any legitimate human competition.

The Davenport bank robber had come as a surprise to Cofgod. A footprint at the scene proved that it had been a human involved in the robbery and had to be a professional to destroy a demon summoned from the Void. Cofgod was still cursing the demon he'd placed there to guard the vault. Demons were fickle, avaricious and self-seeking by nature and it had been Cofgod's mistake to believe that his power over it would ensure its loyalty. The demon had obviously wanted the case for itself and paid the ultimate price for its failure. The hidden alarm placed beneath the case had alerted Lord Cofgod's minions but they'd arrived too late. Since then his redcaps had been busy trying to locate the source of the telephone call made to the Davenport Bank.

They knew that two members of the Flintstaff family had evaded them in the1980's. Maud Flintstaff had managed to take her niece out of school after her parents had been murdered whilst sailing. The two had disappeared, or changed identity. It had been a mistake not locating them and those responsible had been liquidated. Maud Flintstaff was now either dead or ancient and still in hiding. Either way she was of little threat. The niece however may well have bred by now and that was of greater concern.

The Cramp family had, by all accounts, died out after they'd taken care of Sergeant Arthur Cramp. He was meant to be the last of an ancient line. Thus it had caused some alarm when Cofgod had been handed a mobile telephone number that was registered to a Thomas Cramp. The target lived on a farm in Oxfordshire with his mother and father. There was also an elder brother who was currently in West Africa teaching permaculture.

It would have been quite simple to drive over to the farm, eradicate the family and retrieve the case. But having lived in a bog for over ten thousand years, preying on unwary travellers, Lord

Cofgod had certainly learned patience. It was better to wait and see what this person might reveal. And he was proved right. Cofgod had been alerted this very afternoon that Tom Cramp was on the move. He listened with increasing interest from the comfort of his offices in Mayfair as three teenagers boarded an express train for London Paddington, took the Circle Line to High Street Kensington and walked to The Royal Geographical Society. Cofgod had called for his chauffeur and a team of zealous minions trained in the delicate art of massacre.

A motorbike had followed the three teenagers and two scientists from the R.G.S. to a house in Albion Street. The targets were now ensconced within one of the houses as Cofgod's Bentley pulled into the quiet street with the large black van following closely. The mirrored glass dividing his chauffeur slid down silently as the driver inclined his head towards his lord.

'How would you like this done, sir?' asked the driver.

'Keep one of the children and the two scientists alive. The priority is the case and the journal... everything else is of little interest.'

'And in which dimension would you like our lads to go in, sir?'

'Oh, I think they should see what we really look like, don't you? After all, an enemy surprised is half-defeated,' said Cofgod as he picked up the in-car telephone.

NINETEEN

Tom rifled through his pockets and grabbed his phone.

'Hello?' said Tom and then frowned. 'What d'you mean: 'Gotcha'?'

Charlie glanced across the table towards Shini. The temperature in the house had dropped by ten degrees. He felt the skin tightening around the base of his neck and goose bumps appeared on his skin. Tom put the phone back in his pocket.

'Well weird,' he said. 'Some upper class bloke just said, 'Gotcha,' and hung up.'

'I'm sure there's nothing to be concerned about,' said the professor as he re-lit his pipe and puffed it into life.

'Have you got a back door?' asked Charlie as he fumbled for his kukri once more.

There was a crunching thud from the hallway, like the sound of an axe smashing into wood. Dr. Frobisher cursed as he leapt from of his chair. He raced out of the room into the hallway. In an instant he rushed back through the sitting room door, slammed it shut and began dragging a leather armchair across the room to bar the door. 'We're being attacked by stunted goblins!' He shouted. 'They're hacking through the front door.'

'What?' asked Charlie running over to help the doctor.

'They're called Redcaps.'

'What're Redcaps?'

'Splat!'

'Those.'

They all had their first ever view of a redcap. It was sliding unceremoniously down the glass of the bay window. Charlie could only describe it as the type of goblin he'd seen in fantasy movies and role-playing computer games. It was green-skinned, shod in iron boots, wore torn and ancient clothes and had a bloody red cap on its head. It must have been all of four feet in height with clawed hands. As it slithered down the window the cap it was wearing left a bloody smear. The first redcap was followed by another as it thumped against the window but failed to break it.

'Triple-glazing,' said Professor Manly by way of explanation. 'I never thought I'd live to see the day that a fairy story would come true before my eyes.'

'Well, you may not live to see the end of it,' yelled Charlie as the sound of splintering wood grew more intense. 'How do we get out of here?'

'Don't you know?' asked Dr. Frobisher as he ran over to the fireplace and grabbed a brass fire-poker. 'Legend says you can't outrun a redcap.'

'What d'you mean?' asked Shini. 'They've got stumpy little legs. We must be able to…'

Another redcap thudded against the window and managed to hold onto the frame with one hand. It opened its mouth and snarled at the people inside, showing off its cracked, yellowed teeth and blackened tongue. In one hand it held the business end of a medieval pike which it battered against the window. A crash at the front door was enough to spur the humans into action.

'To the back door,' shouted Dr. Frobisher. 'Follow me.'

Charlie grasped the case and leapt over the sofa following the professor and Shini into the kitchen. Tom dragged the coffee table over towards the living room door and upended it. Just as he pushed it tight against the door frame the point of a rusty old pike smashed through the door barely an inch from his face. Tom jerked his head

146

back as it came through again but this time he grabbed the shaft and pulled as hard as he could. His effort was rewarded with a satisfying crunch and a curse as he pulled the pike through. The pike was only a few feet in length and he spun it round and thrust it back through the hole in the door. There was a yelp. Tom roared with a mixture of joy and fear, and then he ran.

'Come on, Tom,' yelled Charlie from the kitchen door.

Once inside the kitchen, Tom found Shini tapping away on her phone as Charlie was helping Dr. Frobisher drag a Welsh dresser in front of the door leading to the hallway. Professor Manly was peering out of the back door that led down to a small garden surrounded by a five foot close-board fence.

'I got one of them,' shouted Tom as he brandished the pike. He glanced over at Shini and added: 'Is this really the time to be texting?'

'I'm not texting, you idiot. I'm looking for ways to stop them.'

'Well, they don't like it back at them,' said Tom brandishing the pike.

'The journal mentions sea salt,' said Dr Frobisher as he dragged the kitchen table over with the help of Charlie. 'They're called redcaps because they dye their caps red with the blood of their victims. If their cap dries out they die too.'

'I have salt,' said the professor. 'Second cupboard on the left. Above the kettle.'

Shini flung open the cupboard and rifled through the contents until she found a kilo bag of Atlantic sea salt.

'I think you should leave now, while you have the chance,' said Professor Manly as wood splintered from the kitchen door. 'I'll hold the fort. Come on, you don't have much time left. They'll find the garden soon enough. Get outside and jump the fence into the neighbour's garden and so on until you reach the Bayswater Road. If you can hail a taxi then get the hell out of here. I'll hold them back for as long as I can. You too, Dr. Frobisher. You must continue the good work.'

'I'm not leaving you, Professor,' stated Dr. Frobisher.

'Then you'd better take this,' said Shini handing him the sea salt.

'Shini,' said the professor grasping her shoulders. 'You have to listen to me. If they followed you here then they know who you are, which means they probably know where you live. That tells us they have substantial power. Do you understand what I'm saying?'

'I'm not sure...'

'You have to disappear. Completely. You won't be safe at home.'

'But...'

'Now go. Flee!'

Charlie grabbed Tom by the arm and pulled him towards the back door. Shini followed. They raced down the short flight of steps and into the garden. Tom scrambled over the fence first, still armed with his pike. Charlie watched Shini vault the fence before he passed her the case and hauled himself over. They scrambled through rose bushes, tripping over children's toys and barging through hedges. Up and over, up and over they went. After they'd vaulted the third fence Charlie heard the scrabbling sounds of pursuit. He stopped and glanced back over the fence. There were three redcaps. One was hanging over the fence hauling one of his comrades up while another was below him hanging on to his feet. Tom came up beside him.

'If we can't outrun them then we need to stop them here,' said Charlie. 'They'll be at a disadvantage getting over the fence.'

'Right,' agreed Tom hefting the pike.

Spying through a knot hole, Charlie watched as the redcaps hurried towards the fence separating them. They each carried a pike and clumped along in their iron boots. Two of the redcaps held their pikes together while the third stepped onto the shafts. The two holding the pikes heaved their comrade into the air.

'Now!' shouted Charlie.

Tom stuck the pike into the frosty grass with the iron blade pointing skywards. It all seemed to happen in slow motion as the redcap catapulted over the fence and then realised that its landing was not going to be a soft one. In mid-air it attempted to fly backwards by wildly flapping its arms. It did little to reduce the impact. With the sound of jelly hitting a marble floor, the redcap kebabbed itself on Tom's iron pike. Another redcap scrabbled to the top of the fence and peered over at its lifeless friend before the corpse fizzled into dust. It hissed in rage and then turned to find Shini suddenly appear next to it. She smiled and grabbed its bloody hat from its head. The redcap howled in despair, dropped from view and vanished in a cloud of fug. The last redcap charged straight through the fence. It used its teeth, talons and pike to smash its way through.

Shini, Tom and Charlie ran through the tangle of the small wood before reaching the Bayswater Road. They helped each other straddle the railing and just as Charlie dropped the other side he saw the redcap hurtle towards him from the darkness. He dodged to one side as the redcap thrust the pike through the railings, missing him by inches. It hissed at him and clambered over the barrier. Charlie didn't think. He grabbed Tom and Shini and sprinted across the road, oblivious of the cars and buses swerving this way and that to avoid them. As they reached Hyde Park Charlie spun round to see the redcap sprinting at astonishing speed towards them; its iron-shod boots clanking across the road until a No. 53 double-decker bus crushed it beneath its wheels. In a moment it was gone. The bus screeched to a halt. Other cars were stopping and people were getting out and looking under the bus. There was a dent at the front of the bus but no body. Only ash.

'Let's not hang around,' said Shini. 'Too many questions.'

'What about the professor?' asked Charlie.

'Call the police, mate,' said Tom. 'It's the best we can do. Let's move it.'

TWENTY

'How... how did they find us so quickly?' asked Charlie. He stared at his hands; they wouldn't stop shaking. The train was packed with commuters and they were standing between two compartments as it rattled westwards. Charlie felt claustrophobia clawing at his heart. He couldn't breathe. He wanted to scream.

'The professor told me the Shadows have power,' said Shini. 'If they can raise demons and own banks then it looks like they can track a bunch of teenagers.'

'What do we do?' asked Tom as he checked through his phone.

'You need to dump that for starters,' she said nodding at his Strawberry.

'No way! That cost me four hundred quid.'

'Listen to me, both of you. How did they find us?'

'No idea,' said Charlie looking down at his phone. He'd only just got it.

'Either they had cameras in the bank and can do some sort of face recognition, or they traced the call we made to the bank back to Tom.'

'You mean they've been watching us?'

'It's that, or they have some darker power to find us...'

'What're we going to do?' asked Charlie. He'd been listening to them but felt a million miles away, like he was on another planet. Nothing felt real anymore. Had Tom really skewered an irate goblin with a pike? What the hell was going on? He wanted to faint. He wanted to go home, sit upstairs in his bedroom and play stupid computer games for the rest of his life. He wanted to go back to school even.

They stood in silence for a while, swaying back and forward with the motion of the train. They were all nervous; in shock. Tom was still holding his phone which was shaking. Shini was playing with a strand of her hair, winding it round and round her index finger. Charlie realized he was clenching his hand around the handle of the case. He looked down at the battered thing with all its strange post marks and bills of lading and felt a degree of calm fill his being. They had the case and they had the journal. They did have hope. If they could learn to use what they'd fought so hard for then they might just beat the odds so heavily stacked against them. And then it came to him.

'I... I think I've got a plan,' he said. 'We're going to upset a few people but it's the only way we can do it. Unless anyone else has a better idea.'

'Go for it. But Tom, you have to ditch your phone,' said Shini.

'Okay. Okay. I can always get another one.' He took the sim card out of the back and went into the toilet of the train. Charlie and Shini heard the toilet flush and Tom reappeared.

'What about you two?'

'My turn next,' replied Charlie. 'So here's what we do...'

*****

They walked to Shini's house first as it was the closest to the train station. It had turned into a misty night as the frigid air hit the warmer water of the River Thames; it spread across the land like ghostly tentacles. There were lights on around the house. Raj's car was gone but her dad's Aston Martin was parked on the gravel drive. Shini said her dad would probably be in his study, on the phone to one of his associates trying to hammer out another deal on an exotic car. They left her by the gate and walked a little way down the road to wait for her.

Twenty minutes later Shini's eased her way through the front gate again carrying a rucksack on her back

'Everything okay?' asked Charlie.

'No problem,' she replied. 'I told him I was going to stay with a friend for the weekend.

'He was okay with that?'

'I told him my friend's dad was a priest.'

'Ah,' said Charlie, grateful it was dark and Shini couldn't see the colour of his face.

'Who's next?'

'Me,' said Charlie. 'Tom's parents are used to him being in the den til late. They won't know he's gone till morning. Come on, it's a good couple of miles so we better get a move on.'

Tom and Shini waited a hundred paces from the cottage in a turn-off to one of the surrounding fields. Leaving the case with them, Charlie clambered over the gate and walked through the grass towards the dark silhouette of the church. He skirted round the field until he could approach his house from the back. It would mean going through the graveyard but it was the least likely way he would be spotted if anyone was watching the house. He hunched down and jogged towards the fence. At the ancient, ivy-covered iron railings of the graveyard, he stopped to catch his breath and scout the area. Charlie scanned the tombstones. This was where dead people were put in the earth to rot and become soil. That was all. Or at least it had been. Now was a different story…

Charlie took a deep breath and wedged his foot between two railings and hopped over the fence. He landed amongst frosty leaves and grass, making little sound. There was a light on in his parents' bedroom and one downstairs in the kitchen. He crept beside the graves, using them for cover. Over the next fence, he walked past the burnt remains of the shed and up to the corner of the house. It looked clear. The front door was open and he pulled upwards on the door handle, knowing this would stop it squeaking when it opened. He went through the hall and up the stairs, treading in a tried and tested pattern to avoid the creaking steps in the old house.

Once inside his bedroom he pulled a bag out of from the closet and filled it with clothes, a pair of walking boots, a torch, batteries, matches and a Leatherman's multi-tool. As he made his way past his parent's bedroom he placed a note on the floor by their door. He crept back to the kitchen but stopped as he passed the living room where his mum performed some of her healing ceremonies. A glint of light had caught his eye from the collection of semi-precious stones his mum had on display. He went over to the table and examined the stones. He'd seen them a million times and some of them were beautiful to look at but he'd never bothered to learn what his mum actually did with them. To one side, next to a large polished Tiger's Eye, was a finger-length piece of translucent crystal. His mum said it was all the way from a special mountain in Brazil. She'd told him it was a self-contained generator. It had power. Charlie frowned, slipped it in his pocket, and left the house.

Tom was last. It took twenty minutes to walk to the dirt track that led to the back of the barns and the old stables. As they approached the buildings, Charlie hissed for them to stop. Up ahead was the silhouette of a large car parked at the end of the gate. There was a single orange glow inside from someone smoking a cigarette.

'Shit!' said Tom. 'What do we do? I have to warn my dad...'

'Listen, Tom. They're here for you,' whispered Shini. 'It's your mobile they traced, remember? That's why they weren't at Charlie's or my house, because they don't know who we are yet.'

'But we need the pick-up...'

'Maybe we should come back later,' said Shini.

'No way. I'm going home now and getting my stuff and getting the pick-up,' said Tom. 'We'll never make it without transport.'

'Then we need a plan,' said Shini.

'We could sneak round,' said Charlie.

'It's only one of those stupid redcaps. We'll do it together,' replied Tom.

'Hang on,' said Charlie unsheathing the kukri. He looked up and down the track before selecting a stand of hazel. As quietly as he could he sawed through two lengths and sharpened an end of each. Testing the points he passed one to Shini and one to Tom. 'If we get into trouble you'll have something to protect yourselves with.'

'Both of you take some of this,' said Shini. She pulled a bag of sea salt from her rucksack and poured some in their hands.

Charlie and Tom left Shini with the case and crept down the track towards the vehicle. Tom took the right side of the track and Charlie the left. There was only a slither of moon and some starlight but the lights in the farm cast a silhouette of the figure in the black Range Rover. At the last moment, beside the door, Tom stood up and tapped on the driver's window. Charlie could see the figure jerk in surprise and wind the window down. Then time seemed to slow. Tom threw his handful of salt straight into the man's face and as he did so Charlie wrenched open the passenger door and threw his too.

The man was certainly surprised by the assault but he failed to disappear in a puff of ash. Instead he looked down at his suit and began brushing the salt off. Very slowly he turned towards Charlie. His eyes were golden and he smiled, revealing two very sharp fangs.

'Hmm, salt,' he said licking his lips. 'It goes so well with a pint of blood.'

'It's not a bloody redcap!' Charlie yelled as he turned and fled down the track.

'It's a bloody vampire!' yelled Tom as he followed.

Charlie heard the car door open and he pumped his legs as fast as he could down the track towards Shini. His feet had turned to lead and he was sure he was moving backwards instead of forwards. Tom caught him up.

'He's after us.'

'I bloody know,' said Charlie stealing a glance back. 'I can't see him... he's... he's not behind us.'

And then he heard the beating of wings. Charlie strained to catch sight of Shini but he couldn't see her. He hoped that she was wise enough to hide so that at least one of them might survive to tell their story. Something swooped overhead, the flapping wings almost knocked Charlie over. He felt his ankle turn on a loose stone and then he was over, the kukri flying from his grasp, the frozen ground ripping into his hands and knees. He tumbled to a stop, with agonizing pain where stones were buried in his skin. He rolled over and searched the night's sky for the vampire. He saw Tom running back towards him. But it was too late. The vampire appeared as if by magic, its lucent wings folding behind it. It was as grey as granite and its face was pinched and bloodless. Charlie struggled to back away but the vampire stepped on one of his legs.

'Aaaargh!' shouted Tom as he charged at it with his hazel spear thrust forward.

The vampire stepped to one side and swatted Tom across the back of the head as he passed. Charlie watched Tom crash into a hedge beside the track and collapse motionless. The Shadow turned and stared into Charlie's eyes, boring into the depths of his soul, seeing everything; every thought, every desire and every weakness. It laughed as it bent over him.

'Before I eat you alive, boy. Tell me where the case is and I promise I'll kill your friend quickly. If you don't, I'll make him one of my minions and I'll spend a thousand years tormenting him. He'll be my pet. Do you want that, boy?'

'Please... please don't hurt us,' said Charlie. 'It's up the track, with the journal. You can have it back. We didn't mean to get involved...'

'Show me,' said the vampire grabbing him by the collar. It hauled Charlie to his feet with one hand, half dragging him along the track. They reached the area where Tom and Charlie had left Shini but there was nothing; no sign of her or the case. Charlie looked around desperately.

'We left it here, I swear.'

'Time to die, fool,' growled the vampire. It pressed him against the trunk of an oak and pushed his face sideways to reveal his neck.

156

'You might think you can stop me, but you can't. You're weak. Pathetic. I've lived for millennia and I will have what I desire.'

'Desire this, dick!' said Shini stepping round from behind the tree and smashing the case into the face of the vampire.

There was a high-pitched screech that clawed at their ears followed by a puff of ash. Charlie slid to the ground. He looked up at Shini and burst into tears. She crouched down beside him.

'It's okay, Charlie. You're alright. It's gone now. You're safe.'

'It's not okay. Don't you understand?' he said looking in her eyes. 'I would've told it anything it wanted. If I'd known where you were, I would've told it. I can't do this anymore. I just can't.'

'It's alright. Look, Tom's coming down the track. Come on. Wipe your face. That's it.'

'What happened?' asked Tom. He looked groggy and unsteady on his feet. He rubbed the back of his head. 'Where is it?'

'I whacked it with the case. It seems even touching it is enough to ash them.'

'Wish we'd known that before,' said Tom 'You okay?'

'Yeah, I'm okay,' said Charlie getting to his feet. He looked at his bloody palms and winced as he tried to pull out some of the grit lodged beneath the skin. 'You?'

'Feel like I've been in a rugby match against the All Blacks...'

'Come on, let's stick to the plan,' said Shini.

They all walked back down the track. Charlie hunted around in the undergrowth until he found his kukri. When they reached the car Charlie peered inside. He took the keys out of the ignition, put them in his pocket, and closed the door quietly. They climbed the five-bar gate and crept around the back of the barn until they reached the stable block. Tom stood one side of the den, Shini and Charlie the other. Tom lifted the latch and pushed the door inwards. It creaked horribly but no demons leapt from the room, so Charlie and Shini went in to gather what tools they might need while Tom went to the farmhouse.

A while later Tom appeared carrying a rucksack and a long leather bag strapped across his back. Charlie faced Tom and nodded towards the bag; Tom, grim-faced, nodded at his friend. He beckoned Charlie out into the night.

'Everything okay?' asked Shini.

'Fine,' said Tom unslinging the leather bag. He pulled the zip open to reveal a twelve-bore 'up-and-over' shotgun.

'Now we're talking,' said Shini. 'I've been thinking. Let's take the Range Rover instead of your dad's pick-up. It'll take longer for anyone to know we've run away.'

'Good idea,' said Tom. 'But I still think we should warn our families.'

'No. Shini's right, Tom. The more they know the more they're at risk.'

'If you're sure. Okay. Let's move.'

Charlie handed Shini the keys as they dumped everything in the back seats. Tom pulled the shotgun free of the bag and slipped two cartridges into the barrel before snapping it shut and checking the safety. Charlie sat in the back with the luggage. Shini started the engine and slipped it into reverse. She leant over and peered backwards as she reversed the car up the lane. Charlie watched her, noting how beautiful she looked when her hair fell across her face as she frowned with concentration. All he could feel was shame.

Once on the road, Shini drove through the dark country lanes following the directions given by Charlie. Charlie and Tom knew all the tiny back roads that wound their way through the countryside. They'd spent summer holidays cycling along every lane just to see where they went; escaping the chores doled out by parents. Shini drove up a steep hill and Charlie told her to take a left onto a farm track once she'd reached the crest. They were now deep in the Chilterns and heading further and further from any sign of village or town. There was not a single light on as far as they could see across the countryside; only the deep orange glow of distant towns on the horizon. After one more turning Charlie was relieved to see that his memory had not failed him as they bounced down the dirt track leading to Aunt Maud's farmhouse.

TWENTY ONE

Saturday 14th February. After Midnight.

The Lee Enfield .303 rifle pointing at Charlie through the letter box was hardly the welcome that he was hoping for from Great Aunt Maud. The fact that she was ancient, a bit wobbly and slightly mad didn't fill Charlie with confidence as he stepped out of the Range Rover with his hands in the air. He walked into the headlights that were shining at Aunt Maud's front door.

'Hello? Auntie Maud? It's me, Charlie. Your great nephew,' he said a bit desperately.

'Who's with you?' Aunt Maud shouted above the barking of Ruben behind her.

'Friends, Auntie. My friend Thomas Cramp and Shini. Friends from school.'

'What are you doing here in the middle of the night? Apart from scaring the living daylights out of an old woman?'

'Auntie, you're the one pointing a gun, not me…'

'It's not a gun, it's a rifle,' she said. 'Now then. Let's see these friends of yours, and I want them to move very slowly into the light next to you.'

'Come on you two,' said Charlie.

'I'm not going out there,' wailed Tom. 'She's a nutter, Charlie. Let's get the hell out of here.'

'Don't be ridiculous, Tom,' said Shini as she climbed out of the driver's side and walked up beside Charlie. She smiled at the barrel of the rifle that was still waving through the letter box.

Tom reluctantly followed suit. The barrel withdrew after a moment's pause and the front door opened. Ruben bounded out into the frigid night air and promptly thrust his head between Charlie's legs. Charlie grunted and ruffled Ruben's head and ears. Aunt Maud was dressed in a faded pink nightdress that became terrifyingly transparent as she stepped into the lights of the Range Rover.

'Oh my god,' said Tom and ran round the side of the car to kill the headlights. 'That's the scariest thing I've seen all night,' he whispered to Charlie as he walked past. Charlie laughed for the first time that day.

'Come on, you lot,' said Aunt Maud. 'Before you catch your deaths.'

'We need to hide the car, Auntie,' said Charlie as they grabbed their stuff out of the back and carried it into the kitchen.

'Into the barn, left-hand side, next to the old tractor. It should fit. And watch out for the cats…'

Shini went back outside with Charlie to hide the car. Tom leant his shotgun against a corner of the room before placing his hands in front of the Aga to warm them. Aunt Maud eyed him curiously. Tom went red in the face.

'Know how to use that?' challenged Maud as she glanced over at the shotgun.

'Since I was twelve years old,' replied Tom as he stared at the rifle Maud was holding. 'What about you?'

'Cheeky blighter,' she muttered arching an eyebrow. 'I may be old but I can still hit a tin can at a hundred paces.'

Shini and Charlie bustled through the front door with Ruben in tow as they carried the last of the bags into the kitchen. Maud peered outside one last time before sliding the bolts across the door. She placed the rifle against the welsh dresser and filled the kettle with water before placing it on the Aga. The three friends collapsed onto chairs around the kitchen table looking exhausted. Maud asked no questions as she cleared the table and placed four cups, a bowl of sugar, a jug of milk and a tin filled with biscuits in front of them.

Once the kettle had boiled she made them all a cup of strong sweet tea and sat herself at the end of the table in her favourite chair. From there she administered first aid to Charlie.

'Is it the police?' she asked sounding hopeful. 'Or the Shadows?'

'Uh?' grunted Tom half-asleep.

'Well, you're obviously on the run from someone and I'm rather hoping it's the police…'

'Sorry, Auntie,' said Charlie looking up from his tea. 'The Shadows have tried to kill us. More than once. If we go home they'll probably kill Mum and Dad too. I didn't know who else to turn to…'

'Despite being very angry,' began Maud. Glancing at the teenagers she changed tack, 'not with you three mind you, I'm very relieved you've made it here. You've done the right thing. Now, from the beginning. From the moment I last saw you. Tell me everything…'

Aunt Maud listened to their story intently, allowing the three of them time to add forgotten details and snippets of information that might be vital in the greater scheme of things. Once they had finished it was late into the night; they were physically and emotionally exhausted.

'I know you're all very tired,' she said. 'But I have some questions. Then I'll show you to your beds and run a hot bath for Shini. My first question is about the Ouija board. You say that it told you Henry Flintstaff and Arthur Cramp were defeated in India?'

'That's right' said Shini. 'And that we had to help save humanity. Then everything went crazy.'

'What do you think that means?' Maud asked. 'And it didn't say how you could do it?'

'No. But it gave us the code for a bank in London where the case was.'

'Unbelievable,' said Maud and sighed.

'Where we fought a demon and took this case which belonged to Flintstaff and Cramp and is meant to be a magical weapon against the Shadows. Now? Now I believe that goblins, vampires, demons and a magic suitcase really exist,' said Charlie. 'But two weeks ago I'd have said you were mad.'

'I did, actually,' said Tom. 'All that stuff about your brother in the war... I said you were senile. Sorry.'

'It's alright, young man, it's part of the curse our families carry; not to be believed. It's called the Cassandra Complex.'

'I don't think a Ouija board can lie, can it?' asked Shini.

'Probably not,' agreed Maud. 'We just have to find a way for you to save the world.'

'We could use the Ouija board again,' said Charlie. 'To see if we...'

'Too risky,' said Shini. 'The Shadows were on to us the last time.'

'Agreed,' said Maud. 'So, if we believe that the case can instantly transport a person to a given destination then getting it working must be top priority.'

'I agree,' replied Shini yawning.

'Enough for now,' said Maud standing slowly. 'I'll make up your beds and run you a bath.'

*****

Charlie woke from a wonderful dream about swimming in a perfect pool of water surrounded by jungle trees and the squawking of parrots. Then reality hit as Tom opened the bedroom door and flopped back onto the bed next to his. Charlie groaned as memories from the night before came crashing back. Images of the dying vampire, the clunk of redcap boots close behind him, the crash of doors being smashed from their hinges. He sat up and rubbed the balls of his hands hard into his eye sockets. Lights exploded behind his eyelids and then he turned and peered through the curtains behind him. The window looked out the back of the house onto the frozen fields as they climbed up to the copse of beech at the top of the rolling hills. The sun shone on a glorious cloudless day. He could see a couple of pheasants wandering across the field as crows swirled around the beech trees on the hill.

Charlie rifled through his bag and slipped on a clean pair of jeans, a t-shirt and hoodie. The house was surprisingly warm considering how run down it looked. He walked down the narrow passageway past the bathroom and the tiny sewing room Shini had slept in. Her door was ajar and he just glimpsed a bed with the covers pulled back and a crumpled pillow. His heart beat faster as he went downstairs, through the living room and into the kitchen. He found Shini sat next to Aunt Maud with the journal opened in front of them. Maud was wearing her usual array of oversized jumpers and corduroy trousers while Shini had her hair tied back and was wearing a V-neck sweater and tight leggings. She glanced up as he came in and gave him a smile that lit up his world. Maud caught the look on Charlie's face and nudged Shini in the ribs. They looked at each other and giggled. Charlie went red in the face as he turned to fill a mug with hot tea.

Once Tom had woken up they all ate breakfast. Afterwards, they cleared the kitchen table and placed all the items they'd acquired over the last couple of weeks. There were the two journals, one belonging to Maud's brother, Robert Flintstaff, dating 1942, and the other written by Sergeant Cramp and Major Flintstaff, dating 1865. There was also the letter from Agnes Cramp written in June 1923 and the case itself.

'Now then,' said Maud looking at each of them in turn. 'How're you going to deal with your parents once they find out you've not gone away for the weekend and you'll not be home on Monday morning?'

'I'm going to call Mum and tell her the truth,' said Charlie. 'Well, most of it. I'll ask her to go round to the Cramps and to Shini's dad and try to persuade them not to call the police or the newspapers.'

'What are the chances of that working?'

'It's our only option.'

'Once we get to a town we'll buy some cheap phones and call them,' said Shini. 'There's not much else we can do. Just hope, really.'

'I'll give you two days before your mum phones, Charlie. It'll be difficult to convince her that you're not here.'

'But you have to,' begged Charlie.

'And I will,' Maud replied. 'Our next concern is those hunting you. How much do you think they know so far?'

'They know where I live,' said Tom looking concerned. 'They won't try anything though, will they? I mean, against my mum and dad?'

'It's unlikely. They were watching your place, but that was it. They'd be stupid to attract the attention of the police,' reasoned Shini.

'Agreed,' said Maud. 'We've been gifted one or two days, I believe. Let's use it wisely. We need to be sure of a secure perimeter, a lookout, a full study of both journals and an attempt to work out how to use this case of yours.'

'I'll read the journal from 1865 and note down anything I think is relevant, especially types of creatures we may encounter and the methods Flintstaff and Cramp used to combat them,' said Shini.

'I'll walk the perimeter first and then read Robert's journal. It's been years since I did that and although I'm not sure it's going to help our current situation I may find something,' said Maud. 'I think you two boys should look in the tool shed for anything useful and make sure you cover up that car. There should be an old tarpaulin in one of the sheds.

Aunt Maud tugged on her wellies and great coat and marched out of the kitchen but not before Tom handed her his shotgun. She stopped for a second, snapped the break-action open and checked it was loaded before snapping it shut again. She smiled at Tom and hefted the weapon into the crook of her arm before marching out the door with Ruben in tow. Tom grinned at Charlie and shook his head. While Shini located a pad of paper and pen, the two boys laced up their walking boots and went outside into the yard. The sunshine and bright blue sky chipped away at some of the horrors of the night before. It was still freezing outside but the day held hope. Hope, and a single purpose that Charlie had never felt before; there was no more school and no family, just a mission to prepare and to survive. The farmyard was built in a 'U' shape with the house in the middle, a wood shed and coal store to the right of the house and the small barn and workshop to the left. The open side of the yard was sealed with a stone wall and the farm gate that lead up the track to the world outside. The track was the only way in for anything other than a tractor.

'Where first?' asked Tom.

'Coal shed, wood shed, tool shed and barn,' said Charlie pointing at each in turn.

'Sounds like the start of a farmer's rap song,' said Tom.

The coal shed had little of interest except a wide-bladed shovel, two buckets, half a ton of coal briquettes and a mummified rat. The door to the wood shed was half off its hinges as they entered the next building. Maud had done well with her wood scavenging; adding to the pile Charlie had chopped, the room was three quarters full. In the corner was a heavy-bladed log axe with an ash handle worn smooth from use. Tom swung it in his large hands and grinned. Sitting on a small shelf on the wall was a whetstone which Charlie put in his pocket.

They walked past the house and opened the tool shed. The room was covered in cobwebs as they pushed the door open. It groaned alarmingly and motes of rust and dust erupted into the air. Inside the shed it smelt of diesel and dust and oil and bird droppings. It was a decent size though, with a long table running down one side with a large vice bolted at the near end. Rusted tools hung from nails along its length. Pieces of pipe and broken farm equipment, electrical wire and bailer's twine, old tobacco tins and jars filled with rusting screws and nails covered the work bench. A billhook caught Charlie's eye and Tom pulled a garden fork, spade and scythe from one corner. A large canvas sheet mouldered away in one corner which Charlie dragged out while Tom hefted his axe in case any rats jumped out, but only a small field mouse skittered away squeaking in anger at being woken from its hibernation.

By midday the two boys had covered the Range Rover with the canvas, sharpened the billhook, scythe and axe to a razor's edge and piled together a collection of tools, fencing wire, barbed wire, hammers, nails and anything else they thought might be of use. They searched the Range Rover thoroughly in case the vampire had left his mobile phone inside the vehicle and disconnected the car battery just in case the Shadows had some way to track the vehicle. They found the registration papers inside the glove box along with the insurance documents; both gave a company address in Central London. The barn had an ancient tractor inside with flat tyres, bales of hay and some old pallets stacked in a corner. They were just dragging the pallets out into the yard when Shini opened the kitchen door and called them in for lunch.

Maud had made a huge veggie casserole that would last them both lunch and dinner with a mound of mashed potato on the side. The mash was drowned in butter and salt and tasted fantastic. After a second helping Charlie cleared the plates away and washed up while Shini did the drying. Maud put the kettle on and told them about the farm and used a framed aerial photo from the 1980's to write down the names of the surrounding fields and woods. Maud hung it next to the Aga so they could all use it for reference. Afterwards, Tom placed the case on the table and opened it carefully.

'Have you found anything that might help?' Tom asked Shini.

'Yes, I think so. Sergeant Cramp does mention powering the engine inside the case. He says it's powered by carbon and the more compressed the carbon the longer it runs.'

'But the hole to put the carbon in is tiny,' said Charlie frowning as he gently opened the miniscule brass door to the engine. 'What on earth can we use?'

'Er,' said Tom hesitantly. 'I might have something…'

'Like what?' asked Shini.

'Give me a second,' he said as he left the table and ran upstairs. Two minutes later he sat back down and cleared his throat uneasily. 'I want you all to promise not to be angry with me.'

'Why would we be…' began Charlie.

'Just promise,' interrupted Tom.

'Okay. We promise,' said Shini.

Tom dropped the velvet bag from his clenched fist, undid the tie, and poured out a pile of cut diamonds. There was absolute silence in the kitchen. Just at that moment the winter sun poked through the kitchen window and a single beam of sunlight hit the small pyramid of gems. Light refracted off a thousand facets and sent rainbow colours spinning around the room. Tom looked around at his friends. All three of them were gazing at the diamonds.

'What?'

'How?'

Tom held his hands up. 'Davenport Bank,' he said by way of explanation. 'I was the last to leave, remember? There was that cabinet by the door and as you two were running down the passageway I just had to take a look. The key was on the same chain as the vault key. There were quite a few metal trays and this bag was on the top. I didn't know what was inside but I grabbed it all the same. I didn't tell you because I thought you might think I was stealing them, you know – that I was a thief.'

'How many are there?' asked Charlie as he poked the mound of diamonds with his finger.

'One hundred and eighty-two.'

'That's a lot of diamonds,' said Shini.

'That's a lot of money,' said Charlie.

'Well, if you lot have finished gawping at them,' said Maud breaking the spell. 'Maybe we can see if one of them will power up this case of yours.'

Tom pulled out a pair of tweezers from his Swiss Army knife and picked up a single diamond. It was a few millimetres across and oval in shape. He placed it inside the brass door and pushed the door shut with a faint click. All four of them gathered round the open case and waited. And waited. And waited. And then it happened. A wisp of steam vented from the side of the brass case, a dull glow emanated from the valves and the bulb, and Charlie felt a soft vibration coming from the case itself. However, the case remained empty. Charlie noticed the disappointment on Shini's face.

'Maybe it's a bit like a computer,' he said closing the case and snapping the fasteners shut. 'Maybe it needs to kind of re-boot itself or warm up. Remember, it hasn't been used for a hundred and fifty years.'

'Or maybe they just left it empty,' Shini said. 'While we wait, I want to show you what Charlie discovered inside the journal.' Shini peeled back a small flap that Charlie had found when they were in Professor Manly's house in London and removed the thin finger of broken crystal which she placed on the table. 'The journal mentions that travel glyphs or runes only appear with the use of the crystal and the case combined. It utilizes the power of sunshine or moonlight and can be used as a sort of pen. There are different sets of glyphs for different parts of the world. The journal also mentions a map that has the locations of every travel portal on the planet, but in the last pages Major Flintstaff reveals that the Shadows stole it from their house in London. Flintstaff seemed undeterred by this because he remembered many of them off by heart.'

'I knew it was important,' said Charlie handing Shini the crystal he took from his mum's collection. 'And I knew my mum had one just like it at home; she uses it to realign a person's energy... or something'

'How does it all work though?' asked Tom. 'We have the journal, the crystal, and the re-booted case, so we should be able to travel like they did.'

'Except we don't have the map, or the memory of Major Flintstaff,' said Shini.

'But we do have the address of our enemies,' said Charlie waving the registration document of the Range Rover.

'But that's crazy!' exclaimed Shini. 'We're trying to avoid them, not walk straight through their front door.'

'As the Americans like to say,' said Tom in a cheesy accent. 'Offence is the best defence.'

'Ah,' said Shini. 'You mean like Vietnam, Iraq and Afghanistan, do you?'

'Exactly,' agreed Tom enthusiastically.

'I was being sarcastic, Tom,' said Shini shaking her head. 'They hardly won.'

'Depends how you look at it,' said Tom. 'The States has never been invaded by any of those countries, have they?'

'Yes, but...'

Charlie shook his head and pulled the case towards him, the argument dissolving into a background hum. He flicked the two catches and took a deep breath before opening the lid. The argument stopped abruptly as they saw Charlie's expression change. Maud, Tom and Shini jumped to their feet and hurried to Charlie's side. Sitting inside the case was a pile of carefully folded tweeds.

'Where the hell did all that come from?' asked Tom as he prodded a tweed jacket.

Charlie tentatively poked his hand inside the case, past the folded clothes, deeper and deeper as his hands brushed against a multitude of textures and shapes. He just wanted to touch the bottom...

'That's incredible,' whispered Maud. 'Look at your arm, Charlie.'

Externally, the case was no deeper than twelve inches, and yet Charlie's arm had disappeared up to his bicep and he still hadn't reached the bottom. At his maximum reach Charlie grasped something cold and hard. It was a Victorian ceramic toilet brush holder with 'Le Hotel Des Royales' printed on the side. Tom grinned and plunged his hands inside the case and dragged out a wooden pole which he continued to pull hand over hand until all ten feet of it had been revealed. The steel tip of the Cuirassier's lance was as keen

171

as a razor. Shini took a turn and pulled out a feathered headdress from the Matsés tribe of the Amazon jungle. Maud clapped her hands with joy, dug into the case and pulled out a beekeeper's bonnet.

'Pretty random, man,' said Tom pulling out a preserving jar with a dead frog floating in it.

'Its spatial dimension is all wrong,' said Shini. 'How's it possible?'

'I think we should be worrying about how this case is going to be any help in defeating the Shadows,' said Charlie. 'Although it's obviously magical it seems to be filled with junk.'

'I think we need to stay on track,' said Maud. 'You boys need to finish the wooden stakes while I organize the house. And put that lance somewhere safe.'

'There's no internet coverage here,' said Shini closing her laptop. 'We really need to get to town.'

'Well, Shini, I think we should go on a girls' day out tomorrow,' said Maud prodding the pile of diamonds. 'There are a few things we need to stock up on, or you three will eat me out of house and home.'

*****

Charlie hacked away at another stand of ash pollards as the sun dipped beneath the saddle of the hill to the west of the farm. Plumes of foggy breath erupted from his mouth as he used the billhook to remove unwanted side branches from the poles he'd been cutting. He couldn't stop thinking about his mum and dad. Were they in danger? He felt rotten that he was doing this to them. Tom said he felt the same and he was swinging his axe like a Viking; lopping the pollards with a single swipe. Once they'd collected thirty or so poles, each about as thick and long as a broom handle, they bundled them together with rope and hefted them onto their shoulders for the walk back to the farm. They clumped across the ploughed field as their mud-encrusted boots got heavier and heavier. Darkness crept across the field as they walked, snapping at their heels. Even though the temperature was freezing, both of the boys were sweating by the time they reached the farmyard.

They dropped the pile of wood beside the workshop and decided on a cup of tea before sharpening them into stakes. Aunt Maud was busy hanging their washing on a rack beside the Aga, humming away to herself. The kettle was gently steaming on the hot plate. There was no sign of Shini or Ruben, so Charlie popped his head into the sitting room and saw that like Ruben, she had been seduced into sleep by the warmth of the open fire. The journal was in her lap with one hand still holding it protectively. Charlie watched her sleep for a moment. He noticed that Shini slept with a hint of a frown creasing her forehead, as if she were solving a problem. Her eyelashes rested upon her high cheek bones and her lips were slightly parted as she breathed. He sighed at his own cowardice and closed the door gently behind him.

'Aunt Maud?' said Tom as he dumped another spoonful of sugar into his tea cup and stirred vigorously.

'Yes, dear,' replied Maud as she shook out a duvet-sized pair of her underwear before hanging them up.

'What are those symbols etched above the front door?'

Charlie took a cup from Tom and sipped the hot tea loudly as he sat at the kitchen table.

'They were one of the few things my father learnt during his time in the army. He said he met a mystic during his time in Hong Kong. They advised him to carve the symbols above his front door. They're protective symbols, or for concealment. Something like that.'

'Do they work?' asked Tom.

'Who knows...' said Maud as she hung a g-string of Shini's on the drying rack. Both boys stared wild-eyed at the tiny black garment until Maud glanced up from her work. Tom and Charlie instantaneously began a thorough study of their cups of tea. 'But nothing has bothered me here apart from some unruly teenagers.'

Charlie was suddenly hit with a realization that shook him so badly he could barely breathe.

'They're never going to stop looking for us, are they?' he asked.

Maud looked at the two of them and smiled sadly. 'No,' she said. 'They won't. That's why I've lived alone ever since your mother left, Charlie. I've been a terrible coward, really: too crippled by fear to take the Shadows on. Too scared of dying.'

'We'll get them, Maud,' said Tom grimly. 'Don't you worry about that; Charlie'll come up with a plan. Won't you, mate?'

'Er…' replied Charlie trying not to vomit.

TWENTY TWO

Sunday 15th February.

'I know…' said Count Strigoi into the receiver. 'Of course. We tried. I know it wasn't. Of course I can deal with it, what do you take me for? How dare you! It wasn't my fault. Then send some… I know it's only two weeks before the meeting. I understand.'

Lord Cofgod watched the count's face pale with rage as he fended off the caller. He knew who was on the phone and he couldn't help smirking at the count's unease. It was a Shadow of equal power, and some whispered, even greater than the count's. Cofgod glanced at the pile of dandruff on the shoulder of his jacket and brushed it off just as Count Strigoi turned and caught the action, grimacing at him in disgust.

'If you could decompose elsewhere, I would appreciate it,' said the count.

'Oh, don't mind me,' said Cofgod genially as he brushed off his right shoulder too. Count Strigoi glared balefully at him. 'I assume that was the Duke, was it not?'

'Yes, it was. He's sending one of his minions.'

'I thought he was busy setting up the summit of the cabal in Davos.'

'He is. But he said he wants to keep an eye on what's going on over here. Anyway, they may well be of help.'

'Doesn't he trust us to do the job?' asked Cofgod.

'Why should he?' stated the count angrily. 'You lost them.'

'We lost them, yes,' agreed Cofgod.

'I seem to remember ordering *you* to clear this mess up, Lord Cofgod, and all I hear is your complete failure to execute your duty.'

'I seem to remember you *requesting* me to complete a job which is still in progress. I don't remember any time limit being put upon it,' said Cofgod casually. 'I also hear whispers that one of your minions was not only eliminated at the farm but had his vehicle stolen too... can that really be true? Do you think your minion might have *helped* them escape?'

The temperature in the room dropped by thirty degrees; frost crept across the glass table top and ice crystals sprouted from the chairs. Count Strigoi's eyes narrowed as he grew in stature. Two inch fangs slipped past his lips like vicious stalactites and razor-sharp talons sprouted from his fingers. Cofgod arched an eyebrow and began whistling a tune while checking his suit pockets. Cofgod grunted in satisfaction as he brought out a clove of garlic and bit into it. Garlic juice trickled down his chin as he munched on the herb. Strigoi hissed in anger and retreated.

'Now then,' said Cofgod as he picked at his rotten teeth. 'If we can stop playing: *I'm scarier than you* games, we can get down to business. We know who we're dealing with at last and, although we've been taken by surprise, we should at least be content that we're only dealing with three children.'

'Continue,' muttered Strigoi as he took a seat.

'Our main target is Thomas Cramp who called the Davenport Bank with his mobile.'

'A Cramp?' said Strigoi. 'I thought we'd finished them off by eliminating the sergeant?'

'Seems like one slipped through the net.'

'Hunting a teenage Cramp should be good sport,' said Strigoi. 'So what happened last night?'

'Through his mobile number we managed to dig up his address which you know, of course. We tracked his phone and discovered him on the way to London with another boy and a girl.'

'Do we know who they are yet?'

'No. But we will. Anyway, I was informed and told my minions not to attempt anything until we knew their destination. We followed them to the Royal Geographical Society at around five o'clock where they met a Professor Manly and a Dr. Frobisher. They left the R.G.S. and took a taxi to Professor Manly's house in Albion Street where my minions assaulted the house…'

'Hardly subtle about it, were they…' added Strigoi.

'If you want subtlety, you don't call on redcaps,' explained Cofgod. 'The children fled with the case while Manly and Frobisher remained behind.'

'And what of these scientists?' asked Strigoi leaning forward.

'We have them,' said Cofgod with his black eyes gleaming. 'They are helping with our enquiries.'

'How much help?' asked Strigoi.

'Actually, not that much at the moment. They keep asking us questions… scientists, you know. Born inquisitive.'

'I'll send you someone. They'll talk. Continue with the night's events.'

'We searched the house in Albion Street and found papers pertaining to the journal. It seems that Dr. Frobisher has been studying the journal in secret for quite some time…'

'So the journal was never inside the case?' asked Strigoi.

'That is what we must assume. At some point Agnes must have split the case and the journal; hiding the case in that tenement in the Isle of Dogs and the journal with the R.G.S.'

'How did we miss the R.G.S.?' mused Strigoi.

'For some reason, it has been impossible to infiltrate the place. It's something about their scientific nature. It's as if they have a sixth sense...'

'What happened after Albion Street?'

'The children made their escape, resulting in the death of a number of my minions. We lost them after they crossed into Hyde Park. We traced Thomas Cramp's mobile phone to a train in Bristol, but it was a decoy. As far as we knew they were still in London until

I heard a report that one of your minions had disappeared at the farm of Thomas Cramp.'

'It's true,' admitted Strigoi. 'I sent one to watch the farm.'

'To watch the farm, eh?' said Cofgod. 'Or watch me? Do I sense some trust issues between us?'

'We're all involved in this, for the good of the Shadows.'

'My minions discovered his remains this morning,' continued Cofgod. 'We found a set of tyre tracks, footprints and a pile of ash.' Cofgod leant back in his chair and scratched his head; another small avalanche of dandruff drifted to the pristine floor. 'I suppose the only thing to do now is to kill young Cramp's family and wait for the children to give themselves up...'

'It is tempting,' agreed Strigoi. 'However, they are children and I'm inclined to wait. If we kill the parents first the police will get in the way and it saps our resources to deal with them. No, we'll send out minions to scour the area. I want the Cramp family followed. I want to be assured that if the children poke their heads out into the world for a second they'll be located. They'll make a mistake, get homesick, call a friend, or something. They still have no idea who they're dealing with.'

'But if they have the journal,' warned Cofgod, 'we must assume they will know soon enough.'

'No, I think you overestimate their abilities because of your failure to capture them. A hundred and fifty years ago we defeated the two greatest opponents of the Shadows with relative ease. We were still forming the cabal back then, we had limited resources...' Count Strigoi waved a hand around him. 'And look at us now; a global and dimensional unification has occurred. Even the great Flintstaff and Cramp would be powerless against us now. Three children cannot stop us. They may have the journal but they don't have the ability to use the case. We'll roll over them like a... like a...'

'Lawn mower?' suggested Cofgod enthusiastically. He liked riddles.

'No, a… you know, it flattens things…' struggled Strigoi.

'Ooh, I know. An elephant?'

'No, it makes roads flat…'

'Oh, you mean a steam roller,' said Cofgod.

'Yes, that's it!' exclaimed Strigoi.

'Hmm,' murmured Cofgod. 'They're a bit slow.'

*****

Cofgod descended to the ground floor of the Ellipse and strode through the bustling forum as humans and minions hurried to their work stations in order to make Count Strigoi even richer and more powerful than he had been the day before. It was almost frightening, the ease in which one could ensnare even the brightest of humans into focusing on the sole issue of accruing money and scrabbling towards an illusion of power.

'Security' was another magic word to be wafted under the noses of humankind; its scent was enough to drive normal people into a blissful ignorance of the darker truths. Weapons companies were the prime example, and money-maker, of this all-powerful word. To be 'secure' a nation needed to build very large and very dangerous bombs… so far so good. The same nation then sold those bombs to another nation; odd… because surely that nation could use them on the nation that built the bombs in the first place. In response to this new threat, the weapons companies designed even bigger bombs to out-bomb the bombs they originally built to be secure. It was fantastic, especially if you owned a weapons company – of which the Shadows had a leading interest in most.

What Cofgod found to be the most fascinating part of this process was that one would assume the ideas, ways and means of building weapons of mass and minor destruction would come from the Shadows themselves, but it wasn't the case. Humans had an infinite imagination when it came to visiting misery, death and destruction upon its own kind. The humans building and designing the bombs were rewarded with the illusion that they were protecting their loved ones and their country.

Cofgod actually enjoyed the arms conventions he attended, and had even questioned a lead designer of nuclear weapons on how he felt about it. At first the designer had no idea what Cofgod was talking about but when he finally did, he laughed and told him: 'I only build them, I don't press the button.' And that was how the designer of weapons of mass destruction lived with himself and that was why the Shadows would always be victorious.

Lord Cofgod had no idea how long he'd been alive. He remembered small groups of nomads long ago, dressed in furs crouching around fires, knapping flint and peering into the night with fearful eyes. They had been right to be scared because he had been out there, waiting for one of them to venture into the dark alone. He had watched them roam the land free; harvesting what they found and moving on. They had been a wiser people back then. They had worked together, everything for the common good, and had reached a pinnacle of understanding and reason. Every animal was revered. Every plant, rock and stream had its place, every mountain, every forest and every star in the sky had its story. Each member of their tribe understood everything around them. For Cofgod those had been the lean years, hidden away in swamps, awaiting the lame or the weak to pass him by. And then things had changed, not overnight, but it had felt like it. The people began building villages and discovered methods of planting crops and processing metals. People specialized and were ignorant of everything else; gifts became barter and barter became trade and trade meant money and money meant enslavement. Cofgod's days of plenty had arrived. He fed off the people's desire for individuality, their ignorance and their blood too.

Lord Cofgod left the Ellipse and waited for his chauffeur to open the door to his Bentley. He sat in the back and was driven through the streets of London. Continuing his train of thought, it was in the mid-nineteenth century, with the industrial revolution in full swing that had propelled the Shadows towards their true destiny. Most of the Shadows had spent millennia stuck in one place or another, feeding off humans with varying degrees of success. As civilizations advanced so did those Shadows that could follow in its wake. Duke Lycaon, Strigoi, and he were good examples of gaining positions of power. Australian Bunyips, along with various Asian, African and South American Shadows had remained less powerful because it took longer for the 'advances' to reach them. With the building of the first steam ships and locomotives a new age of travel had dawned and the unification of the Shadows of the Void had begun. Once isolated in power and knowledge, the shift in influence had transformed them.

And yet, thought Cofgod, nature always attempted to balance power and through the ages the shaman of the nomadic tribes had learnt, sometimes through disastrous trial and error, how to thwart, combat or quell the Shadows they came across in their wanderings. Weaker shaman often relied on human sacrifice to placate them, or they made deals, and those that did became the minions of the Shadows. There were always humans willing to deceive and betray their brethren in return for a little power. Those shamans that fought the Shadows dwindled in influence as the major religions were created and used to manipulate and control the masses. However, some survivors passed on their knowledge down the ages, nurturing new generations of shamans ready to take the fight to the Shadows and their ever-increasing minions.

The Shadows of the Void had never learnt how a shaman passed on such a mass of knowledge, but it had culminated in the rise of Major Henry Flintstaff-Membrayne and Sergeant Arthur Cramp. These men had single-handedly endangered everything the Shadows had been working on, and with their defeat in 1865, the Shadows had finally triumphed; their ability to pass on their knowledge had ceased to be possible and had let the floodgates of evil open.

The Bentley pulled up outside No. 35 Chepstow Villas. Cofgod smiled to himself as the chauffeur opened his door. He stepped out into the sunlight and trotted up the stairs to the front door. A minion opened the door and took his coat and hat as he entered. There was a certain satisfaction in owning the house of Flintstaff and Cramp, he thought, as he passed through the kitchen and into the scullery.

What Lord Cofgod truly desired was to learn how to use the case and the journal. If he could extract information from the two captive scientists then he would be damned if he was going to pass on that knowledge to the likes of Count Strigoi or Duke Lycaon. It was time for his own ascendance as the greatest Shadow of the Void. A redcap minion bowed his head and unlocked a heavy oak door, allowing Lord Cofgod to enter. He walked very quietly down the stairs to see how his chief torturer was getting along.

'Aaaargh!' gurgled Professor Manly as he slumped forward. 'You see?' he said to the redcap in front of him as sweat coursed down his face. 'That is far more painful than sticking needles through my hand. The mechanical nociceptors are far more acute through a wide incision than through a small puncture wound like a needle.'

'Wait!' whispered Dr. Frobisher just as the frustrated redcap selected a different scalpel. Dr. Frobisher was strapped to an iron chair next to his colleague. They were both the worse for wear, having been incarcerated for over twelve hours. Frobisher's shirt had been torn open and he had blood encrusting his lips and nose. One eye was swollen shut.

'Talk,' rasped the redcap.

'What I'd like to know is a little bit about the history of your evolution... I mean, do your own people have a history of origins? Do you have writing, or is it a verbal history? Where do you think you come from... on a personal level.'

'Well,' said the redcap leaning against a table laid out with a plethora of sharp instruments and gardening tools. 'My old Nan used to tell me about her love of those little blonde babies from the northern tribes in the forests of Germania and up into Scandinavia... you couldn't make a better soup, she said...'

Suddenly the redcap stopped talking mid-sentence, wailed mournfully and slapped himself in the face. He trudged towards the stone wall of the cellar, cuffing Dr. Frobisher as he passed by, and then banged his wide green forehead against the wall. Tears rolled down his face as his bloody cap flopped backwards and forwards each time he struck his head.

'Take a rest, Grott,' sighed Lord Cofgod from the stairs of the cellar. 'I'll deal with them from here.'

'I can't take it boss,' wailed the redcap. 'Bloody scientists. I torture them and they tell me I'm doing it wrong. Say I don't no nothing about pain neurons. Then they ask me about me Nan... I can't help talking about her. Haven't seen her since we left the Old Land and you know how much I miss her.'

'Now, now,' said Lord Cofgod as he patted the crying redcap. 'There's a fresh bucket of blood upstairs in the kitchen. Go and soak your cap; you'll feel a lot better.'

'Thanks, boss,' sobbed the redcap before stomping up the stairs.

Once the recap had disappeared Lord Cofgod took a seat from the table and dragged it before the two scientists. He made himself comfortable, lit a cigar, and leaned back in the chair. Both scientists stared back at him with curiosity, though bloodshot and bruised. Lord Cofgod actually found himself in a state of surprise. Usually, in this situation, the torturer struts around arrogantly dealing out pain on a whim and after a certain amount of terror and agony has been suffered by those being tortured, they tell you everything. And yet these damned scientists were so deeply imbued with a sense of discovery that he could see, even now, the questions forming an orderly queue in their heads. Combining this with the inherent connection between egoism and evil meant that most Shadows and their minions *wanted* to talk about themselves. Clever buggers, he thought.

'Gentlemen,' he began. 'Today you get to choose between life and death. Between answers and questions and between, and between...'

he forgot what he was going to say because Professor Manly had begun discussing Lord Cofgod's height with Dr Frobisher.

'He does seem slightly taller than his minions, perhaps an inch or two, but not by much,' replied Dr. Frobisher.

'And yet being so short, I would assume it does make a difference...' replied Manly.

'Excuse me,' said Cofgod turning purple with rage. 'But...' was all he could manage before transforming from the short, rotund gentleman the world saw him as. His tuft of white hair suddenly spiked amid boils and sores, his eyes had turned jet black and his jaw stretched to accommodate a row of dagger-like teeth. His nose almost disappeared into a snout and his ears became pointed with wiry hairs sprouting from them, his skin took on a grey-green tinge covered in warts and pustules and his fingers grew into hooked claws. From his mouth green saliva dripped onto the floor. The whole transformation took less than three heartbeats and the effect would have been mind-bendingly terrifying if only Lord Cofgod had been a little taller than four feet six.

'That's got to hurt,' Frobisher said with feeling.

'It has to. Just look at the difference in jaw line and the number of teeth. Why don't you ask him? Grott's response was a little too emotional.'

'Enough of your questions,' glowered Cofgod. 'Time for some answers.'

*****

Monday 16th February.

Lord Cofgod sat in Henry Flintstaff's former study facing a tall, elegant young woman with pale skin, wearing an expensive suit and shoes to match. Her platinum blonde hair was tied up, leaving delicate ringlets to fall about her long slim neck. She stared into him with ice-blue eyes. She was an executive minion sent from Strigoi to help extract as much information as she could from the two scientists. Cofgod found her alarmingly attractive and this was only exacerbated by her cutesy French name; Mimi. Cofgod was well aware of a vampire's ability to charm their victims into a willing death, but that did little to affect the more carnal thoughts that popped into his brain.

'You're late,' he said gruffly in an attempt to hide his inner thoughts. 'I was expecting you yesterday.'

'Then we should get down to business directly,' she purred.

'You're too late. We broke them late last night. I have everything there is to know here,' he said pushing a file across the desk.

'Broke them?' she asked raising one delicately plucked eyebrow.

'Into little pieces,' stated Cofgod.

The vampire leant forward and picked up the file. There was a single typed page within. Her eyes darted across the script before she looked back down at Cofgod.

'That is all?' she asked.

'Everything,' stated Cofgod. 'You can inform your master that we're doing everything we can to bring this operation to a successful conclusion. It seems that Manly was the guardian of the journal and Frobisher had made some cursory investigations into the legitimacy of the journal. From what we found at the professor's house in Albion Street, he was in the early stages of his research. I sent those papers to Strigoi this morning.'

'All of it?' asked Mimi.

'Of course,' said Cofgod.

'You're quite sure?'

'It would be unwise to question my loyalty,' growled Cofgod.

Mimi smiled with no emotion before bowing her head. She dropped the file back onto his table before turning and gracefully walking to the study door. Just as she was leaving she turned her head and looked directly into Cofgod's piggy eyes. 'Yes,' she replied. 'It would be very unwise...'

The door closed softly behind her.

'Bloody vampires,' muttered Cofgod. He heard the front door shutting and the clomping sound of very short legs wearing iron boots heading towards his study door.

'Sir?' said Grott.

'Call Babba Belani,' ordered Cofgod. 'And gather the troops. It's time for a different approach.'

TWENTY THREE

Shini and Maud left the farm in the morning, promising to return later in the day once they'd got everything they needed. The night before they'd all contributed to an ever-increasing list of stuff. Maud knew a jeweller there and took a few diamonds to sell to raise some much needed cash. Charlie and Tom spent the day fortifying the house and the surrounding area. They split the sharpened stakes into bundles and used old pallets and any other spare wood that could be used to build and test some traps they'd devised. They dug holes and looped rusting coils of barbed wire along the walls to create choke points. Maud had impressed upon them how important it was to make the farm look as normal as possible. If anyone came visiting they didn't want to raise suspicion. Anonymity was their first line of defense.

It was past eight o'clock in the evening when Charlie spotted the headlights in the distance from his lookout in one of the bedrooms. The lights appeared and disappeared behind hedges as the vehicle bounced along the dirt track towards the farm. He shouted down to Tom in the kitchen before opening the window; felt the cold blast of air hit him in the face before he hefted the .303 onto the window ledge and tried to work out if it was the Range Rover or someone else. Once he was sure it was Shini and Maud he flicked on the safety catch and went down to the kitchen. By the time he got there Tom was already piling bags of shopping on top of the kitchen table.

'They bought Oxford,' he said to Charlie.

'What did you get?' Charlie asked Shini as she hauled another load of bags in.

'Just help Maud,' said Shini breathlessly.

Maud put away the food shopping as the three teenagers sifted through the pile of other bags. Shini handed out a brand new Strawberry 'Krush' to both of the stunned boys. It was the latest model.

'Oh my god,' said Tom. 'How the hell did you afford these?'

'My friend in Oxford bought five stones. Says they were of the highest quality he'd seen in years.'

'We're no longer blind,' said Charlie placing a micro-sim inside the phone.

'Just remember,' warned Shini. 'It's only for calling each other and using the internet. No emails and no social media. No addresses given; nothing.' She then pulled out a new laptop and a box containing four wireless night cameras. 'Security,' she stated. 'We can rig these up on the roof and fix motion sensitive lights around the perimeter.'

'Nice,' said Tom still grinning as he plugged in the phone charger. 'Charlie and I'll sort that out.'

'We also traded another diamond for a kilo of silver which will need melting down and forging,' added Maud.

'Excellent,' said Charlie. 'I always wanted to do a bit of smithying. We'll need to use your Aga, Auntie.'

'There's a good set of bellows in the sitting room and coal in the shed. It'll be hot work,' said Maud. 'I see you've been busy around the house. I hope you haven't made too much mess.'

'Just a few traps here and there,' said Tom. 'And we've boarded a few of the windows as well as some nasty surprises if anyone decides to climb through a window. We've left these planks here to nail to the door, just in case.'

'Right,' said Maud. 'To work everyone. I'll cook dinner.'

*****

Tuesday 17th February.

Tom stared at the screen of the laptop, his mouth open and slack. His eyes moved from left to right as he read the leading article from a prestigious news website. Shini sat beside him biting her lip. She knew what it said and had passed it over for Tom to read. Charlie was oblivious, making a cup of tea and some toast on the Aga. He and Tom had rigged up the cameras and lights on the roof of the farm. By the time Tom had finished reading his jaw had clamped shut and his hands had balled into fists. Charlie glanced up and saw the look in his friend's face and knew that something was terribly wrong. Tom's face contorted and tears pricked his eyes as they darted around the kitchen until they fixed upon the shotgun leaning against the wall. Tom barged past a chair and grabbed the shotgun. He checked it was loaded, grasped a handful of cartridges and stuffed them into his army jacket that was hanging on a hook next to the front door.

'Where are the car keys?'

'Tom, wait,' implored Shini with tears in her eyes.

'Where are the bloody car keys?' he roared. 'If you'd never come to our bloody school this would never have happened.'

'Whoa!' said Charlie. 'What the hell's wrong with you, Tom? Shini hasn't done anything wrong.'

'You're just as bad,' yelled Tom. 'I spend my life looking after you, Charlie Lawrence, and what do I get for it? My mum and dad treated you like a son and now, because of your stupid aunt and that stupid Ouija board, the Shadows have taken them...' Tom couldn't restrain himself any longer and he let out a gasping sob as tears coursed down his face.

Shini stood, pushing the laptop in the direction of Charlie. She moved over towards Tom as Charlie scanned the text on the website. It described how the parents of a missing teenager called Thomas Cramp had disappeared yesterday. Police had found blood at the scene and signs of a struggle. It was believed by the newspaper that

189

the son was now a suspect in the disappearance of his own parents. There was even a number for the general public to contact if he were seen.

Charlie felt faint and sat down hard on the chair behind him. The world was spinning out of control and he was not only caught up in the vortex, but was responsible for creating it in the first place. He watched as Tom pushed Shini away from him. What little control they'd forged out of this mess was falling apart in front of his eyes. He stood and stumbled towards Tom.

'Listen, mate,' pleaded Charlie, 'We can sort this...'

'Shut up, Charlie, or I'll shut you up,' warned Tom clenching his fist. 'Give me the keys to the car. I'm going home and I'm going to find my mum and dad.'

'I'm not giving you the keys,' said Shini. 'Not until you calm down.'

'Give me the keys,' said Tom swinging the shotgun towards her.

'No,' stated Shini. Her green eyes flashed with an inner fire and her jaw jutted out toward Tom. 'Go ahead. Shoot me. What've I got to live for anyway? My only friends are an idiot and a wimp, and my mum disappeared years ago because she couldn't stand to be with me. So, go ahead, Tom. Finish it.'

'Please,' whimpered Charlie. The roaring of an ocean filled his head, ripped through him, leaving him weak and powerless. Where was Aunt Maud? Why did she have to go for a walk when she was needed most? 'Please stop this,' he begged.

Shini glanced across at Charlie and the look of disdain in her eyes crushed him. Shini backed away from Tom as he let out a roar of frustration. Tom grabbed his army jacket, put it on and went into the sitting room. Shini sat back down and grabbed the laptop, punching in text, opening new windows, scanning and typing some more. Charlie stood in the middle of the kitchen unable to make a decision; mind focussed only on what Shini had said. Was he the idiot or the wimp? And it hit him hard when he realized that no one in their right mind could call Tom a wimp. Tom had spoken the truth; he had looked after him since primary school. And Shini had called him a wimp; the one person in the whole world he wanted to impress, to show he was worthy of her friendship, of her love...

Tom stormed back into the kitchen with the shotgun now in its bag. He opened the front door and stepped outside into the freezing day, ignoring his two friends in the kitchen, he slammed the door behind him.

'I knew it. Wait!' shouted Shini. She looked up at Charlie. 'Read this.'

Charlie sat down numbly beside her and read the page on the laptop. It was a business website showing the major stock holders of the media conglomerate that owned the newspapers. The Cramp story was only being run by a few national papers whose majority stake was owned by a Mr. Belani, an executive of the O'Void Corporation.

'The O'Void Corporation own the newspaper, television stations, publishing houses, magazines... everything,' said Shini.

'So?' asked Charlie.

'The same company that owns the Davenport Bank... the same one that owns the car outside. No other news site is telling the story.'

Charlie glanced up at Shini. 'It's a trap!'

'Exactly,' agreed Shini. 'They want us to react because they'll be waiting for us. We have to stop him.'

'That won't be possible,' said Charlie. 'I've known him all my life and when he gets something in his head, he won't let it go. It's his family. We can't stop him... but we can help him.'

'It'll take him a while to reach the end of the lane. You grab some stuff we might need and I'll write a note to Maud. I think we need to call our families, Charlie. We need to find out if they're okay and tell them they need to disappear for a few days.'

'How are we going to convince them to do what we say?'

'Call your mum, she's our only hope.'

'That's not going to be a nice phone call.'

'Better that than what Tom's going through. We'll call after we've dealt with Tom.'

'What about the case?' asked Charlie. 'Should we take it?'

'It's our only bargaining chip if we're caught,' reasoned Shini. 'I think it's better we leave it here until we know how to use it.'

Ten minutes later, Shini drove along the track. Tom was ahead, marching down the lane with his new telephone pressed against his ear.

'Oh, no!' shouted Shini as she put her foot down on the accelerator. 'What's he doing? He'll blow our cover!'

By the time they reached Tom he had thrust the phone back in his pocket.

'Don't say anything, Shini,' said Charlie. 'It's too late now and it won't help.'

Charlie leaned out of his window. Tom's face was set and he refused to look at the vehicle. Shini 'tutted' and drove a little way ahead. Charlie leant back and opened the rear passenger door. Without a word Tom got in the back and shut the door behind him as Shini accelerated down the track. They drove in silence through the tiny back roads, their hearts jumped every time a vehicle passed them.

'Drop me at the railway bridge,' said Tom. 'I can go down the bank and cross the tracks. From there I'll go through the field that we planted with trees last year. That should give me enough cover to get close to the farmhouse.'

'I'm coming with you,' stated Charlie.

'What about me?' asked Shini.

'There's an old curtain shop before the turning into the lane. It's empty and has parking. Wait for us there and make sure your phone is on. We'll call you, okay?'

'Okay,' she said. 'Just watch out for police. If they see you carrying a shotgun all hell will break loose.'

Charlie and Tom wriggled through the hole in the fence and slid down the embankment next to the railway bridge. Checking left and right they hopped over the tracks and clambered into the field of saplings. The grass had grown long and covered their advance as they crouched low to the ground. Tom hefted the shotgun and had the wood axe strapped to his back while Charlie had brought his kukri and the freshly-sharpened billhook. They reached the fence line adjoining the vegetable garden. They could see the kitchen and the conservatory from behind cover and all looked quiet. Tom sat and listened for what seemed like an eternity; if the police had been there then they'd already left.

'Let's go,' said Tom.

They scrambled over the stock fence and through the kitchen garden where Tom led them to the garden shed. Opening the door Tom slipped inside and motioned for Charlie to follow. He opened an old cigar box and glanced at Charlie.

'Crow scarers,' said Tom pulling out a rope of ten bangers. 'Where's the bag of salt?'

Three minutes later they emerged from the shed and crept towards the kitchen door. Peering through the glass Tom slid back down and nodded grimly at Charlie.

'Redcaps. It's a trap,' whispered Tom.

Charlie pointed at the cat-flap and Tom gave him the thumbs-up. Tom lit the fuse and Charlie pushed the salt bomb through the cat flap. For added effect Tom knocked on the door. They heard the clomping of metallic feet, excited whispering, followed by a thunderous explosion. The small window set into the top of the kitchen door splattered with a redcap that slid out of view.

Tom readied his shotgun as he pushed open the door. Charlie stood back armed with his billhook and a handful of salt. The door swung inwards to reveal the shattered remains of what was once a kitchen. Flour, rice and broken glass was scattered across the floor; cups and plates were smashed, kitchen units, chairs and the dining table had been splintered. There was ash everywhere. Tom growled, swinging the shotgun to and fro as Charlie followed him into the house. Charlie looked around the kitchen and frowned.

'This was definitely a set-up,' he whispered.

'What d'you mean?' asked Tom.

'Where are the police? They should be here, or at the very least there should be police tape or, or something showing they've been here. This is meant to be a crime scene. But all we find are redcaps.'

'We have to find Mum and Dad...' Tom swivelled the barrel of the shotgun towards the door leading to the sitting room. 'What was that?'

Charlie swallowed, his mouth dry, as he moved beside Tom. They both walked as quietly as they could amongst the wreckage on the floor. Charlie stood beside the door as Tom stood back, pointed the shotgun at the door and nodded.

'Don't bloody shoot me,' mouthed Charlie as he reached for the door handle.

'I won't,' mouthed Tom.

Charlie turned the handle and gave the door a push before darting back against the wall. All he saw was a look of sheer horror on Tom's face before Charlie's world was enveloped in flame and noise. Tom loosed both barrels simultaneously. Charlie reeled away from the splintered door frame, dropping the billhook from numbed hands, deafened by the blast; he felt blood running down his cheek. He saw Tom desperately trying to reload his shotgun just as a figure lurched into the room. It was missing quite a lot of its face and its left arm, but still managed to inform them of its one desire...

'Braaaaaiiiiinnnnns!' it said.

Tom backed away but dropped a shotgun cartridge he was trying to slide into the barrel. As he stepped backwards he trod on a can of beans and went crashing to the floor. The shotgun skittered away from him just as the figure bent down and grasped his right foot. Tom yelped, trying to kick the hand away. And then another figure staggered into the room, followed by another, and then another.

Tom was still kicking at the hand that held him. The half-face of the corpse loomed over him, with grey-green teeth bared, as it tilted its head to take a bite out of Tom's leg. In a sudden blur of

194

movement the eyes of the undead stared wildly at Tom before the head fell from its shoulders and landed in Tom's lap. Tom rolled away from the collapsing body and scrambled towards the dropped shotgun. Charlie roared with a mixture of anger and sheer terror as he swung his kukri through the neck of another brain-sucking...

'Zombie!' shouted Charlie. 'Go for the head.'

Tom managed to jam a single cartridge into the shotgun before he was set upon by a female zombie that looked like she might have been a punk once upon a time. She tried to grab him with black-laced gloves as he shoved the shotgun against her throat and pulled the trigger. The head, with its black crimped hair, flew into the air with such force that it hit the ceiling before ricocheting into another zombie, knocking it to the floor. Charlie hacked off an arm and kicked a zombie backwards before racing over to Tom and helping him to his feet. With only a glance, both Tom and Charlie saw that the living room was packed with zombies pushing their way towards them.

'Braiiiiiiiiiins,' they groaned. And poured through the door.

Charlie and Tom raced out of the kitchen door with Tom leading the way.

'I need more cartridges,' said Tom breathlessly. He was trying to load as he ran.

'What kind of zombies are they?' asked Charlie following his friend.

'What?'

'I mean lumbering zombies or running zombies? If they're lumbering then we can outrun them, if they're running zombies then we might be in the...'

'Shit!' shouted Tom, picking up his pace.

Charlie glanced behind him and saw that there was a fair mixture of zombie types. Some were just staggering around the farmyard while about ten had begun loping after them and were picking up speed. Tom and Charlie vaulted over a farm gate and ran across a field towards the village green. The front two zombies hit the gate with such force that it buckled and swung open allowing those following to run straight through.

'How many shots you got left?' gasped Charlie.

'Damn it,' cursed Tom feeling in his pocket with his free hand. 'I must have dropped some in the kitchen. I've only got five left.'

'Well, you might have to use them soon because those two in front look like they were athletes before they became zombies.'

'I gotta hit them from point blank to take their heads off. If we stop, the others will catch us up.'

After another two hundred paces they reached the far end of the field where the barbed wire fence was lined with a stand of ash trees. On the other side of the trees was the village's community playing field, bowling green, tennis court and playground. Tom clambered over the fence followed by Charlie. Charlie ducked between two strands but felt one of the barbs tear into his jacket and rake down his back as he struggled to get through. He couldn't free himself. Tom pulled him but it was making it worse. Charlie looked back; the zombies were coming straight at him, running full tilt with cracked and broken teeth bared through loose flaps of decaying skin. Their eyes were wide and glaring as they pitched towards him. Charlie struggled desperately.

Tom timed it with precision. Leading the target, he pulled the first trigger and knew it was a direct hit without even checking before swinging the gun and pulling the second trigger. The second zombie was so close that the shot ripped through its head and shoulders, spinning it in a backwards somersault before it hit the ground and slowly fizzled into ash. Tom didn't stop for a second as he levered the empty cartridges clear and reloaded.

'You better do something fast, Charlie Lawrence,' warned Tom. 'I've only got three shots left and there are at least eight more heading our way.

As the roar of two more shots echoed through the woods, Charlie realised it was his belt that had become entangled and he fumbled with the buckle until he fell through the barbed wire as Tom fired his last shot. He scrambled to his feet just as another zombie hit the barbed wire at full speed. The zombie must have been in the ground a good long time before being raised from the dead because the inertia split the zombie in three. Charlie and Tom were splattered with decaying gore and they reeled back as four zombies struggled over the fence. Charlie and Tom ran through the stand of trees into the wide open playing fields. The car park and exit were a good three hundred metres away with the bowling green and playground between.

Tom and Charlie sprinted towards an elderly couple playing a quiet game of bowls. They were glaring at the teenagers. The two friends ran towards the green and onto the manicured grass. The zombies were not far behind. Tom and Charlie grabbed a bowling ball each and turned.

'I say,' shouted the astonished old man. 'Get your hands off my balls.'

'Get out of here,' shouted Charlie as he launched the bowling ball at the nearest zombie.

'Isn't that Mrs. Braithwaite?' said the lady, grasping her partner's arm and pointing at one of the zombies.

Tom hurled the bowling ball at the lead zombie but missed, Charlie hit it in the chest slowing it for a moment. Tom swore and kept running alongside Charlie as they headed towards the playground. They could still hear the elderly couple deep in discussion.

'That young man just hit her with your ball, dear.'

'But she's been dead since last June...'

Two hundred metres from the playground, gasping for breath, Charlie let out a gargled moan. Standing on the half-burnt fort of the playground stood Jack Marvin with his posse of followers, their scooters lined up in the car park. Jack was stabbing his finger at Tom and Charlie. Immediately eight teenage kids were leaping from swings and slides and ladders onto the safety surface. As one, they raced towards them with Jack Marvin in the lead. They were whooping at the prospect of catching their sworn enemies in their territory.

'That's all we bloody need,' gasped Tom as the distance between them diminished. 'Use the old rugby swerve to get past them,' said Tom still brandishing his empty shotgun.

Charlie managed to dodge and veer past two teenagers but caught a ringing blow against his left ear from a thrown punch. Tom scattered them by brandishing the shotgun as he ran between them. Suddenly the two friends had broken clear, with the village gang behind them and the playground and car park before them. Using every last ounce of energy they pushed ahead. There was a scream behind them, then yelling and shouting and the sound of many feet sprinting up behind them. Charlie glanced to his side and saw that Jack Marvin was alongside him, his face a mask of uncontrollable terror. One hand was trying to keep his trousers up while the other pumped up and down in time with his legs. Jack glanced across at Charlie.

'Alright?' asked Charlie.

'What the fu–'

'Zombies,' replied Charlie. 'You gotta take the heads off.'

'Fer real?' wailed Jack. 'I knew I should'na smoked dat blunt dis morning... my brains is melting.'

'We've already killed about ten of them, but we've run out of shotgun shells,' Charlie glanced behind him and could make out the remaining four zombies. They were catching up with the least healthy of Jack's gang.

'Dammit! They're going to get him,' said Charlie stopping.

Jack Marvin and his gang kept running, leaving Charlie on his own. Tom didn't look back. Charlie hefted the kukri in his right hand, wishing he hadn't dropped the billhook. The last of Jack's gang members waddled past him. Fear poisoned the blood in Charlie's veins as the first zombie ran straight at him. Charlie ducked to one side and swung the kukri with a back-handed stroke that took the top off the zombie's head. It stumbled to the ground as

198

brains spilled onto the grass. The zombie leant forward and began scooping it up and pouring it back through the top of its skull. It licked its fingers and then must have decided that brains tasted far too good and began eating what was left on the ground. In an instant it fizzled into dust.

As Charlie was recovering his balance from his death-dealing blow he was knocked to the ground by a fresh-looking zombie that still looked human. The zombie was female and wearing a fancy business suit. She raked her hands across Charlie's throat as she struggled to hold him down. Charlie squirmed with all his might as she fought to stay on top of him and tear his neck out with her nice white teeth. He managed to grab hold of her neck with his left hand but her strength was unbelievable. He could feel his muscles straining and he was still losing. The kukri had fallen beside him and his right hand searched blindly in the wet grass around him. Charlie struggled as best he could but his resistance was failing and her clacking, grinding teeth were inching towards his throat. He could see two more zombies running towards him. It was all over. He was going to be eaten alive by a zombie businesswoman.

For a few seconds the world closed in on Charlie as he lost the battle to survive. He shut his eyes as the last molecules of strength fled his body. There was a strange noise invading his ears as the end of his life approached. It was an odd mechanical wailing noise and it was not something he expected at the moment of death. He felt a wash of gore spray across his face and the weight of the zombie above him disappeared. He opened his eyes but was blinded by ash. Wiping it away he saw what looked like a jousting match between Jack's gang who were all riding two-up on their scooters, wielding broken wooden staves from the playground and circling the two remaining zombies. Jack Marvin skidded the scooter next to Charlie's head; riding pillion was Tom wielding his axe.

'That was close, bruvva,' said Jack as he looked down on Charlie.

'You came back?'

'Yeah man, this is the best fun we had in years, innit,' said Jack as he leaned forward and held out his hand. 'You got any more of 'em?'

Charlie took his hand and pulled himself upright. There were no more zombies emerging from the field and the ones that had chased them were now piles of ash gently dissolving into the grass. Tom hopped off the back of Jack's scooter and thumped Charlie on the back.

'Thought I'd lost you there, mate,' said Tom. 'Why did you stop running?'

'They were just about to catch one of Jack's mates. I couldn't let that happen.'

'Nice one,' said Jack. 'What's going down?'

'It's a long story, mate.' said Charlie. He pointed towards Tom's farm. 'But there are more of them over there.'

In the distance they could see a black Range Rover hurtling across the field towards a gap in the ash trees. The vehicle slammed through the fence dragging yards of wire and fence posts in its wake, until it hit the small retaining wall of the bowling green, became airborne for a split second and slammed back down onto the manicured lawn. Slewing across the grass, leaving the wire and posts in a tangled heap behind it, the Range Rover drove straight at them at full speed. The elderly couple were still stood gaping at the destroyed green. The car braked and Shini leapt out of the driver's door brandishing a hammer.

'You touch either of them, Jack Marvin and I'll bash you,' she yelled.

'Whoa, Shini. They're with us,' said Charlie. 'They helped us.'

'Well, this is all very nice,' began Tom pointing towards the hole in the fence, 'but I think we need to leave before those old people call the police.'

A cluster of the shambling zombies had made their way down the field and were now staggering into the playing fields. The pensioners had finally decided to leave the green. Otherwise the group of teenagers were the only ones there.

'Leave them to us, bruv,' said Jack revving his scooter. 'We is going to smack them down.'

'When you're done,' asked Tom as he handed Jack his axe. 'Could you feed my cows?'

'Cows, bruv? Them's well dangerous, no? I 'int getting in no field wiv cows in.'

'They're in the cow shed. You can throw bales of hay in over the rails.'

'Oh. Right. Nopraw, bruv.'

TWENTY FOUR

The helicopter circled slowly at an altitude of ten thousand feet. Lord Cofgod had no need of binoculars as he watched the debacle unfurl below him. Babba Belani was sat beside him tapping the silver head of his cane with an immaculately manicured fingernail. Neither of them had spoken to the other since they had spotted the two teenagers crossing the railway track. Their satisfaction at the plan to bring the children out had slowly evaporated. When the two boys had fled the farmhouse, Cofgod was sure his fleet-footed redcaps would catch them within a few hundred paces. Belani's zombies were there to add to the terror aspect and had on many occasions in the past caused such fear in their victims as to cause paralysis. The plan had started to unravel when not a single redcap had emerged from the house to pursue the boys. Instead, a few zombies had taken up the chase, while most of them had wandered around the farmyard with their arms outstretched, bumping into things.

Cofgod sighed. It wasn't surprising that Duke Lycaon with his werewolves and Count Strigoi's vampires had taken most of the power in the world. Here he was trying to team up with Belani, who, although a master of the media world could only create zombies. And zombies were renowned for being the dumbest of all minions; that was why they were chosen to run the television shows.

Cofgod's hopes were raised momentarily when he saw one of the boys turn back to fight off the last remaining zombies, but his hopes were dashed when the rest of the kids rallied and returned to rescue him. It was this brave disregard for personal safety that bewildered

Cofgod most about humans. They seemed to be totally selfish, money-grabbing imbeciles most of the time until there was a crisis and then, somehow, they forgot about their habitual greed and self-centeredness and risked life and limb to rescue people they never even knew, and sometimes people they even hated. If he lived to be ten thousand, no, twenty thousand years old, he would never understand humans.

Belani nudged him and pointed with his cane towards a black vehicle crashing through the gates to the farm and race across the fields towards the group of teenagers on scooters. Any lumbering zombie in range was flattened. Leaving the kids on the scooters, the targets hopped into the battered vehicle before driving into the village.

'Follow that car,' said Cofgod leaning towards the pilot. 'Stay behind them.'

*****

Cofgod and Belani were drinking a 1947 Petrus in the study of Chepstow Villas. Both of them were happier than they had been earlier in the day. The helicopter had kept its distance as they followed Count Strigoi's stolen car back towards the village of Cholsey, along back roads and farm lanes it had driven, before heading across the Ridgeway. There, in the middle of a huge expanse of farmland, lay the tiny farm and outbuildings where the kids had been hiding out. Cofgod did not want to alert them so he'd tapped the pilot on the shoulder and told him to head back to London to fetch reinforcements. At last Cofgod could feel he'd progressed. He knew where all three of them were and that meant they had to have the case and the journal with them. He could almost taste the power that would soon be his and his alone. Belani would remain useful with his media empire, but he felt it would soon be time to clip the wings of Strigoi's vampires and leash Lycaon's werewolves.

Not one Shadow of the Void had managed to learn the art of instant travel across the planet. It had remained the singular ability of those blasted adventurers, Flintstaff and Cramp, known within the cabal as the 'Enemies of the Void'. But that power would soon be his. Cofgod had imagination, and that was far more important than intelligence because it could take you to places no one else dared to believe. With the journal he'd learn how to use the case. With such a skill he could appear anywhere at any time and with that sort of advantage he could seize control across the globe...

A knock on the door snatched Cofgod away from his reverie. It was Grott. He poked his head round the door and opened his mouth to speak. Before he could utter a word, a delicate hand appeared above his head; it was cupped and as it turned downwards a small pile of white crystals fell onto Grott's bloody cap. Grott's eyes turned upwards, he squawked once and disappeared in a pile of ash. The door swung open and Mimi walked in. She raised a finger to her perfect lips.

'Oops,' she said fluttering her eyelashes at Cofgod.

'It's very tough to vacuum that up, you know,' replied Cofgod hiding his anger. He'd quite liked Grott.

'I'm sure it is,' said Strigoi as he appeared at the doorway. He glanced down at the pile of ash and carefully stepped over it. He gestured behind him: 'This is Oleg, Duke Lycaon's personal assistant.'

The massive, feral-looking man behind the count placed a large boot onto the pile of ash and ground it into the Persian carpet as he entered. He was built like a train and uglier than a baboon's bottom but carried himself in a way that warranted extreme care.

Cofgod took a sip of wine and swirled it in his mouth before swallowing. It didn't matter what humans did to the grape, it would never be as satisfying as fresh blood. Cofgod leant forward and filled two more crystal glasses. Babba Belani sat in his chair with a smile upon his dark features. He pulled long and slow on his cigar and blew the smoke out in a thin stream as he whispered under his breath. Strigoi walked over to the desk and took the glasses of wine, handing one to Mimi. He turned towards Babba Belani.

'Don't worry, Belani. You won't be needing any protective spells from me. I'm not here for your head.' Strigoi then turned towards Lord Cofgod. 'But I'd like a reason *not* to take yours…'

'Well, before you do, Strigoi, I'd like some answers myself,' replied Cofgod calmly. 'What did you do with the Cramp family?'

'You should know,' said Strigoi.

'Well, I don't.'

'Cofgod,' replied Strigoi as if talking to a wayward child, 'we know you took them.'

'I most certainly didn't,' replied Cofgod heatedly. 'I admit Belani and I used the false newspaper trick to draw out the teenagers, but when we arrived the Cramps were gone.'

'Maybe,' said Babba Belani in his thick velvety voice. All eyes were irresistibly drawn to him. 'Maybe the children warned them.'

'I don't believe either of you,' said Strigoi. 'I think it's time we took you back across the sea, Lord Cofgod. It's time to send you back to that stinking bog you came from.'

'Oh, I don't think you'll do that,' replied Cofgod as the room filled with Strigoi's minions. 'You see, I know where the children are hiding. With the case and with the journal.'

'Oh, do you now?' replied Strigoi. 'And I wonder at what point in time you were going to inform the Shadows of this vital piece of information?'

'I'd say about now,' replied Cofgod smugly. He could do 'smug'. Cofgod had the right face and build for smugness. In fact, he took smugness to a new level where any other synonym, like 'vainglorious' or 'haughtiness' was devoured and assimilated. He had first practiced his smug look in the dark pools of his victim's blood in Scandinavia and had been refining it ever since. Seeing the suppressed rage building within Strigoi was so rewarding. 'Perhaps you'd like to pay the children a visit?' asked Cofgod. 'But of course you can't, can you? Because you don't know where they are.'

'No, he doesn't,' rumbled Babba Belani flashing his snow-white teeth. 'But I do.'

'Alright! Alright,' replied Lord Cofgod raising his hands and glaring at Belani. 'I'll tell you. It was only my little joke. Ha ha,' he finished weakly.

*****

Wednesday 18th February. Just after Midnight.

Lord Cofgod, Babba Belani, Count Strigoi and Mimi were all wearing new green wellington boots bought from a store in Chelsea. They were stood at the edge of the copse overlooking Maud's farm. If a passing poacher, perhaps called Dibber, had seen them, he would have assumed that four property developers from London had arrived at midnight to survey a recent land purchase; probably to build a completely unsafe nuclear reactor on a piece of greenbelt. For some reason these suited people would have set the poacher's teeth on edge. He would have avoided them and crept around the copse they were standing in and made his way down the hill using the hedgerow as cover. He would have done all of that if only they had been unscrupulous property developers from London. Instead, the poacher found himself bumping into a tree trunk that hadn't been there a second ago. He knew because he'd been poaching these woods and fields for thirty years and there had never been a tree in that spot before, and secondly, a tree always had bark on the outside, not fur. Mammals had fur; Dibber knew that because he'd skinned every mammal known in the United Kingdom. He was a master of the gin trap and snare. Dibber's last emotions were mixed between the excitement of seeing an enormous wolf in southern England, shock that it knew how to walk on two legs, and fear that it was in the process of biting his head off.

'Stop eating him, Oleg,' ordered Strigoi. 'I don't want you ruining your appetite before the main course.'

At the bottom of the hill, across a ploughed field, the farm nestled within its surroundings. There were lights on in most of the windows and smoke trailed into the windless night from two chimney pots. The cold snap still gripped the country and frost glistened from every twig, blade of grass and clod of mud in the light of the quarter moon. Behind the Shadows were ranks of minions. At least, all of them were in ranks except Belani's zombies, which were bumping into trees and getting caught up in the brambles. Count Strigoi sighed. He turned towards the waiting minions.

'Surround the farm before you go in. I don't want anyone escaping. There are three things I want,' he began. 'I want the case. I want the journal and I want one of the children alive. I repeat, alive. Do any of you *not* understand my orders?' Ignoring the forest of arms raised by the attending zombies, Count Strigoi turned to Belani. 'For Heaven's sake, you explain it to them.'

Everyone around Count Strigoi raised an eyebrow.

'What?' he asked and then he realized what he'd just said. 'It's only an expression, for God's sake. I don't believe in Heaven any more than the rest of you...' Strigoi counted to ten. 'Just get on with it.'

TWENTY FIVE

Wednesday 18th February. A bit more after Midnight.

'What have they done with them?' said Tom once more. He wouldn't stop pacing around the kitchen.

Charlie looked up from the silver point he was fastening to a piece of wood. He didn't know what to say. Tom was still in a total panic at not finding his parents. He was convinced they were both dead and flitted between crying and demanding instant revenge. Charlie and Shini called their parents as soon as they left the village. Mr. Nair yelled at Shini for running away, threatened Charlie, begged her to come home and not end up disappearing like her mother. Shini replied with steel in her voice and hung up. Charlie's mum reacted differently. She was relieved that Charlie was okay and listened to his story concerning the Shadows. It took ages to convince her but finally she agreed to take his father out of harm's way for a few days, whatever it took.

Back at the farm dinner was muted and Maud, sensing the three friends were in need of some space, retired to bed early. Ruben the Alsatian sensed something first. Normally, at this time of night, he would have been fast asleep, singeing his fur next to the fireplace in the sitting room. But when Charlie popped outside to the wood shed to bring in some night-burning logs Ruben followed him.

Charlie filled the wood basket, a torch stuck in his mouth so he could see what he was doing, when the hackles rose on Ruben's back and a deep guttural growl broke from his chest. Then, in the distance, he heard a noise that instinctively sent a bolt of primeval terror through his very core.

'Aaaaaaaaaaroooooooooooooooooow!'

The torch fell out of Charlie's mouth and broke leaving only the monochrome of starlight. He hauled the basket out of the wood shed and burst through the kitchen door.

'They've found us!' he yelled as he jammed the wood basket against the door. He grabbed the planks of wood leaning against the wall next to the front door. 'Tom, help me, quick.'

Tom dropped his mug and ran over to where Charlie was holding a plank of wood against the front door. Tom grabbed a hammer and nailed the planks to the door frame.

Shini ran into the kitchen followed by Aunt Maud who appeared wearing her pink nightgown. Maud was carrying the .303 and a box of cartridges. Shini hit a key on her laptop and the screen showed images from the four cameras they'd positioned on the roof of the farm. One by one the motion sensors on the LED security lights flipped on. Shini used the mouse to adjust the cameras and then cursed loudly.

'Oh my god, there are hundreds of them. We're surrounded.'

'What are they?'

'From the south a large group of zombies; a mix of 'chasers' and 'lurchers' by the looks of it. Both are having difficulty getting across the ploughed field. Coming from the east and west we have a lot of redcaps, between twenty and thirty in each group.'

'Bloody hell!' said Tom as he hammered the last nail in. 'We need everyone at a window.'

'That's not all,' said Shini. 'I think they've brought vampires. Coming down the track.'

'That still doesn't account for whatever made that howling sound,' said Charlie.

'Cramp and Flintstaff's journal mention fighting a werewolf in Transylvania. They killed it with silver,' said Shini as she pulled a shopping bag onto the table and up-ended paper bags filled with salt. 'How many shotgun shells have we got?'

'There's only three left,' said Tom pointing at the shotgun in the corner. He placed the last shell on the kitchen table before Maud handed him the Lee Enfield rifle and the box of bullets. 'You'll have to hold the downstairs for a moment. I'm going upstairs to see if I can take out a few before they reach the house,' added Tom.

'Where's the case and the journal?' Charlie asked as he placed bags of salt next to each window ledge. He then used all his strength to arm the window traps they'd built.

'Upstairs in Maud's bedroom. I still haven't worked out how to use it. It's too complicated and every time I pull something out of there it just seems to be random antique rubbish.'

Charlie came back into the kitchen just as Shini was coming the other way. They found themselves squeezing past each other in the narrow doorway. Despite the rush, despite the terror, Charlie looked into Shini's eyes and smiled nervously. He swallowed heavily and bent forward to kiss her. Shini's eyes half-closed as she kissed him back.

'For luck,' she said.

An explosion of rifle fire from upstairs, followed by a whoop of joy from Tom shattered the moment.

Shini squeezed Charlie's hand.

'I didn't mean to call you a wimp. I'm sorry.'

'You did, but it's okay,' said Charlie. 'Let's just get through this.'

The window in the kitchen shattered first followed by the cracking of wood as something heavy hit the front door. Shini grabbed the shotgun, checked it was loaded and poured a bag of sea salt down each barrel before facing the kitchen door. Charlie grabbed the shortened Cuirassier's lance which had received a 'weapons upgrade' as Tom described it. A hissing vampire poked its head through the broken window and was pulling the frame away so it could climb through.

The problem with killing a vampire, thought Charlie, was that it could look human as long as it didn't open its mouth. Killing zombies and goblin redcaps hadn't been easy but they didn't look like your next door neighbour either. A vampire did, and worse, they were very good-looking and charming with it. There was something about their eyes that pulled you in, made you want to please it, to serve it, to welcome it into your home...

The vampire was almost inside the house when Maud marched into the kitchen, cuffed Charlie round the back of the head and knocked the trigger stick to the dead-fall trap suspended above the window. A hinged wooden board weighted with books and bristling with a variety of sharpened spikes swung down into the face of the vampire. A howl was followed by a flash as the thing turned to ash. Charlie rubbed the back of his head and smiled weakly at Maud.

'Never look a vampire in the eye, Charlie,' she said marching back to the sitting room with a lethal-looking sickle in her hand. 'I'll guard the case, Charlie. When it looks too rough, make sure you all get back upstairs.'

The front door was taking a terrible pounding and whatever protective runes had been placed above the door seemed to be having little effect. Shini was waiting grimly with the shotgun levelled. Charlie had an idea, stuffed some bags of salt into his pockets and ran upstairs. He passed Shini's bedroom where Tom was picking off zombies still struggling across the field and went into the bedroom that overlooked the yard. Peering out the window he felt his stomach twist and bowels loosen. There was an army of minions outside. Too many – way, way too many. They weren't going to get out of this.

A group of redcaps were directly below him, smashing the door with their pikes. Charlie was just about to place the lance beside him when he heard the flapping of leathery wings. A vampire landed on the tiles directly in front of him and hissed at him. Unfortunately for the vampire, the pitch of the roof made it difficult to stand and it had to keep flapping its wings to stop itself from sliding down the tiles.

212

Charlie rammed the lance into the chest of the vampire as hard as he could and yelled as it flashed to ash. Grabbing the bags of salt he hurled them down onto the redcaps below and watched the assault on the door falter.

Charlie had to warn the others about the flying vampires or their final line of defence would be compromised. He threw his final bag of salt and took a last look down into the courtyard. The werewolf that leapt over the farm wall had to be eight feet in height with muscles rippling across its vast body. The beast's arms were as thick as Charlie's waist and its head must have been bigger than a male lion. With teeth and talons like daggers it raised its thick neck and stared at Charlie with glowing red eyes. It howled.

'Shini!' yelled Charlie sprinting from the room.

He was too late. Charlie heard the front door splintering, followed by a roar of triumph from the redcaps and vampires waiting outside. Charlie raced downstairs, yelling at Tom to follow him. Tom shot a zombie crawling through a broken window in the sitting room as Charlie leapt into the kitchen. There was an awful noise as Ruben and the werewolf thrashed around on the floor tearing lumps of flesh and fur from each other. Shini was lying stunned next to the broken table with the shotgun next to her. She had blood on her face and was trying to get to her feet. The doorway filled with redcaps and zombies. Charlie hurled his lance into the face of a vampire crawling through a window and then grabbed the fallen shotgun. He pointed at the door and pulled both triggers. The shotgun roared and leapt in his hands, bruising his shoulder and deafening everyone in the room. Tom emerged from the sitting room, shot the werewolf and yelled.

'We have to get back to Maud's room. They're coming through the windows.'

The front door had been cleared by both barrels but they only had a second or two to flee. Ruben was still struggling with the gigantic werewolf and there was blood everywhere. Charlie dropped the shotgun and hauled Shini through to the sitting room and dragged her half-stumbling up the stairs. Tom guarded the bottom of the stairs as the werewolf hurled Ruben's limp body to one side. It turned its head towards Tom and leapt through the sitting room door. The .303 bullet ripped through the werewolf's shoulder, spinning it round as it slammed into the banisters. Tom raced up the stairs as the sitting room filled with minions. Turning right he ducked as a vampire swiped at him from the upstairs corridor. Charlie drove a sharpened ash stake through the chest of the vampire from behind, giving Tom enough time to bundle into Maud's bedroom. They slammed the door and levered the huge antique wardrobe across the door.

'Where's Ruben?' asked Maud as she helped wedge the chest of drawers against the door.

'I'm sorry, Maud,' said Tom as he reloaded the rifle. 'He saved us from the werewolf.'

Charlie grabbed the case and opened it just as the bedroom door crunched with a blow from outside. He opened the journal and flicked through the pages desperately looking for some inspiration. There was a scratching noise at the window they'd boarded up the day before. The glass broke and they could hear something tearing away at the planks nailed across the frame. Maud leant over Shini and wiped at the blood on her face. Another crash against the door - the hinges were slowly bending out of shape.

'There must be something!' shouted Charlie. He flicked through the book unable to see through tears of frustration. Charlie tried to think. If Flintstaff and Cramp knew they might be sacrificing themselves for Agnes, the case and the journal then surely they would have written something that would help members of their families in the generations to come. Had they been so pre-occupied that they'd left out such an essential piece of information?

The noise outside the door was getting louder and the minion at the window managed to pull one of the planks free. A vampire stretched an arm into the room trying to reach Shini's foot that dangled off the bed. Charlie used his kukri to take it off at the elbow. The vampire howled and disappeared only to be replaced by the snarling green face of a redcap. Shini sat up and swayed before steadying herself. An iron pike broke through the top of the bedroom door and the wardrobe was being slowly pushed back. Tom placed the barrel of the rifle next to the hole and pulled the trigger. It did nothing to stop the door being torn to pieces.

'We need the bed! Pull it over here!' said Tom reloading the rifle.

They all dragged the bed across and wedged it between the splintering wardrobe and the far wall. Shini pulled a bag of salt off the bedside table and 'ashed' the redcap crawling through the window. As the redcap disappeared the slightest gleam of starlight struck the floor. Charlie glanced at the floor and flipped to the last page. What had Dr. Frobisher said? There was some Latin or something that he mentioned right at the end of the book. It would have been the last thing Flintstaff had written before leaving. He found the last page. *'Eram quod es, eris quod sum. Manus in mano. Quod si inveni placeat reverti transporter.'* Which was followed by three glyphs. What did it mean? Who the hell wrote in Latin?

'Shini, help me,' shouted Charlie as he pulled the crystal free from the spine of the journal. 'What does this bloody Latin mean again?'

A chunk of plaster exploded out of the ceiling, covering them with white dust. Then another chunk and another. They coughed and wheezed as Shini tapped feverishly into her Strawberry Krush. The hole in the ceiling was filled with the grinning face of a redcap. It frowned and then squealed as it was shoved through the gap from behind, wedging it tight. More chunks of plaster fell as pikes were thrust through the ceiling. The bedroom door finally gave way as the werewolf wrenched it from the frame. Tom shot it in the face before retreating.

'It says,' began Shini reading from her phone. 'I was what you were; you will be what I am. Hand in hand. If found please return to sender... no wait it also means 'to transport'.'

'That's it!' yelled Charlie as he knelt on the floor and placed the crystal into the starlight. It glowed blue. Charlie copied the three glyphs as best he could onto the bedroom carpet. He grabbed the case. 'Everyone hurry. Come and hold hands.'

Just as the doorway filled with the enraged werewolf and a redcap dropped from the ceiling, Charlie grasped the case and held hands with Shini who held hands with Tom who held hands with Maud. He read the Latin script: 'Quod si inveni placeat reverti transporter.'

And vanished.

TWENTY SIX

The eastern sky was aglow with the orange light of a new day's dawn. Crows squabbled and bickered from the palms fringing the riverside; every black-eyed bird gazed at the mass of people knee deep in the water. They waited impatiently for the daily routine of chanting and cleansing to abate, leaving them an easy meal at the water's edge. Offerings were left in the form of banana leaf parcels of rice and lentils. Smoke from cooking fires mixed with thousands of incense sticks creating a thin aromatic layer of mist that wafted downriver. Ancient ruins leant towards the water as if in prayer as they slowly subsided into the river. The paving stones were worn smooth by the multitudes of worshippers. To either side of the flood plain great mounds of boulders erupted skywards as if they were piles of marbles left forgotten by a child-god. The rocks were all the shades of umber, sienna and ochre and stood in direct contrast to the piercing blue of the sky above and the velvet green of the rice paddies below.

The little town built amongst the ruins of Hampi was already bustling with life as streets were swept and watered to keep the dust down. Ox carts filled with fresh vegetables and fruit made their way to the market. Outside the front door of every house the female residents of the town trailed coloured chalk dust into beautifully complex symbols called 'Raongoli.' Each symbol beckoned the gods and fortune to enter their homes. Originally, the coloured dust had been made from ground rice and was an open-hearted gift for ants. A few eager tourists were up, snapping photos of the rituals that had taken place for hundreds of years. Others were making the most of the cool part of the morning to climb the surrounding hills where ruined temples topped every peak. Lizards scuttled and snakes slithered from the blood-warming rocks as sweating, red-faced foreigners crashed along the paths in their heavy walking boots.

A gang of monkeys lounged together amongst the rocks, picking nits, grooming, keeping watch for eagles and always, always studying the movement of the tourists. Oblivious to their surroundings, the tourists carried plastic bags filled with fruit to snack on as they trekked across the vast temple area of Hampi. The grey monkeys tracked and ambushed the tourists, mugging them in broad daylight and divesting them of any bags they carried, gorging themselves on whatever food they found within. In the land of Hanuman, the monkey was king.

An ancient sadhu sat under a banyan tree in total silence as he had done for the last fourteen years, observing his surroundings with detachment and equanimity. He started his day by smoking an enormous chillum, a long clay pipe, filled with a mixture of 'charas' and tobacco. Bellowing out great clouds of smoke into the cool morning air he tied his body-length dreadlocks into a bundle and settled himself down to a day's observation of everything around him. Every ant, every lizard or butterfly, every waft of wind, every raindrop, every cloud and every human that passed him he observed with a calm and tranquil mind.

The sadhu was quick to notice the change in the air, like the build-up of static before a storm; quick to notice the gang of monkeys that lived around him become alert and glance around anxiously. Something was happening. The sadhu smiled at himself benevolently for his momentary lapse – there was always *something* happening...

'Shaaaaaaaaaaaaaaaaaatoooooof!'

'Holy Cow!' blurted the sadhu uncontrollably as four people materialized not ten paces from him. He glanced down accusingly at the chillum he'd just finished smoking. 'Fourteen years silence,' he whimpered.

The four travellers were in various states of shock much like that of the sadhu. A large curly-haired teenager was on his knees retching, punctuated by bursts of irrepressible laughter; a rifle at his feet. An elderly lady wearing a pink robe was slumped in the dust crying. Beside the woman stood a beautiful young Indian girl with fire in her eyes, and a bloody gash across her forehead. The last of the four was a blonde-haired youth carrying a battered suitcase that smelt faintly of bananas. He was pale, bruised and battered but seemingly unaffected by his sudden appearance in a strange land. All of them looked exhausted; battle-worn and bloody. Their clothes were torn and stained and they all carried cuts and grazes upon their faces and bodies. The sadhu glanced behind him to see the troop of monkeys sitting in a perfect line, staring at the newcomers in silence.

*****

Charlie took a deep breath. As the scent of spices, wood smoke and dung filled his lungs he knew exactly where he was. He'd seen this place before when he'd fallen off his bike two weeks ago in what seemed like another lifetime. He stepped over to where Tom was busy trying to throw up and patted him gently on the back. It seemed to work. Tom heaved most of his last meal and sat back on his knees, gasping for air. He cleared his throat, spat and allowed Charlie to pull him to his feet.

'It worked, Tom,' Charlie said. 'It bloody well worked!'

'I feel like I've been turned inside out,' groaned Tom. 'Where are we?'

'Vijayanagara,' said Shini helping Maud to her feet. 'Hampi. Flintstaff and Cramp's last stand.'

'They killed Ruben,' wept Maud oblivious to her surroundings.

Shini wrapped her arms around her and hugged her. 'He was a brave and courageous dog, Maud. He saved my life. I'm so sorry.'

219

'Er, Shini,' whispered Charlie. 'There seems to be a naked man covered in ash staring at us.'

'Namaste, Baba,' said Shini turning. She put her hands together and bowed.

The sadhu grinned toothlessly and beckoned for them to come into the shade of the banyan tree and sit with him around his smouldering camp fire. It seemed that his only possessions under the tree were a stainless steel bowl, a water jug, a clay pipe and a stack of dried cow dung. He was covered from head to toe in grey ash that blended with his huge roll of dreadlocked hair and matted beard. He had painted his forehead white, cut across with a great loop of red paint. Next to the tree a long metal trident was stuck upright into the ground with a string of dried yellow flowers hanging from it.

'Thank you, Baba,' began Shini respectfully. 'Kya aap English bolte hain?'

The sadhu nodded enthusiastically. He poured a cup of water and offered it to Maud who sat beside him and was still sobbing. Maud took the cup, drank slowly and handed it back to him. He offered the cup to Shini and then gently took Maud's hand in his own and held it; within seconds Maud's tears stopped and she lay to one side in the dust, closed her eyes and slept. Tom stared in astonishment at the sadhu who looked back and winked.

'Nice moves, Grandpa,' said Tom as he gratefully accepted a mug of water. 'What're we going to do now?'

'I don't know,' said Charlie. 'All I know is we escaped and we're safe. At least for now...'

'That might be about to change,' said Shini. 'We seem to be surrounded by monkeys.'

She wasn't wrong. Charlie's hand instinctively moved to the hilt of the kukri at his side and Tom unslung the rifle. There must have been more than three hundred monkeys sitting in a circle staring at them... or was it at them, thought Charlie. No, it was the case they were looking at. And their look seemed to show expectation, as if they were saying; 'Hey dude, what's in the case?'

Pushing his way through the group was a very large and very obviously male grey monkey. His whiskers were white and one of his eyes had become pearlescent through blindness. A savage scar crossed his face that had removed part of one ear. Charlie couldn't help thinking that if this macaque had been human then he would've had a gold earring and been wearing a pirate's hat. As the monkey moved silently towards them Charlie flinched but felt the restraining hand of the sadhu. The old man smiled at him, patted his hand and wobbled his head from side to side. Charlie assumed that this meant he should stay calm and passive. The macaque sat down in front of the case and stared at Charlie, tilting its head from side to side. The monkey then sniffed the case and tapped it with his long dark fingers.

'I think he wants you to open the case,' said Shini.

'He can probably smell the bananas,' he replied flicking the latches to the case. The case hissed and vented steam making the monkey sit back in surprise, but its curiosity got the better of it and it leaned forward to peer into the case. 'Sorry, mate,' said Charlie. 'Apart from a lot of junk, it's pretty empty.'

The monkey sniffed inside, shut the case and stood up. It grasped Charlie by the hand and pulled him. The sadhu made appreciative sounds and nodded for him to follow. Clutching the case Charlie got to his feet, trying desperately not to be freaked out by the small but human-like grasp of the monkey's hand. Tom rose too.

'Can you look after her?' asked Shini nodding towards the sleeping figure of Maud.

The holy man wobbled his head to and fro, Shini replied in the same manner. The sadhu leant round and pulled the gold-coloured trident from the earth and handed it to Shini. It was poorly made bronze but it was heavy. Leaving Maud sleeping under the banyan tree they set off. The troop of monkeys gathered around them and ambled towards a distant hill.

After an hour's walk across scrubland, past ruined temples, the group of travellers had multiplied somewhat. There were now thirty-eight kids starting at three months old and onwards, two oxen, five jewellery peddlers, a fruit mamma who'd been stripped of her fruit when she happened to walk around a corner to be confronted by three hundred monkeys, a lost Japanese hippy high on bhang lassi and thirteen wild dogs with various stages of mange. Shini had informed Charlie and Tom that being alone in India was a paradox after they had tried to rid themselves of their followers.

The monkey king led Charlie as they climbed a boulder-strewn hill, triumphantly carrying a banana stolen from the irate fruit mamma. He held it out in front of him a bit like a sword. At the top of the hill there was a crumbling temple with a few columns still standing and a single room within the broken walls of a courtyard. There were lewd carvings amongst the shapes of demi-gods on every wall and pillar. The far wall had a single carving of what looked like a multi-headed demon. The faces had leonine features with goggle-eyes, horns and tusks, or sabre-like teeth protruding from its lower jaw.

Charlie ran his hand across the carved red stone of a pillar before turning round to discover that only Shini and Tom and the monkeys were behind him.

'It's cursed,' said Shini.

'How do you know?' asked Charlie.

'You see those jewellery sellers down there?'

'Yep.'

'Only one thing can stop a jewellery seller from selling his stuff.'

'What?' said Tom, sweating profusely. 'A cursed temple?'

'Pretty much. They told me it was very dangerous to go up here. People have disappeared.'

'Yeah, right,' Tom muttered.

'One thing my mother told me about India is that everything happens here for a reason. It is a land of magic and a land of synchronicity...'

'Isn't that something to do with swimming?' asked Tom frowning.

'No, Tom. It means that if the local people say this temple's cursed then we should be careful, because it *is* cursed. It's a lair of the Rakshasa and Rakshasi.'

The male macaque sat in front of Charlie and was somehow managing to express a look of impatience. It still held out the banana in one hand, while the other reached up to Charlie's jeans and pulled him forward into the temple complex. Tom loaded the rifle while Shini held the trident. Charlie unsheathed his kukri and watched as the monkey reached a crack in the floor of the crumbling temple. It was only a small black hole but the monkey obviously wanted Charlie to inspect it. Charlie knelt down and slipped his hand into the crack. The air felt cooler; there was a draft. For some reason Charlie had a moment of vertigo, as if he were standing on a cliff edge. As he pulled his hand free the macaque gently pushed the banana into the crack and dropped it. There was no sound of it hitting the ground. The hill seemed to be hollow.

'This is a door,' said Shini as she trailed her hand around the carving of the demon on the wall of the temple. 'You see? There are cracks in it.'

The scarred macaque hissed and bared its teeth at the image on the door before urinating where it stood and then wandering off to his troop where they all sat in silence, waiting.

'But how do we open it?' asked Charlie standing up.

Shini used the edge of her trident to clear the loose dust around the edges of the door set into the wall.

'What are we even doing here?' asked Tom. 'Following a bloody monkey halfway across India? I'm starving.'

'I don't know,' said Charlie. 'But I agree with Shini. We're here for a reason.'

'What's that noise?' asked Shini pressing her ear to the stone door. 'It sounds like...'

'A telephone ringing...' answered Charlie.

TWENTY SEVEN

'What happened?' growled Count Strigoi.

'They vanished, master,' hissed one of his vampire minions. 'All of them.'

'So they've learnt to use the case... the question is: where did they vanish to?' said Cofgod.

Count Strigoi was standing in the ruined kitchen of the farmhouse. Amongst the shattered crockery and broken furniture were numerous piles of ash and the torn and bloody corpse of a dog. The house was filled with redcaps rummaging through draws and upending furniture, hunting for clues. Babba Belani was still trying to round up his remaining zombies in the courtyard but they kept wandering off across the muddy fields or getting caught in barbed wire fences. Lord Cofgod found the last remaining kitchen chair and was smoking a cigar quietly in the corner. He was just positioning his face into his smug look when he caught a threatening glance from Strigoi. The count walked into the sitting room, broken glass crunched beneath his green wellington boots. Mimi was just coming down the stairs. She stopped halfway down.

'You should see this,' she said.

Booting a redcap out of the way, the count climbed the stairs and was led by Mimi across piles of ash to the last bedroom where the remnants of a smashed barricade lay strewn across the floor. Lying on his back amongst the broken furniture was the colossal form of Oleg the werewolf. He was breathing in short ragged gasps and his tongue lolled to one side between massive blood-encrusted incisors.

Along with various bite wounds from the dog, there were two bullet holes through his chest and another in the side of his head which oozed ichor. One particularly brave redcap was dipping his cap into the pool of blood on the carpet left by the wound. At the sound of Strigoi and Mimi approaching, Oleg managed to turn his massive head and fix them with one dull red eye.

'Gone,' rumbled the werewolf. 'We failed.'

'But where?' asked Mimi.

'Spoke Roman,' grunted Oleg. 'Remember those days. Good days...'

'Do you know what they said?' asked Strigoi stepping closer.

'Must report to my lord. I must speak with Duke Lycaon. We failed. Must warn him.'

'Now, now Oleg. Let's not be hasty. You're in no shape to go anywhere...'

Before Strigoi had even finished his sentence the werewolf moved with unnatural speed just as the satisfied redcap had flopped his bloody cap back on his head and turned to resume the search, a taloned hand grasped him round the throat.

'Telephone, give me,' growled Oleg holding the struggling recap off the ground.

'I'm not sure there's any signal here,' replied Count Strigoi as he glanced over at Mimi and nodded. 'But you're welcome to use Mimi's phone, if you like.'

Mimi moved towards the prone figure of Oleg with her hand inside her suit jacket. She smiled menacingly, revealing her curved fangs. The werewolf growled from deep within his belly and clenched his fist. The redcap squeaked once before his head popped from his neck like a champagne cork. In a blur of movement Mimi whipped a silver-tipped knitting needle from her jacket and plunged it into the bloodshot eye of the werewolf. She used such force that it broke through the back of Oleg's skull transfixing him to the floor. The werewolf's maw opened once to roar in pain but lay silent and open. The body began its mutation from wolf to human.

226

'Well, well, well,' said Lord Cofgod leaning against the banisters at the top of the stairs. He was now wearing his smug look with great pride as he puffed away on his cigar. 'Poor Oleg. Dying like that in the call of duty. How did those children manage to defeat him, I wonder? I'm sure Duke Lycaon will be most upset.'

Count Strigoi and Mimi hissed in surprise and anger. Cofgod strolled down the passageway towards them, smiling. He looked down at the body that had once been the most terrifying creature ever created by Duke Lycaon and dropped the butt of his cigar before grinding it out with the heel of his wellington boot. He walked past the bed and standing on his tip-toes peered out of the window.

'It seems like I'm back on the team, does it not?' he stated. 'I'll bring a few of my lads up here to bury him nice and quietly, if you'd like.'

'Then enough of your little schemes,' said Strigoi. 'From now on we work together.'

'Oh, I always had our best interests at heart, Count Strigoi. Honestly.'

'Then it's time to tell us everything you know,' demanded Strigoi.

'We should head back to London. There's something I want to show you.'

'What do you want me to do, lord?' asked Mimi as she slid the deadly needle back into her jacket.

'We need to make a few phone calls,' said the count. 'And fast.'

TWENTY EIGHT

'Shhh, I can hear someone talking,' said Charlie waving his hand frantically.

Tom got down on one knee, flicked the safety off the rifle and pointed it at the stone door. Shini moved to the left and Charlie to the right. There was the sound of muttering behind the door and then the grating noise of stone against stone as the hidden door slid open. The sun was shining directly onto the doorway. A man appeared shielding his eyes from the glare. As he caught sight of Tom, grinning madly with a rifle, the man stepped back into the shadows instantly transforming into a Rakshasa. It was a single-headed demon with burnt skin, bulbous yellow eyes and sharpened teeth. Around its head, it wore a necklace of human skulls. It had stubby horns sprouting from its maned head, long sinewy arms and was wearing a loin cloth. In one hand it was carrying a glaive – a long-handled and wickedly curved blade made from black steel.

Charlie expected an attack any second and was confused by the demon's next move. Seeing Tom with the rifle and three hundred monkeys behind him, all hissing and baring their teeth, it tried to close the door. Tom fired the rifle into the retreating Rakshasa with little effect.

'Quick!' yelled Tom reloading. 'Before it closes the door.'

Charlie was the closest to the door and didn't have time to think. He rammed the case between the door and the wall. The door alone must have weighed a ton and Charlie realised he'd made a monumental error. The door would crush the case into nothing and they'd be stuck in India. It was too late to pull it free as the door jammed against the case, trapping it there. It creaked and groaned under the immense pressures but held. Instinctively, Charlie still held onto the handle of the case and as Tom and Shini came forward to help him push the door open, the Rakshasa bit into Charlie's hand. Charlie wrenched his hand free, letting go of the case and dropping his kukri as he staggered backwards. He dropped to his knees, clenching his injured hand to his chest. Black stars erupted in his vision as he fought the urge to pass out from the searing pain. He glanced down at his hand and sobbed as he saw that he was completely missing his little finger, his index finger had a gash all the way down it, and when he bent it he could see the tendons flexing.

Shini yelled in defiance as she thrust her trident into the gap in the door. The Rakshasa flicked her trident to one side with his glaive and grabbed the handle of the case. Tom charged forward brandishing the rifle. The Rakshasa grinned in triumph and then stared down in horror as it watched the case vent off a little steam and turn its hand to ash, spreading up the demon's arm, chest and head...

Shini ran back to Charlie slumped on the ground. He was pale and sucking on his ruined hand. She grimaced as she gently pulled his hand free and inspected it. She took her shirt off, grabbed the kukri and cut a strip from the hem. Charlie looked at her in confusion. She was unaware of Charlie's gaze until she began tenderly winding the cloth around his bleeding hand. She smiled.

'You'll be okay, Charlie. We need to get you to a doctor as soon as possible though. You can stay here. Tom and I can handle it from here.'

'I'm coming with you. Just wrap it up good,' Charlie replied weakly. Everything had become a dream now for him. Everything was detached from reality. 'Funny, but I don't feel pain anymore. It just throbs a lot.'

The sound of the door grinding open made them both look up. Tom poked his head out from inside the temple; he had the case in his hand. Once Shini had finished tying the bandage she put the remains of her shirt back on and knotted it around her midriff. She helped Charlie to his feet, gave him his kukri and picked up her trident. Together they walked into the shadows of the hidden temple.

The interior was cool and dry, lit by a single beam of sunlight coming from a fissure in the ceiling. The room was ten paces across and empty, except for a small pile of bleached bones in one corner next to a stone stairwell. There was no skull but the ribcage made it clear that the remains were human. Shini pressed her finger to her lips and beckoned for Tom to open the case. Shini removed the journal and flicked through the pages until she found Rakshasa and Rakshasi. Sergeant Cramp had made it clear that they ate human flesh, preferably alive. They were able to shape-shift, were magicians, illusionists and some could even fly. Tracing her finger down Shini pointed to the section on killing a Rakshasa. It didn't look good. The best way to kill one was with a crossbow bolt blessed by a Brahmin priest, or a weapon made of bronze.

The stairwell was partially lit by clay bowls filled with oil and a simple string wick. They smoked and flickered, casting shadows down the steep stone steps. Tom led the way, followed by Shini and then Charlie. Charlie walked in a daze, concentrating on placing one foot in front of the other. He held the case in his right hand with the kukri tucked into its sheath. They tried to take the steps as quietly as possible but any noise they made echoed around them. Charlie counted four hundred and nineteen steps before he reached Tom in a vaulted area at the bottom. The coolness this far down gave him goose bumps as sweat evaporated on his skin. The room was about twenty paces square with a single passage leading into the darkness. Otherwise, it was empty. The journey had increased the throbbing in Charlie's hand; pain was shooting through his arm in a series of spikes making him feel faint. He sat on the last step.

'Do you want to stay here?' whispered Shini squatting beside him. She swept a lock of hair out of Charlie's eyes.

'I'll be alright in a minute. I just feel a bit dizzy after doing all those stairs. You go on. I'll catch you up.'

'Shini,' hissed Tom. 'I think I heard something up ahead.'

'Okay. Let's go.'

Charlie rested his head against the wall, closed his eyes, and tried to breathe normally whilst concentrating on the pain. His mum had taught him that it helped. It wasn't working. Shini and Tom had disappeared down the corridor and his body felt utterly without energy. He couldn't even open his eyes. He felt waves of exhaustion wash through him, sending him deeper and deeper into oblivion.

Charlie's eyes snapped open as he gasped for air. He'd been dreaming of being crushed, suffocating under the weight of a mountain. The first thing his eyes focussed on was the sandy floor. There were footprints in the sand; bare feet with claws. The prints had been trodden over by Tom and Shini on their way down the passage. However, there was a single set of prints that went diagonally across the room and seemed to stop at the far end of the wall. Charlie had played a hundred different 'shoot 'em ups' on his computer and knew there were always hidden rooms in temples. He picked up the case and walked over to study the prints on the ground. There was the proof. A half print disappearing *under* the wall. He put the case down and moved his uninjured hand across the dressed red sandstone. All of the blocks were hand chiselled and smooth; their joins were so tight that mortar was unnecessary. But there had to be a way in. And then he saw it; a small raised carving of a gecko no bigger than the little finger he was now missing. He pushed against the carving and felt it shift inwards. With a soft grinding, part of the wall slid open on metal rollers embedded in the floor.

Charlie drew his kukri before peering into the dimly-lit room. Lying on the floor was an ancient man, withered and stick-like, wearing torn trousers and the rags of a shirt. The wizened creature had pale white skin, long grey hair and a beard of rattails. He was breathing. Just. Charlie checked behind him before sheathing his kukri and taking the case. He stopped at the doorway. This was a prison cell. And he was about to walk right in. Charlie walked back outside to where the gecko was carved and used the blade of the kukri to chip an arrow into the stone pointing at it. He then scuffed an obvious trail towards the door from the stairwell. If someone locked him in then at least Shini or Tom would notice this.

'Hello?' said Charlie peering into the gloom.

The old man grunted in surprise.

'What trickery is this?' said the old man as he dragged himself upright against the far wall. 'What fresh torment is this?'

'Er, hello,' Charlie whispered nervously. 'What are you doing down here? Who are you?'

'My name is Major Henry Flintstaff-Membrayne and I've been entombed in this place since 1865. Who might you be?'

'I'm, I'm Charlie Lawrence...' said Charlie crouching down beside the skeletal figure. 'I think we're related.'

'I need help, young man.'

'You're not the only one,' said Charlie holding up his left hand. Blood was already seeping through the bandage and just looking at it made him feel dizzy. 'I don't understand... How are you still alive? Where's Sergeant Cramp?'

'Never made it. Only me. Some kind of magic, torture even, to keep me alive,' wheezed the old man. He glanced at the case and pointed one withered hand toward it. 'Is that it? You found the case? Does it have the journal?'

'Of course, I'm sorry,' said Charlie. He laid the case down and slid it towards the old man. 'We've only managed to... to teleport? Once. We don't really know how it works. I'm afraid every time we open it we just find junk inside, but the journal says you always find what you need in there.'

'It's true, Charlie,' said the old man as he placed an ice cold hand on Charlie's leg. 'Open it for me, will you? There's a good lad.'

'You'll have to help me,' Charlie replied as he knelt on the floor. 'The catches are a bit stiff and I can't open it with one hand. If you just hold the case steady...'

'Too weak, Charlie,' groaned the old man. He slumped forward with his hands dropping to the floor. 'I'm dying. I can feel it. There's something in the case I have to show you, before I go... it's vital in your fight against the Shadows.'

Charlie moved over so he could lean against the case and open the catches with his right hand. The movement made his head reel and the sickening feeling of vertigo washed through his body again. Time seemed to funnel into a tight vortex and as he blinked rapidly to stay conscious, he noticed the foot prints he'd followed through the hidden door. They led this way but not back out again...

Charlie swung his head round just in time to see the ravenous gleam in the old man's eyes as he was grabbed by the throat. Charlie beat ineffectually at the man's hands. The skin of the old man sloughed away like molten wax to reveal the cruel visage of a Rakshasa. Horns sprouted from his skull and teeth grew into savage tusks, the skin darkened and blistered as claws dug into Charlie's neck. But it was the eyes of the demon that brought desolation to Charlie's soul; the bulbous, jaundiced eyes were so bloated they looked sure to burst.

'Open the case!' demanded the demon, squeezing tighter. 'And give me the journal.'

'Can't breathe,' said Charlie clawing at the demon's hands.

The demon responded by grasping Charlie's injured hand and yanking it hard.

'Now!' hissed the demon. 'Or I will eat your hand.'

Charlie scrabbled blindly for the case and fumbled with the catches. In agony, he flicked one catch open and then the other. He grasped the lid and opened it. There was a hiss of steam; strapped to the interior of the lid was the journal. The Rakshasa glanced at the case and then turned its baleful eyes back to Charlie. Charlie fumbled with the straps, finally freeing the journal but it slipped from his fingers and fell inside the case. The Rakshasa hissed and gripped Charlie's wounded hand even harder.

'Please, I'm getting it,' he screamed. Charlie scrabbled inside the case feeling all the strange items hidden within. Nothing seemed to be of any help from the feel of them until his hand brushed against something cold and hard. It felt like a statue. He gripped it and swung the makeshift weapon in a wide arc to catch the Rakshasa across the side of its head. Or that had been his hope, only the demon caught his hand in mid-air. It swung a fist into Charlie's jaw knocking him onto his back. The Rakshasa grabbed Charlie by one of his feet and opened his mouth to bite into his ankle. Charlie wriggled and kicked, glimpsing something whistle past him. There was a roar followed by a burning sensation in his leg as the demon combusted and fell to ash.

Lying on his back he saw the upside down figures of his best friends come over to help him to his feet. Charlie staggered and Tom held him up as Shini picked up her bronze trident.

'We heard you scream,' said Tom. 'Bloody lucky we came back when we did.'

'Find anything?' Charlie managed.

'A lot of passages. A lot of empty rooms. A lot of bones. Human bones.'

'I found a secret door. Look for a small carving of a gecko on the walls.'

Charlie leant against the wall clutching his hand while Shini and Tom moved their hands across the stone blocks.

'Here,' said Tom excitedly next to a carving. 'How does it work?'

'Push it in.'

Tom pressed against the carving and whistled between his teeth as part of the wall swung open without a sound. Ahead was a yawning darkness. Tom took out his Strawberry Krush and activated the torch; holding it high, the three friends entered the passageway. Moving the phone from side to side, Tom went ahead checking for traps or any more stone carvings that might open other doors. Fifty paces on, they stopped abruptly as a hideous cackling echoed down the tunnel. Shini swung round to see the entrance of the passageway they'd used was now blocked by a female demon; a Rakshasi.

'All together now,' crowed the demon. And she swung the door shut.

The noise echoed down the corridor. Utter darkness crowded around the pale beam of Tom's phone.

'We're trapped!' said Tom heading back. 'We have to get that door open.'

'No,' said Charlie firmly. 'There still might be a way out ahead. We have to go on.'

'But this battery won't last much longer...'

'All the more reason to get moving,' said Charlie. 'If there's nothing we'll head back.'

Another thirty paces brought them to a solid iron door. Rusted deadbolts ringed the door along with strange runes and glyphs, drawn in what looked to be blood.

'What do you think?' Charlie asked Shini. 'Will we get vaporized if we touch it?'

'I don't know. But this door is meant to be opened from this side and stop whatever is on the other side from coming out.'

'That doesn't sound good,' said Tom.

Shini took a deep breath and touched the door. Charlie and Tom looked on. Nothing happened. Shini grasped a deadbolt and wiggled it open, followed by another and another. With the last bolt pulled free, she shoved against the door. It screeched in protest and in a cloud of rust swung open.

Tom and Charlie stepped into the room behind Shini and gasped.

TWENTY NINE

Charlie stared at the sight confronting him, the case forgotten in his hands. The cell, about ten paces across, resembled the base of a dried-out well. The room was a giant funnel that stretched more than fifty metres upwards towards a pin prick of light. It was exquisitely built without a single indent where the blocks of stone joined. Apart from the door, there was no way in or out, unless you were a sparrow perhaps. Across every available space within reach were scratch marks, formulae and equations carved into the stone. And yet the prison was hardly the most unusual thing behind the door Shini had just pushed open.

A blonde, middle-aged man wearing Victorian military rags sat with his eyes closed in the Yogic asana of 'The Lotus,' floating two metres off the ground. At ground level sat a slightly more rotund man with unbelievably long hair and beard to match. He was humming to himself as he plaited a hank of hair shorn from one side of his head onto a coil of rope.

'Well, well, well,' said the man as he stopped plaiting and got to his feet. 'What have we here?'

'Who are you?' demanded Tom brandishing the rifle.

'My name, young man, is Arthur Cramp. And if I'm not mistaken, you're a Cramp too, if ever I've seen one.'

'I think the case brought us here to rescue you,' said Shini. 'My name's Aghanashini Nair, this is Thomas Cramp and this is Charlie Lawrence, a direct descendant of the Flintstaff family.'

'Aghanashini Nair?' asked the gentleman as he raised an arm to gently tap on his cellmate's toe. 'The day has finally come.' He turned back towards the three teenagers and bowing slightly said, 'I'm honoured to make your acquaintance.' The effect would have been more impressive if the sergeant didn't have over a metre of hair flopping about one side of his head while the other side was neatly trimmed. 'And this here is Major Henry Flintstaff-Membrayne.'

'Harumph!' grunted the figure floating in the air. He opened one piercing blue eye overhung by a bushy eyebrow and glared at the gathering of people below him. He spotted Charlie holding the case and opened his other eye in surprise. His balance seemed to waver as his body slid to one side and crashed to the sandy floor.

'Whoar! Ooof!'

Sergeant Cramp helped his partner to his feet and brushed him off as best he could while being batted away by the major. Flintstaff stood to attention, gave a crisp salute and then came forth to shake hands with the three friends. 'Pleasure to meet you, young lady. Fine family, the Nair's. I'm sure they're very proud. And you must be a Cramp, if ever I've seen one,' he continued as he shook Tom's hand. 'And you, young man, must be a Flintstaff,' he said grasping Charlie's hand and pumping it furiously. 'Knew you'd get here in the end. And you brought the case too. Jolly, jolly good.'

Charlie picked up the case and offered it to the tall, lean man standing in front of him. He knew this was his relative, knew the same blood flowed within them, but he had to be sure. The man smiled warmly at him, making his moustache lift theatrically at both ends. He looked down at the case and grasped the handle.

'My goodness, it is a pleasure to know our plans came through in the end,' said the major.

'What do you mean: your plans?' asked Charlie.

'We've been using everything in our power to bring you together... to bring you here.'

'That explains a lot... I don't think,' said Charlie.

'You have her eyes,' said Sergeant Cramp as he held onto Tom's broad shoulders. A look of great sadness passed over his features. 'I can't tell you how happy I am to see you, lad.'

'Um, I'm sorry to hurry this family reunion,' said Shini holding her hand up like she was in school. 'But the Rakshasas have locked us in. I think we're trapped.'

Major Henry Flintstaff-Membrayne walked to the centre of the prison cell carrying the case. He flicked the catches, with a hiss of steam the interior glowed dully. The major plunged his hand inside and rummaged. He pulled out a pair of antique scissors and a gilt-edged mirror.

'Get that hair cut, Sergeant. We're moving from 'Plan M' to 'Plan N'.'

'What was 'Plan M'?' asked Tom as he took the mirror and held it in front of the sergeant. Shini took the scissors and began chopping away at the long hanks of hair.

'We were making a rope from human hair in which to escape,' said Cramp pointing at a coil in the corner.

'That is gross,' muttered Shini. 'What I want to know is how you managed to survive for one hundred and fifty years and, by the look of it, not aged a day since you went missing.'

'We believe it was a certain fungus we ate before our encounter with the Shadows which extended our ability to live so long,' said Cramp.

'But why didn't the Shadows just kill you after they captured you?'

'Because our deaths would have released our accumulated powers into the ether, and this would have allowed our relatives to harness it. By keeping us alive they prevented this happening. What they didn't reckon upon was our ability to sway the destinies of our relatives.'

'*Our* destinies, you mean' said Charlie.

'You were not the first; only the first to reach us.'

'What did you eat while you were in here?' asked Charlie looking around.

Flintstaff glanced up at his young relative.

'A banana,' said Flintstaff as he pulled out a medical box from the case. He motioned Charlie to sit beside him and carefully unwrapped the make-shift bandage. 'And Prana. When we were locked in here... what year is it?'

'February 2015,' said Charlie looking away from his ruined hand.

'One hundred and fifty years... Well, I'll be blowed,' he said shaking his head. He pulled out a silver coin from his ragged trousers and flicked it towards Cramp who caught it deftly. 'I was out by a year, Cramp.'

'I did inform you that your meditation ran over by a little, sir.'

'I was sure it was thirty-two years not thirty-three... Anyway, we live on Prana, the life force that flows through the Universe, as well as sharing one banana a week which was dropped through that hole all the way up there,' he said looking away from the tiny beam of light and pointing at a banana sitting on a handkerchief on the floor.

'Er,' why haven't you eaten this one then?' asked Charlie.

'Actually, we're still full from last week. When we heard the gunshot we knew things might be hotting up. I was trying to levitate to the top to see what was going on but I've never really managed to get past ten feet.'

'I've got so many questions,' said Charlie as Flintstaff uncorked a bottle of foul-smelling liquid.

'Listen,' said Tom. 'I'm really happy we're all here together and everything. But, to be honest, I don't care about any of that right now. My mum and dad have been taken by the Shadows and I want to know how we're going to find them. If you want to sit around here, *stuck in prison* chatting, that's just fine, but you'd better show me how to use that case to find my parents first.'

Sergeant Cramp stood and grinned at his long lost relative. He brushed the cut hair from his shoulders and moved beside the major.

'We can use the case to transport wherever you like,' said Cramp.

'No,' said Shini. 'We left Great Aunt Maud outside with a holy man. They're about an hour's walk west of here.'

'Then you'll be needing this,' Cramp said grasping something in the case and pulling out an antique curtain rail. 'Oh,' he said and dropped it back in before pulling forth a didgeridoo. 'Blast it!' he muttered and bent down to rummage in the case. 'Have you lot been messing around in here?'

'Are you looking for this?' asked Flintstaff as he pulled out a snub-nosed, all-terrain, falconet canon with flowing Ottoman script engraved upon it.

'There it is,' said Cramp. 'Tom, I'll need a hand lifting this thing out...'

'That's more like it!' said Tom. He slung his rifle across his back and helped Cramp lift the canon out of the case. They carried it to the entrance of the cell where they pointed it towards the sealed door at the end of the long passageway.

While Tom and the sergeant got down to the business of trajectory, load and charge, Charlie was watching with an ashen face as Major Flintstaff poured the unguent onto his bloody hand. It fizzed and hurt like hell but he held back the tears. After the initial agony his hand went numb as the major cleaned the wound and put six stitches into his index finger. Shini came over and cut clean bandages from the medical box and passed them to Flintstaff when he needed them. He glanced up at Shini.

'You're next, young lady. That's a nasty gash on your forehead. I'm afraid that might leave a scar.'

'If all I get out of this is a scar then I can think myself lucky,' she replied.

'You do know who you are, don't you?' he asked as he finished the bandage on Charlie's hand.

'What do you mean?' she asked.

'Well, your name, for example... it's a bit of a clue, really. Aghanashini means 'Destroyer of sins' and Nair means 'leader' in

Malayalam and also derives from the Sanskrit, meaning 'Protector of the Land'.'

'Ri-ight,' said Shini. 'So what?'

'Have you ever opened this case?' asked Flintstaff as he wiped away the dried blood from Shini's forehead and face.

'Of course,' said Shini wincing. 'We all have...'

'Which means you're one of us, young lady; a protector of this land. No one else can open this case. Humans can touch it but they can't open it. It's lethal for the Shadows. You're destined to fight the Shadows and the evil they sow – a destroyer of sins... Don't you see?'

'How's that possible?'

'From your mother or father. It's passed down through the generations. Noticed anything unusual about them?'

'My mum went missing whilst trekking in Nepal when I was a kid... she disappeared during a blizzard on her way to Everest... they never found her...'

'Then, young lady, that is something we shall remedy in the near future,' promised the major. 'For I believe your mother was also a member of the ancient order of the Solutrean Guard.'

'Solutrean Guard?' said Tom.

'That's us, lad' said Cramp grinning as he pushed a ramrod into the barrel of the cannon.

'But what's the chance of Shini meeting me and Tom, and us all being these guards? It's not possible,' said Charlie.

'Precisely. There is no chance, Charlie... which means it must be something else, doesn't it?' replied Flintstaff.

'What's that supposed to mean?' asked Charlie. 'And please don't call me Charles...'

'To put it simply: like attracts like. All this time in here has given us time to perfect our powers; ones that have been handed down from generation to generation in our fight against the Shadows. When it all started thousands of years ago, only a few were chosen from the tribes to protect humankind from the Shadows. It was a long and dirty war and I imagine very few still survive today. For a hundred and fifty years we have been sending information out into the ether, manipulating events that might enable our rescue...'

'Is everyone ready?' interrupted Tom excitedly brandishing a match next to the cannon's vent.

'One second,' said Major Flintstaff. He put the medical box away and pulled out a tweed suit for himself and Sergeant Cramp. 'Important to make a good impression after such a long absence.'

When he was ready Flintstaff pulled a large calibre handgun from the case and flicked it open to check it was loaded. He passed this to Charlie, showing him the bullet selector. 'This is the Mark II version. Bronze bullets for Rakshasas, silver for werewolves, garlic-infused gold ones for vampires, dum-dums for zombies etc. etc. You'll get the hang of it. Shini, you can have our modified repeating crossbow,' he said pulling another weapon free. He depressed a green button on the stock of the weapon and steam-powered gears cranked the recurved limbs back as a bronze disc slipped onto the breach. 'Point and shoot,' said Flintstaff by way of explanation. Flintstaff pulled two cavalry sabres from the case, handing one to Sergeant Cramp. He pointed the gleaming blade towards Tom. 'When you're ready, Tom.'

'Fire in the hole!' yelled Tom as he lit the fuse and ran for cover.

'What does that mean?' asked Sergeant Cramp crouching beside him.

'No idea,' said Tom while the fuse sizzled. 'They say it in the movies.'

'What are movies?' asked Cramp nonplussed.

'You've got a lot of catching up to do...'

The roar of the canon blasted around the cell, filling it with roiling grey smoke. The power of the detonation had thrown the carriage of the falconet back against the far wall. Far from waiting for the smoke to clear down the passageway Flintstaff marched forward sword in hand, followed eagerly by Sergeant Cramp carrying the

243

case and his sabre. Charlie looked across at Tom and Shini. He grinned.

'Now it's time to kick some butt, Tom. We're going to rescue your family and put an end to this.'

Tom flicked the safety off his rifle.

'Let's do it!'

The three friends left the cell and followed in the wake of Flintstaff and Cramp. The two gentlemen had reached the shattered stone doorway at the end of the passageway and were busy fighting their way into the room where Charlie had nearly been choked to death. The area was filled with demons. Charlie slid through a gap to the left of Sergeant Cramp, closed one eye and put a bead on a particularly nasty Rakshasi. The female demon had three heads and four arms. She was wielding a variety of evil-looking blades and was managing to hold Cramp at bay as he deftly parried each blow. Sixteen bronze bullets later and there was a small pile of ash where once a demon stood. Cramp doffed an imaginary hat and launched himself at the next demon.

Shini sidestepped Major Flintstaff as he skewered a demon and then fended off a flurry of blows from two demons armed with spears. They were trying to take him from both sides. Shini lifted the crossbow but Flintstaff was in the way. He was moving too fast for her to take a sure shot without endangering him. Thinking back to her hours of online game-playing she aimed at the wall instead, and hoping her geometry was up to scratch, pulled the trigger. The result was more than she'd expected. With an almost unstoppable velocity the bronze disc ricocheted off the wall, instantly beheading a Rakshasa, only for it to whizz straight towards Major Flintstaff's head which he deflected with his sabre. The disc spun through the body of another demon, hit a wall, took an arm off another, hit another wall, narrowly missed decapitating Tom and finally embedded itself into the back of a fourth demon.

Tom, Charlie and Cramp got to their feet, having dived to the floor, to find the room empty bar a few piles of ash. Flintstaff secured the outer door as Shini reloaded the crossbow. Moving towards the circular stairwell they began the ascent. Deep inside the network of passageways they heard a rumbling. Dust fell from the ceiling and the floor beneath them shook. Sergeant Cramp glanced towards Major Flintstaff.

'Thinking what I'm thinking?' asked Flintstaff.

'Thinking it might be a good time to take these young fellows outside, sir.'

'What is it?' asked Charlie as he obliterated a demon coming out of the tunnels towards the stairs.

'It's Ahiravan. They've raised Ahiravan – A King of the Rakshasas,' said Flintstaff. 'Off we go chaps. Quick as we can up those stairs. Sergeant, take the lead. I'll take the rear.'

Charlie glanced back once before he turned the first corner of the stairs and glimpsed a passageway filling with demons. They were moving slowly, deliberately. Behind then came a shrieking that tore at his ears and sent splinters of pain lancing through his teeth. Lethargy filled his body and he could hardly lift his legs, they felt so heavy. He pushed himself on trying to shut out the screams in his head.

'It's magic,' yelled Flintstaff through the noise. 'Keep going. Our only hope is to get outside into sunlight.'

There was a roar as the king of the demons let loose his Rakshasas. They raced up the stairs with weapons and armour clattering as they went. Halfway up the stairs they caught up with the major. He spun round and decapitated the first demon to turn the corner.

'Duck!' yelled Shini.

Flintstaff dropped to one knee as Shini fired the crossbow. The disc hurtled down and around the stairwell slicing through anything that came in its path. Shini reloaded and fired another. The major grasped her by the arm and pushed her onwards.

Cramp, Tom and Charlie staggered out of the temple into the blinding sunlight, closely followed by Shini and Flintstaff. The army of Rakshasas poured up the stairwell only to stop at the entrance, hissing at their enemy and the searing sun.

'That'll slow them down,' said Cramp as he pulled Shini to one side.

Charlie and Tom fired through the doorway taking down a demon about to fire his bow at the major. The shrieking of Ahiravan, echoing up the stairwell, changed into a sibilant chanting. Black clouds boiled and roiled across the sky as day turned to twilight. The group retreated in a semi-circle away from the temple towards the path leading down the hill. The entrance to the temple shifted and collapsed as the giant demon smashed his way into the open, crushing minions in his path. He was a ten-headed demon with twelve arms bristling with weapons. Each head was a horror of horns, tusks and lambent eyes. Rakshasas poured out around him keeping close to their king. Charlie fired off his revolver until it was spent. Pushing the pistol into his belt he ran to Cramp and grasped the case. He needed more ammo. Tom was out of bullets too and was brandishing his rifle like a club. Shini flicked a switch on the crossbow and loaded a bronze boomerang. She went down on one knee and aimed at one of the demon king's heads. She breathed out, steadied herself and pulled the trigger.

As Charlie was rummaging through the case in search of ammo he glanced up to see the boomerang scythe towards Ahiravan. Shini looked triumphant but at the last second the demon caught the boomerang deftly in one of its many hands and hurled it back. Shini stared, frozen, unable to move as the missile hurtled towards her. Charlie used the last of his strength and leapt towards her. There was a loud 'thud' as he rolled in the dust beside her. Shini grabbed him by the arm and pulled him backwards.

'Charlie! Are you okay? Are you hit?'

Charlie struggled to his feet; in his right hand was the case with the boomerang still quivering in its side.

Charlie and Shini turned as a grey wave of macaques flowed across the boulders towards the Rakshasas. The troop of monkeys was led by their scarred, one-eared leader against their ancient enemies. The monkey king stopped beside Charlie and tapped the case insistently. Charlie frowned and opened the case. The monkey pulled a lethal-looking bronze mace from the interior, winked at him, and charged towards Ahiravan. With jagged teeth bared, the monkeys leapt onto the army of Rakshasas, twenty monkeys to a demon. They ripped and tore and pulled and bit their enemy. Tufts of fur and splashes of blood arced into the sky as Ahiravan swatted the monkeys away with a deadly swirling of his twelve arms.

Flintstaff leapt forward with Cramp at his side as they duelled with the demon lord. Fighting off six arms and five heads each, their blades were a blur of bronze-edged steel. The monkey king hurtled out of nowhere and smashed his mace down onto Ahiravan's foot. The demon king roared and hopped backwards, crashing against the ruined temple; stone blocks shifted and gave way. Using many of his arms to gain his balance, Flintstaff and Cramp rushed forward to slice into flesh. Flintstaff darted sideways and sliced through an exposed neck with a long backhand cut. He reversed the blade and sank it deep into the abdomen of a Rakshasa. Cramp took off two arms with a single sweep and dodged out of range of a swinging war hammer. The monkey king leapt into the air with his mace raised high and demolished one of Ahiravan's heads with a crunch.

Ahiravan bellowed in pain. The black clouds above shimmered and evaporated like morning mist. The sun shone bright once more, burning and tormenting the demons. In seconds the remaining Rakshasas were fleeing down the stairwell. Ahiravan lashed out with his remaining weapons causing his three attackers to jump back out of range. A single head glanced behind him as he barged past his minions towards the stairwell. The bulbous eyes opened even wider as a bronze disc sliced the top of the skull clean off.

'Not so fast that time,' said Shini looking up from her crossbow.

The last of the demons fled down the stairwell and the hill became silent once more. The dust settled and birds began to sing. Tom dusted himself off and clapped Charlie on the back. Cramp and Flintstaff walked to the stairwell to check they were safe.

'Everyone okay?' asked Major Flintstaff walking back into the sunlight. 'Jolly good show, chaps.'

'Sir, I think the monkey wants a word...'

The surviving band of monkeys had formed themselves into an organized circle around Charlie and the case. They looked at him expectantly. The leader, now also missing half the other ear, walked over to Flintstaff, took his hand and led him to the case. Once he was there he gently pulled the boomerang free of the case, laid it to one side, and then sat on his haunches waiting.

'One good turn and all that,' said Flintstaff as he opened the case. Gradually a large iron bowl arose with a fuse at the base. Flintstaff struck a match and took a pace backwards. Charlie looked at him quizzically. 'Monkey Mortar,' stated Flintstaff as the mortar erupted in a yellow flash; a hundredweight of bananas leapt into the sky.

The monkey king jumped up and down clapping his hands and did a victory somersault as bananas rained down amongst his delighted tribe.

*****

The sadhu sat under the banyan tree, a wide smile spread across his face. He had spent a pleasant morning tending the needs of this most excellent English lady. After three hours he was still holding her hand, gently patting it in an encouraging way. Flintstaff and Cramp had arrived with the three teenagers in tow along with five jewellery salesmen, thirty-eight children ranging from three months old to adolescent, two oxen, the fruit mamma who had been stripped of her fruit when she happened to walk around a corner to be confronted by three hundred monkeys, the lost Japanese hippy high on bhang lassi and thirteen wild dogs with various stages of mange. The banyan tree had never been so busy.

248

'All I want to know is how we're going to find my parents,' said Tom.

'That is our next course of action, Tom. Of that you can be assured,' growled Cramp. 'I'll not have any of my relatives remain in the clutches of the Shadows. Not again - not ever.'

'Then there's only one place for us to go,' said Major Flintstaff. He was busy drawing a large circle in the red dust whilst trying to shoo away excited children jumping in and out of his drawing. 'Now, if you'd all like to join me in the circle we can be off.'

THIRTY

The old wine cellar of No. 35 Chepstow Villas was becoming a little crowded. Tied to four chairs were the two R.G.S. scientists and Mr. and Mrs. Cramp. The scientists were gagged after two more redcaps had suffered nervous breakdowns whilst torturing them. Mr. Cramp was bruised, bloody and barely conscious while his wife was sitting next to him glaring at Lord Cofgod. Babba Belani, Mimi and Count Strigoi were also present, along with a selection of minions.

'Not quite dead then,' said the count looking at the scientists. 'And the Cramps seem to have miraculously appeared in your cellar, Lord Cofgod...'

'It's a funny old world,' said Cofgod. 'With them in our care we have leverage.'

'What about the other families?'

'We searched for them but it seems they have gone into hiding,' said Cofgod. 'Have we had any word from India?'

'Nothing,' said Strigoi. 'We've sent minions but it'll take time...'

'Then assume the worst,' warned Cofgod.

'I want these four moved to the Ellipse, Mimi. Get a van here as soon as possible. Although the general public have a knack of ignoring each other, make sure it's done without raising too many eyebrows.'

'Certainly, sir,' said Mimi pulling her mobile from her suit pocket. She walked back up the stairs to the ground floor.

Cofgod watched Strigoi take a seat opposite Mrs. Cramp, ignoring her baleful glare. The count closed his eyes and pinched the bridge of his nose. When he looked up her reaction to his gaze was instant. She squirmed in her chair and her breathing became short and ragged but she couldn't break the stare of the Lord of the Vampires.

'Where is your son?'

'Ran away,' moaned Tom's mum.

'Where?'

'Don't know.'

'Does he have the case?'

'Cows? They'll need feeding...'

'Not cows! Case. *The* case...' he turned towards Cofgod. 'Don't they think of anything other than their damned cows?'

'Not really,' said Cofgod. 'I think we should kill the husband... it might make the wife focus a little more.'

'Once we have the case we'll kill the lot of them, but not until I HAVE THAT CASE!' yelled Strigoi.

'Shush!' said Cofgod tilting his head.

'Don't you shush me...'

'Shut up,' snapped Cofgod waving his arms. 'I heard something.'

There was a rumbling sound coming from underground. Cofgod was pretty sure the tube trains were nowhere near this street. He'd never heard them before. Maybe they were working in the sewers... and then he saw Mrs. Cramp's chair tilt backwards as the floor beneath her slid seamlessly away to reveal a set of stone steps descending to a room below. Mrs. Cramp fell backwards but there was no crash as she disappeared; only a gasp as someone below caught her. Cofgod's cigar dropped to the floor unnoticed. That was why he'd found nothing of value all these years. He'd failed to discover the most important room in the house. A secret basement. Cofgod turned and fled.

'Cofgod,' snarled Count Strigoi. 'You fool.'

*****

Charlie wasn't the only one to jump back in surprise as Mrs. Cramp toppled down the stairs. But it was Shini who'd given them fair warning of their enemy. With Flintstaff and Cramp sat beside her under the banyan tree she'd Googled their former residence and discovered that Lord Cofgod had bought the whole street a year after Agnes disappeared. Apparently the house had been broken into and vandalized and then left in ruins until Cofgod purchased it. Both Flintstaff and Cramp had been mesmerized by the smart phone as Shini tapped away at the touch screen. Only Tom managed to keep the two adventurers on track instead of spending the rest of the day looking at cool apps.

The basement in Chepstow Villas was just as they'd left it one hundred and fifty years ago. The group had appeared inside the transportation glyph set into the stone floor; both Tom and Sergeant Cramp seemed to get the worst of the travel sickness as they held onto each other. Major Flintstaff heard the voice of Count Strigoi shouting above them and a look of determination set upon his features. He moved quietly over to the work benches and selected the Cat-o-Vault 3000 from the wall. He opened up the magazine and tipped it sideways. A collection of bones fell onto the workbench causing Sergeant Cramp to grimace apologetically.

'Sergeant Cramp,' whispered Flintstaff. 'You have two minutes to come back with something useful...'

'Right you are, sir,' replied Cramp saluting. He handed Tom the Cat-o-Vault, grabbed him by the hand and took the case. Flicking through the journal he found the glyph he was looking for and used the crystal inside the journal to draw them on the floor. 'Back in a tick...'

While Cramp and Tom were off finding ammo, Flintstaff quietly showed Charlie how to speed load the steam-powered revolver. Shini led Maud to a chair where she sat calmly, still in a state of shock, and then Shini joined the two men. Flintstaff gave her a quick rundown of extras on the self-loading steam-powered crossbow and helped her load a magazine of wooden stakes. Cramp and Tom returned five minutes later soaked to the skin and smelling of rotten seaweed.

'Good hunting?' asked the major frowning.

'We-ell,' began Tom before he was nudged by the sergeant.

'Absolutely, sir. Top class and all that,' said Cramp as water pooled beneath them.

Charlie, Tom and Shini held their weapons ready as Flintstaff and Cramp drew their sabres. Cramp moved ahead and depressed an enamelled button on the wall beside the stairs. Cramp's attempted charge up the stairs was halted abruptly by a woman tied to a chair crashing down on top of him. Cramp managed to break the lady's fall but it slowed their assault considerably.

'Mum!' cried Tom helping drag the chair away from a flattened Cramp.

Flintstaff charged ahead quickly followed by Charlie and Shini. At the top of the stairs they came face to face with three vampire minions. Major Flintstaff thrust his sabre into the thigh of one of them before being grabbed and wrestled to the ground. Shini pumped three wooden stakes toward another, only to find the vampire suddenly appearing behind her. She hadn't even seen it move. But Charlie had. He turned a dial on the handgun and shot a single bog-oak bullet into the back of the vampire's head. The vampire screeched, took flight and smashed into the far wall before turning to ash. Shini swivelled to her left and fired three more stakes at another vampire, managing to pin it in the shoulder. Flintstaff was still rolling on the floor until Shini swung the crossbow round and shot the minion in the heart.

Charlie saw the two R.G.S. scientists still tied to chairs in the far corner, while Mr. Cramp was being dragged up the stairs by a very pale man and a very dark man in expensive suits. A group of redcaps, armed with pikes, were forming a defensive wall of steel before them. They angled their pikes at forty-five degrees and howled and whooped in eagerness. Behind them a couple of zombies came crashing down the stairs in a heap before getting to their feet and staggering towards the scientists, looking for an easy meal.

'Cat-o-Vault. Single shot,' yelled Tom. He fired the weapon from the hip towards the group of redcaps.

Only Tom and the sergeant weren't surprised by the ammo they were using for the Cat-o-Vault 3000. A squid arced across the room and face-planted a redcap. Immediately its tentacles suckered onto the minion, wrapping around its face and squirting its salty ink. Blinded, the redcap dropped its pike and ran round in circles before hitting a wall and collapsing.

'Automatic fire!' yelled Tom. Charlie ducked as the launcher released a barrage of fish, each one about the size of his hand. For a second Charlie wondered what possible use a fish could be in a fight until he focussed on one as it flew towards the redcaps. They were mostly made of teeth. The defensive wall of pikes collapsed as redcaps were hit by famished fanged fish.

Shini beheaded the two zombies approaching the captive scientists and suddenly all the noise of battle ceased. The wine cellar was empty. Piles of ash and broken chairs were all that was left. Shini cut the scientists' bonds and helped them into the safety of the basement. Flintstaff led the way up the scullery stairs, dispatching a zombie on the way. As the group entered the kitchen they could hear the noise of screeching tyres on the road outside.

'To me!' shouted Tom as he sprinted through the house. Everyone followed him out the front door to see two limousines speeding away down the street. Flintstaff and Cramp stood outside their front door for the first time in a hundred and fifty years. It was difficult for them to close their mouths as they gaped at all the cars parked down the street.

'Where does everyone keep their horses?' asked Cramp.

'What happened to all the smog?' asked Flintstaff.

'No time,' said Charlie as he shot the lock off a scooter parked next to a street light.

Tom crouched beside him and tore open the plastic bodywork to reveal the electrics. Pulling two wires free, he twisted them together and the engine spluttered to life. Handing Charlie the Cat-o-Vault, he jumped on the bike while Charlie hopped on the back, and off they went down the street in a streak of blue smoke.

'We have to grab a car,' said Shini looking up and down the street. 'Or a cab.'

'And these are cars?' asked Flintstaff pointing to a parked vehicle.

'Yep.'

Flintstaff walked into the middle of the road and held his hand up. Unfortunately, he was facing the wrong way...

*****

Three minutes later and they were speeding down the road with Shini at the wheel. The front of the car had a deep dent.

'You can't do that,' said Shini as the car slewed to the right and on through a red light. 'People won't just stop if you walk out in front of them.'

'Lesson learned,' groaned Flintstaff from the back seat.

*****

Charlie held his breath as the scooter raced between the traffic. They'd already knocked off three wing mirrors during their pursuit to catch the limousines. Charlie spotted them turning left onto the Bayswater Road, heading into the city. Tom skidded at the traffic lights, pushed it between two cars and mounted the pavement. People yelled and dived out of the way as Charlie shouted apologies in their wake. Bouncing down onto the road again a car slewed beside them, horn blaring, as the scooter shot off in a cloud of smoke. They were catching...

*****

Strigoi, Babba Belani and Mimi were all sat in the back of the limousine with an irate Mr. Cramp sat facing them, still tied and gagged. Two minions employed by Count Strigoi sat in the front. The limousine up ahead had Cofgod and a few of his minions packed inside. At the junction of the Bayswater Road and Lancaster Terrace, Cofgod's limousine followed the traffic left.

'Go straight on,' ordered Strigoi.

The car roared down the one way street against the flow of traffic. Cars and buses skidded out of the way. Babba Belani wasn't smiling as much as usual and he kept glancing behind him as the vehicle swerved this way and that through the oncoming traffic.

'Two of them kids is chasing us,' said Baba Belani. 'On a scooter.'

'Then they'll catch us up and die,' stated Mimi calmly. She leaned forward and opened a panel beside the in-car bar, extracting a machine pistol. She checked the clip, flicked the safety off and opened the window. As the scooter veered past another car she leant out of the window and took aim...

*****

Shini was driving as fast as she could in a car she'd never driven before, down roads she'd never been. She handed Sergeant Cramp her phone and told him to type in the Ellipse building on her SatNav app.

'Ooh, that's new, Sergeant,' said Flintstaff pointing at the BT Tower in the distance. He was still concussed from being run over. 'And look at that. That lady is almost naked!'

'There's no point in trying to catch them,' said Shini. 'But we've got a chance of beating them to the Ellipse if we can find a way with less traffic.' Shini leaned over to Cramp. 'Now press 'enter', see?'

'In fifteen metres turn left,' said the phone.

'Good Lord,' said Cramp holding the phone at arm's length.

'I know, right? Actually, we say OMG...' said Shini swerving left. 'As in: Oh My God.'

'Which one?' asked a dazed Flintstaff.

*****

Charlie watched the Bentley veer left and assumed the other would follow, but the second limousine swerved into oncoming traffic and drove the wrong way down a four lane road. Tom made a decision and slid the bike between two oncoming cars and bumped onto the pavement beside Hyde Park. People jumped clear as the street ahead echoed with the sound of horns blaring. They were catching the limousine even though the bike could barely reach 50kmh. With the road narrowing, Charlie saw Mimi lean out of the right hand passenger window and aim a gun at them. Tom swerved behind the limousine as the first spray of bullets smashed into bushes, trees and ricocheted off iron railings. Tom swerved to the other side of the limousine. Charlie fired the Cat-o-Vault instinctively, loosing off a Snapping Turtle through the open window. He reloaded and fired again. An electric eel shot like an arrow inside the vehicle. Gunshots from inside blew out the rear window and the left-hand passenger door burst open as Babba Belani fell from the speeding vehicle with a twenty kilo turtle attached to his face. Tom swerved round the Vodou King and twisted the throttle. The eel was causing havoc in the back of the car. Blue flashes were followed by more gunshots.

'I thought this was meant to be a Cat-o-Vault...' Charlie shouted in Tom's ear.

'Sergeant Cramp wanted to land at the London Wharf to find street cats but we ended up at the aquarium instead...'

'Watch out!' warned Charlie.

Another body flew out of the open door and this time Tom applied the brakes as hard as he could.

'Dad!' cried Tom. The scooter skidded and wobbled to a stop inches from Mr. Cramp. Tom dropped the scooter as Charlie hopped off the back. They dragged him to the side of the road then Charlie went back to fetch the scooter. The limousine carried on for a few seconds and then shuddered to a stop fifty paces down the street. Mimi got out and walked calmly towards them, reloading the automatic pistol. Tom untied the gag and the rope binding his dad's hands. There was nowhere to run. His dad was semi-conscious and an assassin was on her way. Onlookers scattered and cars emptied as they saw the gun in her hands. A policeman ran across the road and attempted to tackle her to the ground. Mimi moved in a blur and hurled the policeman ten metres across the road to crash against a parked car where he collapsed unconscious. She aimed her pistol just as Charlie grabbed the Cat-o-Vault off the road, rolled once and squeezed the trigger.

It was only a goldfish. And not a big goldfish either. It was the kind that could be won in a travelling fair and died two days later only to be flushed down a toilet. The destiny of this fish was even shorter but far more glorious – it hit Mimi in the eye just as she was pulling the trigger. Bullets sprayed out of her pistol cutting gouges into the road, cars and scooter, whizzing this way and that as she stumbled backwards, shrieking.

Charlie and Tom grasped Mr. Cramp under each arm and dragged him onto the back of the scooter. Charlie held onto him as Tom squeezed up front, grabbed the throttle and off they sped down the street. They passed Baba Belani, still rolling on the road trying to pry an angry turtle off his face.

*****

Count Strigoi's battered limousine pulled up outside the Ellipse. The two minions in the front got out and opened both passenger doors. The count and Mimi stepped out onto the windswept street. Mimi was still clutching her left eye and the count came around to put his arm through hers just as another vehicle pulled up not ten paces away; car doors opened as Shini, Cramp and Flintstaff emerged.

Shini pulled the crossbow out of the car as Cramp placed his hand on the hilt of his sabre. Major Flintstaff, still concussed, wandered off a few paces and stared up at the immense building towering over them all.

'I say,' he said. 'That whole building's made of glass, Sergeant. D'you think Paxton had anything to do with it?'

'Actually,' said Count Strigoi. 'It's mine.'

'Major Flintstaff,' whispered Cramp. 'We have the count.'

Count Strigoi smiled at Cramp. He raised his hand and clicked his fingers. The two minions from the limousine stepped between them. One of the minions spoke into a small microphone which prompted four security guards at the door of the building to walk across the marbled entrance to join them.

Shini raised the crossbow but Sergeant Cramp laid his hand on the weapon and lowered it. There were too many people around, ignorant and innocent of what was happening. Flintstaff stood in front of Count Strigoi, ignoring the security guards. The count's eyes bored into the major who merely smiled in return, but there was steel in his eyes when he spoke.

'Count Strigoi.'

'Ah, Major Henry Flintstaff-Membrayne. We meet again. How was your little... holiday? Did they treat you well?' he sneered as he looked Flintstaff up and down. 'You look like you lost a little weight...'

'It was very instructive, Count. Although a change of clothes would've been nice.' replied Flintstaff. 'And by the looks of it you've been a busy little bat since our absence.'

'This?' asked Strigoi waving at the immense building behind him. His top lip curled, revealing one polished fang. 'This is nothing, Major. *Nothing*. You have a little catching up to do, my friend.'

'And I intend to, Count,' said Flintstaff glowering. 'From what I've seen so far, your ability to defeat three unprepared teenagers tells me everything I need to know about your organization.'

'A hiccup, that's all. Go home and read your history, Major. And when you're ready you can come back and discuss whether your great Age of Steam and your precious Science have benefited humankind like you once believed. I think you'll find we've been very busy indeed while you've been rotting in India.'

'Your time has nearly come, Strigoi. Can you feel it?' asked Flintstaff leaning in close so that his nose nearly touched the count. 'Can you?'

Four bodyguards moved in to protect their lord but the count took a step back, smiled and waved them away. He took Mimi's arm once more and turned towards the entrance of the Ellipse. Flintstaff returned to the car.

'Why didn't you kill him?' asked Shini. The sound of sirens approaching echoed through the streets.

'I'm afraid it takes a little more preparation to kill a Lord of the Shadows, Shini. Nonetheless, it is at the top of my list.'

'Come on,' said Cramp. 'I haven't had a cup of tea for a hundred and fifty years and I'm gasping!'

'I think we should do something,' said Shini as they set off down the road. 'How will our families ever be safe if we don't rid ourselves of Count Strigoi? It's alright for you two; you can defend yourselves. But what about my dad and brother, and Charlie and Tom's?'

'Stop the car,' said Major Flintstaff.

*****

Count Strigoi and Mimi walked briskly through the main entrance towards the private elevator.

'Close the building,' snarled the count as he walked past security. 'Everyone out. And no one gets in, do you understand?'

The guard nodded and hit the fire alarm.

'I'll string him up,' said Strigoi as they waited for the elevator. There was a steady rush of people making for the entrance being herded out by security guards. 'I'll torture him for a thousand years. I'll... I'll...'

'Let me take out Flintstaff,' said Mimi as the lift opened. She pressed the button for the executive suite on the top floor.

'I'm not talking about that twit,' he said. 'Flintstaff has no idea what sort of power we wield in the modern world. He's a spent force. I'm talking about that double-dealing green-skinned runt, Cofgod. He's been playing me all along... making alliances with Babba Belani, trying to get the case for himself, keeping secrets... Who else is he working with?'

'He's working for someone else?' asked Mimi checking her bruised eye in the mirror.

'Who?' demanded Strigoi as he grasped Mimi by the throat and whirled her around to face him. 'Who is it? Lycaon? That oversized dog thinks he can take me on?'

'I... don't know, sir,' said Mimi clutching his hand. 'It was a question. He'd be a fool to break the alliance. We're taking over the world together... what use to split?'

'Can't I trust anyone, anymore?'

'Me, my Lord,' said Mimi. 'Always me.'

The elevator opened and Count Strigoi strode towards his office at the end of the corridor with Mimi in tow. The ebony door opened automatically for him as he approached. Count Strigoi stopped in his tracks.

*****

'Do come in,' said Major Henry Flintstaff-Membrayne of the Solutrean Guard. A single, very rare, Tasmanian Orange-bellied parrot sat upon his shoulder. Shini, armed with the crossbow, and Sergeant Cramp with his sabre stood either side him. The case sat upon the table. He waved a hand languidly around the chrome and glass office. 'A little overstated, don't you think?'

'It's a matter of taste.' Count Strigoi laughed. 'Stupid of me to think you'd walk away from here, even if it was to lick your wounds.'

'I never leave business unfinished if I can help it, Count.'

'It would have been wiser,' added Mimi moving beside her lord.

'Shini's been showing me just how far you've come on your computer thingy,' said Flintstaff. 'It's such a shame you didn't stay in your castle instead of meddling with the affairs of humans.'

'Your sentimentality for your own breed is quite sickening, Major. Humans yearn to be dominated. The Shadows are destined to be their overlords. The fact is: humans cannot live under their own rule. Your so-called 'civilization' is a mask for every foul deed ever perpetrated by one human on another. Look at your history. War followed by enslavement. Enslavement followed by rebellion. Rebellion followed by oppression. And we have guided humanity along this path for thousands of years.'

'And now we're here to put a stop to it,' said Sergeant Cramp.

'You think you are, but you can't. Since you've been gone the world has spun out of your control. Science and religion will destroy each other. The O'Void Corporation will throttle the life from this world, and like us vampires, we'll bleed it dry. There's no turning back. Your Golden Age was twenty thousand years ago, Major, when you were living in caves making stone tools. Our Golden Age is now. And we intend to feed off the misery we've created until the end of time. All humans will be our slaves. Two weeks from now will be the greatest meeting of the Shadows of the Void in the history of the world. Duke Lycaon has organized everything for us in Switzerland. And I intend on bringing you there as my pet.'

Major Flintstaff smoothed down his blonde moustache before twirling each end into a point. He frowned, arched an eyebrow, pursed his lips and squinted. He turned towards Shini.

'Did you get all of that?' he asked.

'Certainly did,' said Shini tapping her phone. 'It's now on the web.'

Mimi snarled as she shred her human form and flung herself towards Shini. Shini dropped her phone as she scrambled for the crossbow but it was knocked from her hands as Mimi crashed into her. Sergeant Cramp rushed to her aid but was knocked aside as if he were a fly swatted by a giant hand. He smashed against the glass wall that looked over London, blood splattering across it from his nose. Flintstaff turned to find Count Strigoi behind him and took a punch that sent him reeling across the table and onto the floor. The parrot squawked and took flight. Flintstaff glanced towards Shini who was struggling to keep Mimi away from her neck. He crawled beneath the table and scuttled down its length until he reached the fighting females. Strigoi was up the other end trying to find where the major had landed after being punched. The major grabbed Mimi's leg and dragged her beneath the table while Shini kicked and thrashed herself free of the vampire's grasp. Flintstaff got a six inch high heel across the bridge of his nose for his efforts but it was just enough time for Shini to find the crossbow.

'Flee, Shini!' ordered Flintstaff. 'I'll take care of these two.'

'No chance,' said Shini as she pointed the crossbow at Mimi and fired. There was a loud 'twang' but no flash of ash as Mimi vaporized... because Mimi didn't vaporize. 'The bolt's fallen out,' yelled Shini. She dropped the weapon and scrambled across the floor towards the motionless figure of Sergeant Cramp. There, beside him, was the wooden bolt...

Flintstaff, dazed by the swinging kick from Mimi, was dragged from under the table by Strigoi. He couldn't hold on to Mimi any longer and he let go as Strigoi bit into his neck. He felt skin and tissue ripped away, hot blood pouring down his chest. Time slowed. He watched aghast as Mimi leapt once more at Shini. Shini turned holding one arm up in valiant defence... Mimi in mid-air reaching out towards her throat and Shini's other hand holding the wooden stake braced against her chest. Mimi landing with a high-pitched scream and then a huge flash as she disappeared in a cloud of ash...

'Noooooo!' yelled Strigoi.

Flintstaff felt the hold on him slacken for a second and then his chin thrust forward as he slammed his elbow into the side of Strigoi's head. He felt the count's nails rip more flesh free as he fell sideways.

'Shini, get out,' ordered Flintstaff. He pressed his left hand against the wound on his neck as he turned towards the count. The Tasmanian Orange-bellied parrot landed on the Major's shoulder and screeched angrily.

Flintstaff flexed his right hand as Count Strigoi stood and shook his head. Shini made it to the door, leaving Flintstaff and Strigoi, a motionless Cramp and the case. Major Flintstaff moved steadily towards the count. Strigoi snarled and stood his ground.

'You cannot defeat me,' said Strigoi as he drew himself up to his full height. 'I am the Lord of the Vampires. I am the darkness. I am eternal. I am a Shadow of the Void. I am...'

'Rather boring...?' said Flintstaff and poked Strigoi in the chest, as if to validate his point.

Count Strigoi swayed backwards on his heels, just keeping his balance. The Tasmanian Orange-bellied parrot flew at his face squawking loudly. It was enough. The count overbalanced and took a single step backwards. He frowned, looked down at his feet, eyes wild, and screamed. He had stepped into the open case.

'No! Please, not like this... I beg you,' wailed Strigoi. He was descending deeper and deeper into its depths. Smoke rose from his fingers as he tried to claw his way out. He coughed ashes from his mouth as black vapour leaked from his ears.

'You wanted the case, Strigoi,' said Sergeant Cramp from behind. 'Well, it's all yours.'

Count Strigoi, the Lord of the Vampires, disappeared into the depths of the case.

That magical, curious case.

THIRTY ONE

Friday 20th February 2015.

Lord Cofgod sat on a bench looking out over the misty dales of the Scottish Borders. The view from here really was stunning when the low cloud cover, blizzards, or fogs were not sweeping through the region. Of course, Cofgod actually preferred the fog; it was his favourite time for hunting as it added piquancy to the whole thing. There was nothing like the thrill of the chase when a young couple, hopefully in love, were lost on the moors and night was drawing in. If you wanted full-bodied flavour then free range was the only way forward. It had been an age since Cofgod had returned to something as simple and peaceful as squatting beneath a bridge waiting for a passer-by. He had been tracking one particular couple since lunchtime when they'd stopped for sandwiches and a thermos of coffee beneath a gnarled oak.

Cofgod picked at a piece of flesh between his teeth using a splinter of bone as a toothpick. He knew things in London weren't looking good. Belani had contacted him that morning and filled him in. Count Strigoi and Mimi had totally vanished leaving a single pile of ash in his office. Count Strigoi's recording about enslaving mankind had gone viral across the planet. The wholesale dumping of shares and boycotts would devastate the O'Void Corporation. Flintstaff and Cramp were back at No. 35 Chepstow Villas. All three of the blasted children were still alive. It was a litany of disasters. Duke Lycaon was hardly going to be happy; especially as his minion Oleg was dead.

Cofgod wasn't stupid. He knew who'd get the blame for all of this. When news got back to the Shadows relating to the loss of the case, the actions of the teenagers, and the escape of Flintstaff and Cramp, everything would point to him. Babba Belani the Bokor would hold Cofgod responsible because that was his speciality – everyone believed what he said, and Belani was too useful with his control over the media to remove. What did Cofgod have to offer? His gamble hadn't paid off and now he was stuffed.

So Cofgod had decided to run. He ordered his minions to head north in the limousine and not stop until they reached his ancestral home of Hermitage Castle. All he'd wanted was a bit more power. Well, a lot more power actually. He couldn't see why the Shadows were so upset with him for having his own secret agenda. Surely that was the whole point in being evil. There was only so much of this hand-in-hand, 'let's all be evil together,' claptrap he could stand. It made sense to look out for oneself to the exclusion of all others. However, all his carefully built dreams were now shattered by a bunch of teenagers. He would have his revenge, of that he was sure. It would take time, but he had lots of that.

As Lord Cofgod finally managed to dislodge the piece of sinew from between his teeth he turned to his right to beckon his minion over with the bottle of wine the hikers had been carrying.

Strange, thought Cofgod, *where on earth is he?* Bloody minions were so unreliable. Cofgod felt the bench beneath him groan under the weight of something very large sitting down beside him. A voice as deep and as terrible as the sins of the world rumbled.

'Good evening, Lord Cofgod.'

Lord Cofgod swallowed once, deeply, before turning his head to the left.

'Good evening, Duke Lycaon.'

THE END...
FOR NOW.

I really hope you enjoyed the novel as much as I did writing it. Please leave a review on Amazon if you want to support a struggling writer! For updates, cut chapters and sneak previews of Flintstaff and Cramp: The Mystery of the Missing Map.
Visit www.flintstaffandcramp.com
or Email me at: Katanaboy@hotmail.com
or Flintstaffandcramp on Facebook.

Many Thanks!

Printed in Great Britain
by Amazon